MW01138528

DEADLY LODE

A Novel

****

Randall Reneau

This book is a work of fiction. Names, characters, places, and incidents either are products of the author's imagination or are used fictitiously. Any resemblance to actual events or locales or persons, living or dead, is entirely coincidental.

Copyright © 2012 by Randall Reneau

All rights reserved, including the right to reproduce this book or portions thereof in any form whatsoever.

First paperback edition September 2012

For additional information, please visit our website at: http://randall-reneau.com/

Manufactured in the United States of America

10 9 8 7 6 5 4 3 2 1

ISBN: 978-1479131792

ISBN: 1479131792 (e-book)

This book is for Lynne, Aimee, and Lacey.

Randall Reneau

Acknowledgements

A very special thank you to Ken Hodgson for reading the manuscript and for his encouragement, enthusiasm, and long-standing friendship. Also, thanks to Sheldon Russell for reading the manuscript and providing a much-appreciated quote.

Prelude

Striking a match with the tip of his blackened thumbnail, the dynamiter knelt down and lit the fuse. He watched the acrid white smoke stream from the combustible cord. Satisfied the fuse was burning properly, he yelled, "Fire in the hole!" And hauled ass back down the drift. Thirty seconds later the blast shook the mine, sending dust roiling out the mine portal.

In the summer of 1891, near the small town of Winthrop, Washington, the Sullivan gold and copper mine operated around the clock. Mine manager Tom Delany worked long hours in the small log cabin that served as both his office and quarters. As he flipped-through the latest assays, a broad grin broke out on his face. The assays were good, damned good. The ore was averaging nearly three-quarters of an ounce gold per ton and 1.5 percent copper.

The only bad news in the assays continued to be the high levels of pitchblende, a uranium mineral discovered about a hundred years earlier. The heavy, dark mineral had no known economic value, and had to be separated from the gold and copper ore. A major pain in the butt, and an added expense. Shaking his head, Tom noted that every single assay contained uranium, often running as high as 10 percent.

"Jesus Maria," Tom said, to himself. "If they ever figure out a use for this damn stuff, somebody could make a fortune."

Uranium aside, he knew the Sullivan was a damned good gold and copper mine, and the assays on his desk proved it. He planned to bring his wife out from back east, buy a house in nearby Winthrop, and finish out his career working at the mine.

Glancing up from the assay reports and looking out his office window, Tom saw his day-shift foreman, Big Jim Maclean, striding toward the office. Big Jim was gesturing with his hands and looked to be talking to himself.

"Damn, this can't be good," Tom thought, as Big Jim burst through the door.

"Boss, two more men are down, and I mean down!" Big Jim boomed, while parking his huge frame into a not-quite-big-enough chair. "Puking their guts out, they are, down on level two."

"What in the hell is going on?" Tom asked, shaking his head in disbelief. "This is getting to be a full-time problem."

"By God, I have nary a clue, Tom. I've checked the mess hall provisions and chewed out the cook, but everything seems according to Hoyle. It cain't be the damn water, either. We all drink the same water out of Montana Creek. It's got to be something in the mine, cause the topside folks are fit as a fiddle."

"Any unusual odors in the mine?" Tom asked, thinking there could be some kind of mine gas present.

"You mean other than from miners that don't bathe real regular and fart more or less continually? Or them damn fumes from the dynamite?"

Tom laughed. "Yeah, other than those."

"I'll tell you what the miners think, Tom. They think the damned mine is cursed."

"Cursed, my ass. Look, Jim, I don't put any stock in such nonsense." Tom replied, then added under his breath. "Of course, neither did the fellow who stole the Hope Diamond."

"Hope, what?"

"Never mind, Jim. We've got to figure out what in the hell is going on here."

They needn't have worried. The mine would soon face a tougher problem than sick miners. It would come to be known as the Great Financial Panic of 1892. By 1893, the financial backers of the Sullivan Mine went bust, the mine closed, and talk of a curse was soon forgotten.

*****

On the morning of June 23, 1946, everything at the abandoned Sullivan Mine appeared normal. Montana Creek gurgled along, the birds sang, and the insects buzzed. At a little past three in the afternoon, the birds quit singing, and the insects quit buzzing. The quake hit with megaton force. In seconds, the rocky slope above the mine avalanched down the hill-side, burying the mine portal under tons of rock and debris. Sealed and hidden, only the pitchblende remained at work, slowly decaying and emitting it's deadly radiation.

Significant events often begin modestly, and so it was with the great flood of 2003. The National Weather Service proclaimed the northern Cascade Range winter snowfall as an all-time record. Even grizzled high-country trappers said they could not recall, or even heard tell of, anything like the prodigious snow-pack now awaiting the spring thaw.

It began simply and gently. A warm zephyr followed by a drop in pressure caused the deer to snort and shake their heads. The rain began to fall, gently at first like a lover caressing a new partner; teasing, advancing, then climaxing in a torrent that consumed everything in its path.

The snow began to liquefy, first into rivulets like so many veins on the back of an old man's hand. Then coalescing into an arterial flow, swelling streams and drainages with a volume of water not seen since the retreat of the Quaternary ice. The deluge continued for days, funneling huge volumes of water, rock, and debris down canyons, reshaping the topography.

Montana Creek, now a raging torrent, began to eat away at the talus from the old landslide, rock and debris slipping inexorably into the muddy waters, no match for the abrasive mixture.

Great chunks of loose rock and soil broke away and disappeared into the morass. Little by little, a structure, not of nature but of man, began to emerge. Sections of square-cut timbers and pieces of worn steel rail were uncovered and pulled into the torrent.

As the flood waters exposed the Sullivan portal, dank, fetid air from the bowels of the mine rushed out. Hissing a warning to those who might seek her riches.

Chapter 1

Sitting with my feet propped up on my old cherry-wood desk, I was deep into re-reading a very hard-to-find copy of L. K. Hodges's *Mining in Eastern & Central Washington.* Written in 1897, it's arguably the best surviving record of mining in the late eighteen hundreds in this part of Washington State. And a book that never leaves my office.

I pulled out a pencil to make a few notes on old mines in the upper Methow River area. I'd just started to write when my desk phone rang. I jumped like a gut-shot bobcat. The pencil lead, leaving a check mark-looking thingamajig gashed across the paper in place of a word.

"Damnation." I muttered, picking up the phone. "Geology office, Trace Brandon speaking."

"Trace, Will Coffee here. Want to grab a beer at five?"

"You bet. Meet you at the First Inn?"

"See you there, amigo."

Will Coffee was a good friend and former classmate at Central Washington University in Ellensburg, Washington. He'd been a star center for the CWU Wildcats football team while pursuing his business degree. After graduation, Will had gone on to get his law degree from Gonzaga, in Spokane. He was a stand-up guy and handy in an altercation.

While Will had been completing his undergrad and law degrees, I had knocked out my BS and MS degrees in economic geology at good old CWU. I had moved away from E-Burg, as the alumni referred to Ellensburg, after completing my masters.

Will had done likewise after passing the Washington State bar exam. Both of us had wanted to polish off any rough edges with a bit of Fortune 500 experience. Will had snagged work in the legal and land departments of Cal-Tex Oil Company in Los Angeles, while I had honed my mineral exploration skills with Continental Minerals Corporation in Denver, Colorado.

About eight years in the corporate meat grinder had done the trick. Now in our early thirties, well-honed, and still single, we'd migrated back to E-Burg and hung out our respective shingles. I had rented a second-floor office in the old Phoenix Building on West Sixth Street. Built just before the great Ellensburg fire of 1889, the building had been resurrected from the ashes and restored. Hence, the name.

At five sharp, I was standing in front of the First Inn, a long time E-Burg watering hole favored by the students at CWU. And by a few of the locals who could put up with them.

"Hey, Trace, how's it hanging?" Will said, ambling down the sidewalk from his nearby law and abstract office.

His office location just up the block from the First Inn, wasn't a coincidence.

"Twitching and slightly to the left, pard," I replied, with a smile.

Will laughed and shook my hand. "Boy howdy, can you believe this June weather?" he asked, glancing around. "Kind of makes you forget about last winter, don't it?"

"Yep, you can't beat E-Burg in the summer and fall," I said, opening the bar door.

The barmaid, Tina Hart, a tall, busty red-head with killer green eyes, spotted me and Will coming through the door and threw us a quick wave. Tina and I maintained an ongoing, semi-serious relationship. Meaning we slept together whenever possible. She often told me I reminded her more of a cowboy than a rock hound. She said it helped make up for me being just shy of good-looking.

I returned the wave and held up two fingers. Tina nodded and went to the bar to get two bottles of Tumbleweed Ale, known to the male student body as simply . . . T and A. Our usual libation.

10

In a couple of minutes, Tina made her way through the happy hour crowd to our table.

"Lordy, Lordy, if it isn't Diamond Jim Brady and his trusted companion, Slick Willie," Tina said, with a chuckle, handing us our Ales.

"I God, but you're sassy, Tina," Will replied, doing his best Gus McCrae imitation.

"Sassy, but damned good-looking," I added, elbowing Will in the ribs.

"You know, Trace, for a guy with no money, you sure got a lot of style," Tina said, with a laugh, before turning to the next table of thirsty customers.

"Yes, ma'am," I called after her. "Thank you."

"So, podjo, what's shaking in the geology world?" Will asked.

I took a healthy pull of my ale and set the frosted mug on the table. "Well, since you brought it up, I have been doing some research on the old Winthrop mining district," I replied. "I think I'll head up that way in a couple of days and do a little prospecting."

"Got wind of something?" Will asked, a mischievous glint in his eye.

"Nothing specific, but after a flood like this spring's, a lot of fresh outcrop is exposed. You never know, a virgin vein might be sticking up shouting, 'Come and get me, come and get me!' " I said, with a laugh, thinking about Curly in *City Slickers II*. "Anyway, it's worth a look."

"Well, keep me posted if you find anything worth staking. We, down at Dewy, Cheetum, and Howe, are always available to handle any legal or title work."

"Roger that," I replied, clinking my beer mug against Will's.

A couple of days later, I packed up my 1976 Ford Bronco with maps, a GPS, a Brunton compass, clothes, boots, claim posts, the full-meal deal. My old Bronco looks a bit worn on the outside, but under the rough exterior she's pure *Thunder Road.* Sporting a high-performance, 302-cubic-inch engine coupled with a four-speed manual transmission and dual chrome exhaust pipes, she's my pride and joy, and a very fast mover.

From E-Burg, I headed up Highway 97 to Pateros, hung a left, and proceeded up Highway 153 along the Methow River. Just south of the town of Twisp, I picked up Highway 20 and rolled into Winthrop.

Too late to start any field-work, I checked into the Winthrop House, known locally simply as the W. The W would be my base camp for the next few days while I scouted out the area.

In my room, I spread topo and mineral management maps out on the bed and planned tomorrow's attack. The area I wanted to reconnoiter lay near the confluence of Montana and Goat Creeks. Historical mine production records from the area indicated good gold and copper values. One mine in particular caught my attention, the old Sullivan Mine.

Production from the Sullivan had ceased rather abruptly around 1893. This could simply be due to ore zones petering out. However, I had a hunch the culprit was the Panic of 1892.

Early the next morning, I gassed up, bought a pound of summer sausage, a six-pack of Tumbleweed, and a box of crackers, the basic field geologist's lunch; and headed out. Driving northwest along the Methow River on Highway 20, I turned off to the right on Goat Creek Road. I'd gone less than a quarter of a mile before the road got bad. I stopped, and locked the front hubs of the Bronco, and continued on in four-wheel drive. About two miles later, I hit the confluence of Montana Creek and Goat Creek. Pulling off the track, I parked and locked the Bronco, grabbed my backpack, and strapped on my Smith & Wesson .357 Magnum. I'd run into bears around here before. This time of year they could have cubs, and be damned dangerous. Backpack on, pistol loaded, I started up Montana Creek.

On the topo map, it looked to be about a mile to the old Sullivan Mine site. However, the spring mega-flood had pretty much destroyed the old mine road, slowing my progress to a snail's pace. After about two hours of working my way up the canyon, I looked up the steep slope to my left and could make out part of a mine entrance. I knew from Forest Service reports that the quake of 1946 had triggered a landslide, sealing the portal. It appeared the talus had been washed away when Montana Creek flooded.

Adrenaline now in overdrive, I worked my way up the slope until I stood at the mouth of the old mine. I took my flashlight, pointed it down the dark adit and thumbed the on button. The adit looked open as far back as my light could penetrate. It's always a strange feeling to light up old mine workings, and the Sullivan was no exception. I could feel goose bumps on my arms.

Normally, I won't go into an abandoned mine when I am working alone. It's just too damn dangerous. I could see the obituary now: Dumb Shit Enters Mine Alone. As usual, curiosity overruled common sense. I needed to see the rocks and hopefully grab a few samples from the lode vein.

I took off my red CWU baseball cap, and dug my hard hat, light, and battery pack out of my backpack. My army-surplus webbed pistol belt carried my Brunton compass, rock hammer, and pistol. I also had a small Geiger counter in my shirt pocket.

Geared up, I started into the mine adit. Most mines have a damp, earthy smell to them. Not this puppy. The Sullivan Mine flat-out stunk. A sickly-sweet smell of death and decay. As I moved cautiously deeper into the adit, I found skeletons of small dead animals I assumed had been trapped by the landslide.

All geologists and miners have a sixth sense about danger, and right now my sensor was in the red. I couldn't put my finger on it, but there was something wrong with this mine. At a bend in the adit, I saw a small alcove and what looked like a bunch of very old sample bags. Kneeling down, I looked at the tags on several of the bags. They appeared to be vein chip samples. The writing by now was too faded to make out the exact sample locations.

Opening one of the bags, I removed several of the larger rock chip samples. Even with my head lamp it was still too dark to identify all the ore minerals. However, I could make out copper oxides, pyrites, and a dark-gray mineral with a dull pitchy luster. The sample felt quite heavy for its size. On a hunch, I pulled out my pocket Geiger counter and held it to the sample. The sample pegged the first couple of scales, each scale being ten times stronger. I went to higher and higher scales until I finally got a reading. Twenty-thousand counts per second. Very, very, hot rock. I re-bagged the rock chips and grabbed a couple of the old cloth sample bags and shoved them in my backpack.

The mine floor was covered with an inch or two of water from seepage. Moving down the adit, I kind of shuffled along. The roof of the working was clean, and I could pretty well make out the vein structure and geology. The pay zone appeared to be a big quartz vein sandwiched between a granodiorite, a type of granite, and schist.

I pulled out my Brunton compass and took a bearing down the strike of the vein. Two hundred eighty degrees to the northwest. I followed the overhead vein, taking Geiger readings and knocking off and bagging fresh samples. I was already spending the money when the floor disappeared from under my feet, and I was underwater.

I immediately knew two things. The first being, that I had stepped into a flooded vertical winze, a shaft connecting one or more mine levels. And secondly, I could be in serious trouble.

Bobbing back to the surface, I managing to hang onto my hard hat and compass. Drown if I must, but no way in hell was I losing my antique solid-brass Brunton. Treading water, I pocketed my compass and adjusted my hard hat and light and looked around. I'd stepped off into a winze all right. Walked right into it like a first-semester geology student. I'd made a classic amateur mistake of not cutting a walking stick to probe for holes as I be-bopped down the mine . . . un-damned believable.

There was only one choice. Pull myself out. I kicked my way to the edge of the winze but couldn't quite get a hold with my fingers. My main malfunction was all the weight I was carrying. The damned samples in my backpack were threatening to pull me under. One thing about uranium; it's a seriously heavy mineral.

I managed to shrug out of my backpack. Kicking as hard as I could to stay afloat, I shot-putted my pack to solid ground on the portal side of the adit. I could stay afloat now, but needed to find a place to crawl out. The water smelled like dead rats and was cold as ice.

Now in full-blown survival mode with Mr. Hypothermia tapping me on the shoulder, I worked my way into a corner of the winze, where I could get some leverage with my steel-toed boots. Using my rock hammer like an ice pick and jamming my toes into any purchase, I managed to pull and crawl my way out.

My ascent from the abyss probably wouldn't have made the next issue of *Rock Climber,* but I made it out. Cold and smelling like week-old kitty litter, I grabbed my pack and headed, a bit more cautiously, back to the portal.

Clearing the portal, I went straight to Montana Creek and cleaned up as best I could. I draped my clothes over huckleberry bushes and laid out my gear and myself over several large, flat, sun-warmed boulders.

I'd nearly drowned in some damned stinking mine, and now, lying bare-assed in the sun, my mind started drifting back to my last date with Tina. Jesus, I thought, guys really are hopeless.

After a nap, I put my mostly dry clothes back on and rounded up my gear. I was anxious to see how the samples looked in sunlight. I opened a couple of sample bags and examined several of the larger rock chips with my ten-power hand lens. I confirmed the presence of chalcopyrite, a copper sulfide, secondary copper minerals, pyrite, and a ton of pitchblende.

Holy moly . . . this could be good, I thought as I bagged up the samples.

Chapter 2

I hardly remember the walk back down to the Bronco. All I could think about was the rich uranium ore. I pulled my cell phone out of the glove box and checked the signal. Barely two bars. I dialed Will's cell phone and managed to get through.

"Will, Trace, here. Are you where you can talk?"

"Affirmative, old man, what's up?"

"I may have found the mother lode, Will. I am going to give you some township and range information. Can you get on the Bureau of Land Management's website and check for current claims?"

"Can do, amigo. Fire when ready."

"Okay, sections sixteen and twenty-one, Township thirty-six north, Range twenty east. Got that?"

"Got it."

"Second thing, Will. Call the county clerk at the Okanogan County courthouse and have them run a claim search on any claims filed in the last ninety days in the sections I just gave you. Also, we need to see if there are any patented claims in those sections."

"Can I get in on this, Trace?"

"You're already in, pard. Just call me back when you have any claim information."

"On it, and thanks, Trace."

Back at the W, I started formulating a claim-staking program. This would have to be kept very, very, quiet. There's no shortage of slimeballs and crooks in the mining game.

I plotted the bearing of the vein and figured about three claims in width and ten claims in length should cover the vein structure. Each lode claim is allowed to be a maximum of fifteen hundred feet in length by six hundred feet wide, equaling a little over 20 acres. In total, I was looking at staking about 619 acres, just less than a full section.

Rather than stake the claims myself, I wanted a registered surveyor to do the job. And I knew just the fellow, Ken Hodges. Ken's office was in Chelan, Washington, only a couple of hours from the Sullivan Mine. We'd worked together on a number of claim-staking projects in the past. He ran a first-class operation and documented everything, including photographing the front page of a local newspaper alongside each location monument. So, there'd be no doubt as to when the monument was staked. Ken also used state of the art GPS equipment and could tie each location monument and claim stake to within about two centimeters.

As an independent third party, Ken would be able to testify to the validity of my claims, should the need arise. I knew of a number of low-life scum suckers who routinely over-staked new claims. They hoped for an out-of-court cash settlement, or, even better, a court-appointed fractional claim interest.

One of the worst bottom dwellers, Cyrus 'the Virus' McSweeny, immediately came to mind. The Virus operated out of Spokane under the name of Columbia Resources, LLC. It was rumored he also owned interests in offshore holding companies.

Cyrus's resume was colorful, to say the least. He wrote the book on pump-and-dump stock scams. And he'd been accused, more than once, of *naked* short selling, selling shares he didn't own, via his offshore accounts. His favorite scam, however, remained over-staking newly staked mining claims.

Always on various agencies radars, his only pinch, so far, was for income tax evasion. The judge gave him five years at the federal pen, in Sheridan, Oregon.

The Virus could smell a new mineral discovery. I figured it was just a matter of time.

Will called back just before I headed down to the W's dining room for a celebratory steak and a good bottle of Washington State wine.

"Howdy, Will. What did you find?"

"Good news, Trace. No current claims in sections sixteen or twenty-one. Sullivan Mining Company staked most of both sections in the late eighteen hundreds, but those claims are all long since closed. No patented ground, either. You're good to go."

"Great news, Will. I'm going to call Ken Hodges in the morning and get him and his crew up here ASAP."

"Good plan, Trace. Listen, if you need me to come up, just give me a holler."

"Okay, Will, and thanks."

The next morning I called Ken's office in Chelan and filled him in on my staking program. I told him I needed the staking done as quickly and quietly as possible, with a maximum of documentation.

"Expecting problems, Trace?"

"Could be, Ken. I always worry about some jerk over-staking me and claiming he was there first."

"Cyrus the Virus?"

"He's on the top of the list."

"Don't worry, Trace. By the time my crew is done staking, we'll have the claims documented to where they'll stand up in any court."

"Perfect. When can you start?"

"Send me the proposed claim locations and give me a few days to get all the location forms and claim tags prepared. Today is Wednesday. How does this coming Monday sound?"

"Sounds good. I'll head back to my office today and e-mail you the claim data. It will also give me a chance to send some samples off to the lab for assays."

"Okay, see you on Monday, Trace.

The next morning I was back in my office, e-mailing Ken the claim data. I picked up the phone and called Will.

"Will, it's Trace. Can you come over for a couple minutes?"

"I can be there in about fifteen minutes. What's up?"

"I want to show you some samples I grabbed at the Sullivan."

While I waited for Will, I split the samples from each bag into two equal parts. One for the lab to assay, and one for safe keeping.

In about fifteen minutes, there was a knock on my door, and Will stepped into my office.

"Take a look at these, Will."

"Holy crap, they look like pure sulfides . . . and man, are they heavy."

"Right on both counts, amigo. According to the old production reports, the Sullivan ran about three-quarters of an ounce gold with about one and a half percent copper."

"What's the kind of pitchy-looking black mineral?"

"That, my friend, is why the samples are so heavy. It's pitchblende uranium."

"Damn, are they hot?"

"About off scale. Best I've ever seen."

Will quickly put the samples down on my desk and wiped his hands on his trousers. "Hmmm, very interesting," Will said, looking at his hands. "I've been reading commodities reports predicting uranium may take off again."

"Yeah, it looks like the beginning of a new cycle. Since Three Mile Island, the price of uranium has been in the crapper. But with all the new reactors forecast to come on-line, the commodity traders are back in the uranium market."

"A perfect time to bring a new uranium deposit on-line."

"Exactly so, pard."

"So, what's the plan?"

"The plan is to meet Ken Hodges and his survey crew on Monday in Winthrop. His crew will get all the claim location monuments staked. And I'll file the location notices at the Okanogan County courthouse. Once we do that, the claims are valid. We'll have thirty days after we file to get the corner posts in."

"Sounds good. So what can I do to participate in this fine new venture?"

"You start looking for a clean Vancouver, B.C., public shell. If this thing pans out like I think it will, I want to vend the claims into a public Canadian company. We'll start trading on the Vancouver Stock Exchange, and raise some serious developmental capital."

Will nodded. "I have an attorney buddy named Wally Wilkins. We went to law school together, and he lives and offices in Vancouver. He does mergers, acquisitions, and securities law. And he always knows of a few good shell companies."

"I'll get you a nice block of shares for your time, and the new company will reimburse your expenses."

"Perfect. Thanks, Trace."

"Hey, that's what friends are for. And you never know. We may need a tough, ex-football player turned lawyer, if we run into any trouble."

"Cyrus?"

"Damn, you're the second guy in two days to mention the Virus."

"Yeah, well, he's always out there, and if he gets wind of a new find, he could be trouble."

"Agreed."

After my meeting with Will, I sent the split rock-chip samples to a lab in Silver Valley, Idaho. I purposely avoided any local labs. If the assays were as good as I expected, I didn't want the Virus alerted.

I drove back to Winthrop on Sunday and checked in to the W. The next morning I was having coffee in the hotel restaurant, when Ken Hodges walked in.

"Hey, Trace, good to see you again."

"Howdy, Ken. Have a seat."

Ken was in his forties, dark haired and stout from years of field work. We both ordered steak and eggs, and got down to business.

"I've got all the claims plotted, including lat-long co-ordinates. We'll be able to put the location monuments and corners in by GPS," Ken said, handing me a spreadsheet.

"Perfect. I want to get all the location monuments in as fast as possible."

"We'll get them all in today. All the claim location notices are signed by me as Agent for Reserve E&P, LLC, as you instructed. Everything is ready to record with the Okanogan County clerk."

Reserve E&P, LLC was a Nevada corporation I'd set up for claim-staking projects.

"Good job, Ken. Let me have the location notices after we finish eating. I'll drive up to Okanogan and get them filed today."

"Okay. Once the monuments are in the ground, the claims are valid. We'll finish staking the corners in a couple of days."

After breakfast Ken and his crew headed up to the Sullivan Mine. I jumped in my Bronco and headed to the County Courthouse in Okanogan.

After a long day, Ken and I met for supper at the W.

"How'd it go today, Ken?"

"No problems. The terrain is pretty steep, but thirty claims are not much for my crew. All the location monuments are in, and even some of the corners. We'll knock it out tomorrow."

"Perfect. I filed all the notices with the county clerk and will send copies of the stamped, recorded, notices to the Bureau of Land Management, in a few days."

"When the claims get posted on the BLM website, the Virus will likely see them," Ken said. "I hear he has a file clerk doing nothing but looking for recent claim activity. I also hear she's damned good-looking."

I laughed. "Well, good-looking or not, they'll have a tough time messing with our claims."

Chapter 3

It had been a couple of weeks since I'd filed the claims with the Bureau of Land Management. The claims were now readily visible to anyone researching the BLM's website.

I'd just gotten to my office when the phone rang.

"Geology office. Trace Brandon, speaking."

"Mr. Brandon, Cyrus McSweeny here."

Jesus, that didn't take long, I thought. "Yes, sir, Mr. McSweeny, what can I do for you?"

"Have we met, Trace?"

"No sir, not officially. But some of my clients have, well, become acquainted with you."

"That's one way to say it. Listen, Trace, I see where your LLC has staked some claims around the old Sullivan Mine."

"Yes, that's correct."

"I thought the mine was closed by a big landslide in the forties?"

"She was, but this spring's flood exposed the mine portal."

"I see. Were you able to get in the old workings and grab some samples?"

"Yes, I poked around a bit and collected a few samples."

"If you don't mind me asking, since you have it pretty well tied up, how's it look?"

"Well, I could only sample the first level. The second level is flooded."

"Are you sure about water in the second level?"

"Yep, pretty sure," I replied, thinking back to my full gainer into the flooded winze.

"Well, how did level one look to you?"

22

"Good enough to plan some core drilling."

"I see. Would you be interested in a partner? I have pretty deep pockets, Trace. I could help defray a lot of the exploration expenses, in return for an interest in the claims."

"I appreciate the offer Mr. McSweeny, but I think I can handle the initial exploration costs."

"Well, what about beyond that? No offense, but I'd be surprised if you have the financial wherewithal to bring a mine into production."

"Probably not. But if the lode grades out, I'll have several financing options."

"Reverse merger with a public shell, eh?"

Damn this guy doesn't miss a thing, I thought to myself. "Well, it's one option."

"The public market can be a damned rough place, Trace, if you don't know what you're doing."

"I'll keep that in mind, sir. Fortunately, I have a damned good attorney to keep me out of harm's way."

"Yeah, well, you'll probably need him. Good talking to you, Trace. I'll be seeing you."

Not if I see you first, I thought, as I hung up.

After his call to Trace, Cyrus made a second call to his right-hand man, Bill Thornton. Thornton, or Thorny as Cyrus called him, was built like a fireplug. Bald with a salt-and-pepper goatee, he stood five feet eight and weighed two hundred pounds. Thorny reminded people of a bulked-up Yul Brynner. Like Cyrus, he'd worked and fought his way out of the mines. He was smart and tough as nails.

"Thorny, it's Cyrus."

"Hey, Cyrus, what can I do for you this fine morning?"

"I want you to find out everything you can on some new claims staked in sections sixteen and twenty-one, Township thirty-six north, Range twenty east. Look for the REP claims, number one through thirty. The locator is Reserve E&P, LLC. I want to know who did the staking and if they're duly recorded in Okanogan County."

"Yes, sir. Standard routine?"

"Yeah, standard routine. If they missed any steps in locating or filing these claims, they may have a new partner. Get back to me as soon as you can, Thorny."

"You got it, boss."

After my conversation with Cyrus, I called Will to fill him in.

"You'll never guess who just called me."

"The Virus?"

"Good guess."

"What'd the jerk want?"

"He said he saw our new claims posted on the BLM website and tried to pump me for information. Hell, he even offered to partner up."

"Holy crap, the guy is friggin' unbelievable."

"I told him we didn't need a partner at this stage, and he immediately guessed we were looking to do a reverse merger with a public shell company."

"He's a bottom-feeder, Trace, but he's nobody's fool. Don't underestimate the bastard."

"Don't worry, I won't. But he'll have a tough time over-staking us. Ken documented and photographed everything, every monument, every corner. I have hard copies and computer files, as does Ken. Cyrus is going to run into a dead end if he tries to mess with our claims."

"Agreed, but he may try another tack."

"Same thought crossed my mind, amigo. In any case, I think you and I should head up to Winthrop on Wednesday. I want to hire a dozer crew to repair the old mine road and put in three drill pads. I could use your help on the permit side with the Forest Service."

"Sounds good. I would love to get out of the office for a little road trip."

"We can get some work started, and we'll be able to keep an eye on the claims. Also, as a precaution, I am going to call Henry Orvis, the Okanogan County sheriff, and give him a heads-up about possible trouble with the Virus."

"Do you have a good relationship with the sheriff?"

"Yeah, pretty good. He's a cousin, on my dad's side."

Will laughed. "Pretty handy. Got any other surprises up your sleeve?"

"Maybe one or two. We'll have to see how this plays out."

After Will and I finished, I called Robert Malott, owner of Chewak Construction Company in Winthrop.

"Bobby, Trace Brandon, down in Ellensburg."

"Yeah, Trace, long-time no hear."

"Yep, last time was when you put in some drill pads for me on the Boulder Creek project."

"I remember, Trace. So, what can I do for you today?"

"I need to reopen the old Sullivan Mine road, from Highway 20, up Goat Creek, to the confluence of Montana Creek. Then about a mile up Montana Creek to the Sullivan Mine. And I need three drill pads built."

"I'm familiar with the Sullivan, Trace. You have claims in there?"

"Just staked and filed thirty."

"Who did the staking?"

"Ken Hodges and Associates, out of Chelan."

"I know Ken. He's one of the best."

"I'll send you maps and a plan of operation. Can you take a look and give me a proposal?"

"I'll need to get on-site and see what we're looking at, work-wise."

"Okay, Bob, today is Monday. How about we meet at your office on Wednesday, and I'll give you the grand tour. I'll bring Will Coffee with me to do the permitting. Do you remember Will?"

"Ugly as sin, broken-down ex-center for Central, turned law dog?" Bob replied, with a snicker.

I laughed. "Yeah, Bobby, the same center who's team beat your team's sorry ass four years running."

"Okay, bring him if you must," Bobby replied, with a chuckle. "I guess I can put up with him for a day or two."

"Thanks, Bob. See you at your yard on Wednesday."

*****

Will and I rolled into Winthrop about ten Wednesday morning. We met Bobby at his office and then headed out to the claims, dropping Will off at the Forest Service office.

Bobby and I drove up the rough road along Goat Creek, stopping where I had parked the previous trip. Getting out of the Bronco, I noticed beer cans and sandwich wrappers on the ground.

"Damn, somebody has been here since my last visit," I said, pointing to the beer cans.

"You'd think they could pick up their damn trash," Bob replied, shaking his head in disgust.

"Tell you what, Bob, I think we'd better check some of our location monuments to be sure no one's messing with our claims."

"Expecting some kind of trouble, Trace?"

"Do you know who Cyrus McSweeny is?"

"Oh, yeah, I know the Virus."

"Well, he called me the other day, pumping me for information. He said he'd be seeing me."

"I noticed you're carrying a shooter."

"Yep, .357 Smith & Wesson," I said, patting my holster, "loaded with 230-grain hollow points."

"Good. Keep it with you when you're up here, especially if you're up here alone."

"Jesus, is Cyrus that dangerous?"

"In his line of work, he's the top of the food chain. Miners I've worked with say he'll take down or move claim stakes and pay off clerks in the courthouse to pre-date his location notices. Hell, he's the full-meal deal of trouble. Don't underestimate him, or his drones."

"Don't worry, pard. I won't."

When we got to the mine, I showed Bobby where I needed the drill pads built. I left him to map out his work plan while I checked the location monuments. I walked down each of the claims, checking the latitude and longitude of each monument with my GPS. All the claim stakes were up and matched the original coordinates.

Returning to the mine, I dug my hardhat and mine light from my backpack. Looking around, I found a sapling and cut a stout walking stick. One mine swim per year is my limit.

Slowly, I began working my way down the adit. It didn't take long to find what I was looking for: a number of fresh gashes in the roof of the adit. Someone had cut several samples from the exposed vein. It wasn't too difficult to guess who. I just hoped Cyrus's man had sampled far enough down the adit to step off into the winze.

On the trip back to Winthrop, I didn't mention what I'd found to Bobby. He had his hands full building the access road and drill pads. I dropped him at his yard, and he promised to have some costs to me in a couple of days.

I met up with Will back at the W.

"How did it go at the mine?" Will asked.

"Bobby got a good look at the work and will have a proposal for us in a couple of days."

"Everything copacetic at the mine?"

"We've had company, Will."

"The Virus?"

"Got to be. Someone's been in the adit. I could see fresh chisel marks where they took samples. Once Cyrus gets the assays back, he'll know uranium is the play."

"Do you think he is going to try something with the claims?"

"I don't think so. The claims are legally located and filed and now in the BLM system. When he finds out Ken did the staking, he'll probably drop that idea. My guess is he'll come at us some other way. Maybe after we're public. He could buy up a large block of shares and demand a seat on our board. Or he could just short the shit out of our stock. In any case, we're going to have to be very, very, careful going forward."

Back in my office the following Monday, Will and I had a conference call with Will's attorney buddy, Walter Wilkins. Wally told us he had a suitable shell company. We agreed to meet in Vancouver just prior to a special shareholders' meeting Wally would call. The shareholders of the shell company would vote to approve vending my claims into the shell company. In return for the claims, I would receive a controlling share position. The process was commonly referred to as a reverse merger.

Will, Walter, and I would be elected directors of the company. As directors, we would appoint the officers of the corporation. I would serve as chairman and CEO, Will as secretary and treasurer. The name of the company would be changed to Montana Creek Mining Corporation. The new trading symbol on the Vancouver Stock Exchange would be MCM.V.

Chapter 4

Cyrus McSweeny's Spokane office was on the sixth floor of the old Inland Empire Building. Built in 1900, it remained one of Spokane's historical architectural treasures.

Cyrus's office was plush, with lots of wood and leather furniture. Photos of various mining operations covered the walls. The only things lacking were diplomas. Like his pal, Thorny, Cyrus had come up the hard way, from working in the mines to investing and promoting penny mining stocks. He was street smart and not afraid to bend or break a few laws. And along the way, he'd made millions.

Now in his early sixties, he was six feet tall, ramrod straight, lean and wiry with a shock of unruly white hair. His cobalt-blue eyes would have made Paul Newman envious. Women still sought his company, and he could still appreciate them.

This particular morning, he was working at his gold-inlayed mahogany desk when his cell phone rang.

"Cyrus, it's Thorny. Got a sec?"

"Sure thing, Thorny, I'm just sitting here looking at some commodity charts."

"Well, this may give you another chart to review. The samples I grabbed from the Sullivan came back, and I have the information you wanted on the those mining claims."

"What did you turn up?"

"On the claim status side, they're tight as a sixteen-year-old virgin. Ken Hodges & Associates over in Chelan did the staking. He's not the expert witness you'd want on the stand. The SOB has never had a claim overturned."

"Okay, so over-staking is out. How about the assays?"

"Gold and copper in line with reported assays back when the mine was in production. Those values alone will make a mine with today's gold and copper prices.

"Anything else?"

"Well, yes. The damned vein carries a lot of uranium. The assays all ran eight to ten percent."

"Uranium, eh? Now I see young master Brandon's interest."

"Uranium's been in the tank since Three Mile Island blew up. Do you think it will come back?"

"Already coming back, Thorny. All the reports indicate utilities are quietly buying up available stockpiles, and looking for more. Price is beginning to trend northward again."

Cyrus paused, drumming the fingers of his left hand on the desk-top.

"Listen, Thorny, I may have underestimated our young geologist friend, just a tad. Get with your contacts in Vancouver and see who's snooping around for a decent shell company. He's going to have to go public to raise enough dough to get rolling."

"Will do, sir. I'll be back to you when I have something."

Cyrus knew a grade of 8 to 10 percent uranium, with any kind of reserves, would put the Sullivan Mine in rarefied air, right up there with the big dogs like Cameco and Rio Tinto.

Will and I drove to Spokane and caught a commuter flight to Vancouver. We met up with Walter Wilkins at the Harbor View Inn, in downtown Vancouver.

"There he is," Will said, waving to catch Wilkins's attention.

Wally waved back and joined us near the hotel's front entrance.

"Hi, fellows. Good flight?" Wally asked.

"Yeah, smooth as a bar-maid's butt," Will replied. "Wally, this is Trace Brandon, my client, partner, and friend."

"Trace, really good to meet you. Will, here, has told me a lot about you," Wally said, extending his hand.

"Walter, good to meet you too, and don't put too much credence in what Will told you about me," I said, with a laugh.

"Call me Wally, Trace. All my mates do. And don't worry. I take all Will's fabrications with a grain of salt."

We grabbed a quiet corner table in the bar, ordered some beers and got down to business.

"So, Wally, you've located a good vehicle to merge with?" I asked.

"Yes, I have. The company is a British Columbia numbered company, incorporated specifically for a reverse merger. One of my associates, Richard Rosenburg, and I control one hundred percent of the five million founder's shares. There's an additional million shares on the street held by investors who bought the initial public offering. Richard and I will give up eighty percent of our shares in return for your vending in all the Sullivan Mine claims."

"So, we'll have about seventy percent control?" I asked, to confirm.

"Correct, Trace. You'll get four million founder's shares. Richard and I will keep one million shares, half a million each. And there will be one million shares of free trade in the float. So a total of six million issued and outstanding."

"What about any funds from the IPO?" Will asked.

"The IPO went out at five cents per share. Netted about forty-five grand, after expenses. Most of the balance has been used to pay small management fees, accounting, legal, filing fees, et cetera, to keep the company current and in good standing. There's thirty-five hundred in the company checking account that will transfer," Wally answered.

I nodded. "What do you think, Will?"

"It's about as tight as you can get and still be a publicly traded entity. It leaves little room for others to gain a significant position."

"True, unless they are able to acquire a significant percentage of the thirty-plus percent we won't control."

"True enough, Trace, but it would take a pretty shrewd trader to do that," Wally replied.

I looked over at Will.

Wally saw the look of concern in my and Will's eyes.

"Is there someone you're specifically worried about?"

"We'll, there is one guy," Will replied. "You may have heard of him. Cyrus McSweeny."

Wally set his beer mug back on the table. "The Virus is interested in your deal?"

"Well, he called me," I replied, "and pumped me for information, even offered to be our partner."

"I see," Wally replied. "Cyrus is well-known on the street up here. And he can play pretty rough. We'll need be very careful not to leave him any openings."

"Agreed and understood," I replied. "But, first things first. We need to get through the special shareholders' meeting and complete the merger. Remember, there's no serum once you're infected by the Virus." I added, with a laugh.

We held the special shareholders' meeting later in the week in Vancouver. All the items on the agenda passed. Montana Creek Mining Corporation was in business.

Wally would start preparing private-placement documents, allowing the company to sell shares to the public in British Columbia, Canada. The company's treasury would issue the shares. Sale of the shares would dilute our control position, but bring in the capital needed to start developing the Sullivan Mine.

It took Bill Thornton about a week to put it all together. He called Cyrus and scheduled a meeting at Cyrus's Spokane office.

"Okay, boss, here's the lowdown. Brandon and his lawyer buddy, Will Coffee, were in Vancouver about a week ago. The Vancouver Securities Exchange filings show they held a special shareholders' meeting and merged their claims into a numbered B.C. shell corp. Looks like they walked away with about seventy percent control. The two founders of the shell company kept five hundred thousand shares each. And there's a million shares in the float. The numbered company was renamed, Montana Creek Mining Corporation."

"Damned fine work, Thorny. I think you'll find a little bonus in this month's check."

"Thanks, Cyrus."

"Who were the original founding shareholders?"

"Walter Wilkins, a Vancouver attorney, who remained a director. And a Vancouver promoter named Richard Rosenburg."

Cyrus rubbed his chin for a couple of seconds. "Okay, Thorny, find out all you can about Rosenburg. He may have some weakness we can exploit. I know this Wilkins character. He's tough, clean, and righteous. No . . . we'll concentrate on trying to acquire Rosenburg's shares.

"We'll need a Canadian entity," Thorny said. "Shares in the private placement will only be available to British Columbia residents, or BC corporations."

"Okay, when Montana Creek Mining's private placement comes out, we buy all the shares we can get through Twisp River Resources. Twisp is a private company, domiciled in BC. I own it one hundred percent though my Cayman holding company, Carib International."

"Perfect, boss."

"Yeah, it's a start. Also, I'll have Twisp River start buying shares in the open market. Not enough to draw attention, just steady buy orders. We'll see how much cheap free trade we can accumulate."

Back in E-Burg, I went to work preparing a three-hole coring program. Wally made it clear we needed some good core assay results to present to investors before we could do a successful private placement. In the interim, the three of us would have to loan the company the money to complete at least the first core hole.

Bob Malott's proposal for building the drill locations and road repair arrived while I was in Vancouver. The drilling locations were one thousand feet apart. If we intersected good ore values, I could extrapolate some inferred reserves. It would be enough to interest the penny stock mine crowd in Vancouver.

*****

I'd been so busy with the claims and merger that I hadn't had any time for Tina. Now, with a few days to kill while Bob's crew completed the mine road and drill pads, I called her.

"Hey, kiddo," I said, when Tina answered the phone, "sorry I've been out of town so much. But getting this mining deal put together turned into quite a chore."

"Uh-huh," Tina replied, coolly. "Are you sure you haven't taken up with another woman?"

Uh-oh, I could be in serious trouble, I thought to myself. "No, nothing like that, Tina. I've been up at the mine most of the time," I said, grasping for traction. "Look, let me make it up to you. How about supper at the Cold Creek Inn?" The quaint little restaurant was located on the outskirts of Ellensburg, on the east bank of the Yakima River, and was her favorite.

"Well, seeing as how I am hungry, and horny, I guess I'll let you off the hook, this time. Pick me up at seven. And you'd better not be late, cowboy."

At seven, straight up, I knocked on her apartment door. Tina opened the door and glanced at her watch. She was wearing tight Wrangler jeans, cowboy boots, and a white blouse with pearl buttons. She looked better than a high-grade assay.

"Damn good timing, Trace," she said, with a husky laugh.

Hot damn, I might be back in the saddle. "Yes, ma'am. Nineteen hundred hours, as requested," I said, with a smile. "And I am at your disposal for the rest of the evening."

"You'd damn well better be," Tina replied, hooking her arm through mine. "To the Inn, and don't spare the horses."

"There's three hundred of them under the hood," I said, as I opened the passenger door of my Bronco. "Just remember to buckle up."

As advertised, the Inn delivered a fabulous meal of Black Angus rib eyes, house salads, baked potatoes, and two bottles of a very limited vintage, commemorative, Central Washington University Cabernet. I found this particular cabernet had a soothing effect on the female spirit. Too bad there were very few bottles of the vintage remaining.

After supper we went back to my place just outside of town. I keep a thirty-one-foot Airstream in an RV park along the Yakima River. The RV park has water, septic, and power, all the comforts of home. Plus, the romantic sound of the Yakima River rushing by.

I don't know if it was the rushing river, the commemorative cabernet, or the RV park ambiance, but something worked. We were kicking our clothes off as we climbed into the Airstream. Horny was the right word. Tina led me, and my erection down the hallway to my queen-sized bed. She pushed me down on the bed, straddled my thighs, and guided me home. It would be a horse race to see who came in first.

I placed, but could barely walk the next morning.

Chapter 5

Bob Malott called and said the mine roads and drill pads were ready to go. After Bob and I were done, I called Chris Blackstone with Blackstone Drilling Company in Oroville, Washington.

"Red, it's Trace Brandon, down in Ellensburg."

Everybody called Chris "Red" because he had a Garfunkel-looking mess of bright-red hair. Fortunately, he also had a sense of humor. A good thing, as he was a big son of a bitch with no neck, a prominent chin, and Popeye forearms.

"Hey, Trace, it's been awhile. What can I do you for?"

"I need to drill three NQ-sized core holes, Red. Angled at forty-five degrees. Total depths will be around four hundred feet. Bob Malott has finished the access roads and pads, and we're ready to turn to the right."

"Sounds good, Trace. Send me a location map, and I'll get a proposal down to you."

"Have you got a rig available?"

"I do. It's a tracked rig. Can go anywhere and makes hole like a two-dollar whore."

I laughed. "Jesus, Red, that's awful."

"Ain't it though," Red replied, with a snort. "All kidding aside, Trace, she's a hole-making son of a bitch."

"Okay, Red, sounds like what I need. One more thing, Red. I need damned good core recovery. So take it slow and easy, and let's try for one hundred percent recovery."

"Not a problem, Trace. We'll do a first-class job."

I sent Red the information he needed and dialed up a conference call with Will and Wally.

"Are you fellows both on?" I asked.

"Will, here."

"Wally, here."

"Good. Okay, fellows, I'm getting a drilling proposal for three core holes. I'll do some calculations and figure about how deep we should intersect the vein. We'll drill using a down-hole hammer to just above the vein. And then we'll start coring."

Wally and Will both agreed.

"As soon as we get enough core assays back from the lab, I'll put together a PowerPoint presentation. Wally, I'll leave it to you to set up meetings with investors and brokers in Vancouver."

"Sounds good, Trace," Wally replied.

Will concurred. "I sure hope the assays are good."

"They will be, pardner," I replied. "We'll be drilling right through the guts of the vein."

"Heard anything more from Cyrus?" Wally asked.

"Nada, fellows. But I know he's out there. It's like an itch I can't scratch."

A couple of days later, I got Red's drilling proposal. The costs were okay, so I signed on the dotted line and faxed a copy of the contract back to him.

Bill Thornton looked at the copies of Forest Service drilling permits and called Cyrus.

"Cyrus, Thorny here. Thought you might want to know. Brandon got drilling permits for three core holes. Blackstone Drilling has a rig on the way."

"Interesting. They haven't done a private stock placement yet, so, they're operating out of good old Hip National. They'll need the core assays to convince investors to buy shares in their private placement. Maybe we should throw a little monkey wrench into their plans."

Chapter 6

I met Red just off Highway 20, at the intersection with Goat Creek Road. He and his crew managed to get the tracked drilling rig and compressor up to the Sullivan Mine and set up on drill hole number one.

Red would use an air-powered, down-hole hammer bit to drill down to just above the vein. At that point, he'd pull out of the hole and rig up the core barrel. We'd cut five-foot cores until we were completely through the vein zone and into footwall schist.

Red maneuvered the drill rig until it was lined up on a 190 degree bearing. This put the drill hole perpendicular to the 280 degree bearing of the vein. Next he locked the rig's mast at a forty-five-degree angle. We would drill all three holes on the same bearing and angle. The vein appeared to be very steeply dipping to near vertical, and we would be coring through it at a forty-five-degree angle. In order to get the true vein thickness, I'd have to do a little trigonometry.

It was nearly six in the afternoon before Red got everything set up.

"Okay, Trace," Red said, looking down at his compass, "she's dead on one-ninety degrees, and the mast is angled exactly forty-five. The night shift will be here shortly, and we'll fire her up and start making some hole."

"Good work, Red," I replied. "Grab a chip sample every five feet. We'll start pulling core at about three hundred feet."

"Sounds good, Trace. You'll be here to start the coring, right?"

"Yes, sir."

Red nodded, but was looking over my head to a point up the mountain.

"Don't turn just yet, Trace. Wait a sec and then look about half-way up the mountain behind you. We're being glassed."

I paused a couple of seconds, did a half-turn and bent down as if tying my boot. Looking up, I saw the sun reflect off glass.

"Got to be binoculars," I said, standing and turning back to Red.

"Huckleberry pickers?" Red said, with a grin.

"Ah . . . I doubt it. I think we may have caught the interest of an old-time mining promoter. Could be one of his drones."

"Anybody I know?"

"Ever hear of Cyrus McSweeny?"

"Everybody in mining knows that slimy so-and-so. I thought he was in prison for tax evasion."

"He was. Did five years and been out a couple."

"Did it temper the old bastard?"

"Not noticeably."

"Okay, so how do you want to play it?"

"Well, with us drilling twenty-four-seven, it will be hard for anybody to stir up much of a fuss. Main thing is securing the core. I've rented a building from Bobby Malott down in Winthrop. We'll split, store, and ship core samples from there. I'll talk to Bob about security at his yard."

"We could be vulnerable when we move the core boxes from here to yard," Red added.

"Good point, Red. I'll transport the cores myself, when I'm here. Otherwise, haul it to Bob's yard with the crew change. I'll call the county sheriff, Henry Orvis, he's my cousin, and tell him what's going on. Maybe he'll run a deputy up here once in a while. Kind of show the badge."

Red nodded in agreement. "For extra security, I'll send Luke Johnson, one of my hands, with you when you're transporting cores. He don't bathe too regular, and he chews old stogies like they was chewing tobacco. But in a fight, he's as mean and nasty as they come."

"Perfect," I said, with a chuckle. "Plus, I'll have Mr. Smith and Mr. Wesson riding with me at all times. I'll see you in the morning."

*****

On my way back to Winthrop, I put in a call to the sheriff's office in Okanogan.

"Sheriff's office, Deputy Haines speaking."

"Deputy Haines, this is Trace Brandon. Is the sheriff around?"

"Yeah, Trace. Hang on and I'll get him."

Cousin Henry Orvis had been sheriff of Okanogan County for about eighteen years, and had always been re-elected by a large margin. Now in his fifties, he had the Orvis side of the family: dark complexion and jet-black hair. Henry was about six feet tall, thin, and wiry with a bushy mustache. He looked a hell of a lot like the actor, Sam Elliott, and he was a dead shot.

"Hey, Trace," Henry said. "Long time no see."

"Yes, sir. How's the sheriffin' business?"

"Never a dull moment. Hell, last week a couple of cowboys got drunke'd up and tried to re-enact the old Omak Stampede Suicide Race. Mashed-hat gallop right through town, down the hill into the Okanogan River, full-tilt kamikaze."

"Damn. Did they make it?"

"Hell no!" Henry chortled. "We had to fish their sorry asses out of the river before they drowned. We're still looking for their damned horses. So, what's up, cousin?"

I gave Henry a brief overview of the Sullivan Mine project, and then got to the Virus.

"I'm sure you know of Cyrus McSweeny?" I asked.

"Yes, is he still causing trouble at his age? Hell, he's got to be in his sixties by now."

"Yes, and yes. He's like a cancer that just won't quite go into remission."

"Is he giving you trouble?"

"Nothing yet, other than his offer to be my partner. But someone is watching the drill site. We saw the sun glint off their binocs."

"Well, cousin, there's not a hell of a lot I can do until they do something illegal."

"Understood. But, maybe you could send a deputy up our way, now and then. Kind of show the badge a bit."

"Be glad to. I'm supposed to be up your way in a few days. I'll give you a holler. You can buy me lunch, and we'll let your audience know the sheriff's in town."

"Thanks, Henry. I really appreciate it. And it will be good to see you again."

On the way into Winthrop I stopped at a burger joint on Highway 20. After eating the best burger I ever sank a tooth into, I headed to the Chewak Construction Company yard to meet with Bobby Malott. We visited a few minutes about security, and then I hightailed it back to the mine.

The night crew was blowing and going. A long line of samples bags were lined up near the rig. Nick Wetzel was the night-shift driller, a rosy-cheeked, heavy-set giant with a bald head and red mustache.

"Hey, Nick," I yelled, to be heard above the compressor, "how's it going?"

"Damn good, Trace. We should be just about to the vein when the day-shift gets here."

"Wow, that's great, Nick. Any problem with groundwater?"

"Not yet. Samples are dry as James Bond's martini."

I laughed. "That dry, huh?"

I opened several of the sample bags and checked the lithology of the rock chips . . . all granodiorite. We were still drilling through the hanging wall above the vein.

I waved at Nick to get his attention. I held up six fingers, then pointed to myself. He nodded, understanding I would be back at six in the morning. I wanted to get back to Winthrop, work on my maps, and get a good night's sleep. We'd start pulling core early tomorrow morning.

At 5:50 the next morning I pulled up to the mine, just behind Red and the day-shift crew.

"Morning, Red . . . fellows," I said, giving the crew a casual salute.

"Morning your own self," Red replied, with the wave of a hand big enough to shag fly balls.

Red and I walked over to the drill, and I checked the latest samples blowing up the hole.

"How deep are we, Nick?" I yelled.

"Two ninety-five, Trace."

"Okay, that's far enough with the hammer. Pull out, and let's start coring. We should be about five feet from the vein."

Nick's crew pulled the drill rods and hammer bit out of the hole, and turned the rig over to Red, and the day shift.

The night crew shoved off while Red's crew set up the wire-line coring system. With a wire-line system, we would be able to pull liners from inside the core barrel without pulling the drill pipe out of the hole. Recovered core from inside the liners would be placed into divided wooden-core boxes. Each core box held twenty feet of core in five-four-foot sections. Markers indicating depths were inserted at the top and bottom of each section of core.

Once the core was boxed, I measured it to determine how much core we had recovered. Next, I described the rock type, noting any mineralization or alteration. And, finally, I photographed the cores to document our work, and for future PowerPoint presentations.

"We're ready, Trace," Red said.

"Okay, Red, let'er rip," I replied.

We cut five feet of core the first run, putting us at three hundred feet. I looked at the bottom section of the core and could see traces of pyrite and other sulfides.

"Red, we're right on the vein."

Red gave me a thumbs-up and ran a liner back down the drill pipe.

It took about an hour to cut the next five feet. When we pulled the liner and laid the core in the box, Red whistled.

"Holy shit, Trace," Red said. It's almost pure sulfides."

I took my rock hammer and broke off about a six-inch section of the core and looked at it with my ten-power hand lens.

"Yeah, it's damned good, Red."

Red and I saw the flash of light at the same instant.

"Our little Peeping Tom is back," Red said, lifting his eyes to the mountain behind us.

"I saw it, Red. Nothing we can do about it. There's no law against watching us core."

The next five cores all cut nearly pure sulfides with just traces of vein quartz. On the eighth run, we cut two more feet of ore and then were into the footwall metamorphic schist.

Red shook his head. "Jesus, Trace, we've cut thirty-two feet of mineralization."

I nodded. "True thickness will be a tad little less as we cut the vein at an angle."

"True enough," Red replied, "but it's still one hell of a vein."

"Isn't she though," I said, looking at the last section of core. "Red, we're three feet into the footwall. Deep enough on this one. Go ahead and trip out, and let's plug the hole."

While Red and the crew pulled the drill rods and core barrel out of the hole, I examined the core in more detail. The ore looked to be comprised of copper, pyrite, and pitchblende. I ran my pocket Geiger counter down the length of several cores.

I looked over at Red, who was watching me with some interest.

"Red, tell any of the crew that handled the core to be sure and wash their hands before they eat, or light up."

"Hot?" Red asked.

"*En llamas*," I replied, nodding. "Very, very, hot rock."

Red and his crew pulled out of the hole and prepared to cement it from top to bottom. The night-shift would likely show up just in time to move the rig to the second drilling location and start drilling. It looked like Red's crew would be doing the coring on the second hole too. Luck of the draw.

We'd cored forty feet with nearly 100 percent recovery. The core was neatly packed in two wooden boxes, twenty feet of core in each box. Luke and I secured the boxes in the back of my Bronco, and I went over to say good-bye to Red and the rest of his crew.

"Super job, fellas," I said. "Nearly one hundred percent recovery—damned good work."

"Looks like we'll be doing the coring on number two as well," Red replied.

"My thoughts exactly. Poor old Nick is getting stuck with the noisy, dusty, hammer drill bit again."

Red and the crew laughed.

"Be careful hauling the core down to Winthrop," Red said. "We don't want to have to re-drill this son of a bitch."

"Don't worry. Luke and I will have this core in Bobby's warehouse and be sipping a cold brew before you can say, 'Jack Dempsey.'"

I drove slowly down the mine road and turned left at Goat Creek. I'd gone about three-quarters of a mile when a man with a bandana across his face stepped out of the bushes and held up a hand. His other hand held what looked to be a 9mm automatic.

I slowed to a stop, keeping the Bronco in first gear with the clutch down.

"Just sit tight, Luke. And hang on," I whispered. "I got this son of a bitch."

"You're wasting your time, bud," I said, as the masked man came up to my open window. "I've only got about twenty bucks on me, and Luke here isn't carrying any dough. You want a stretch in Walla Walla for a lousy twenty bucks?"

"Shut your fuckin' hole. Both of you, get out of the truck."

"Okay, okay, just don't get trigger happy."

Reaching for the door handle with my left hand, I used my right hand to cut the wheel hard and fast to the right. I dumped the clutch and floored the gas, fishtailing the Bronco hard into the outlaw. The Bronco's rear tire caught his right leg just below the knee, snapping it like a twig.

I slammed on the brakes, killed the engine, grabbed my Smith & Wesson from beside my seat, and jumped out. Luke was hot on my heels. The highwayman had dropped his pistol on the road, and Luke kicked it out of reach. The poor bastard was on his ass, rocking back and forth, holding his shattered leg in both hands. The break was a compound fracture, and bone was sticking up through his torn jeans.

"Okay, amigo," I said, "who sent you, and what were you after?"

"Fuck you, you son of a bitch. You busted my leg all to hell."

I kneeled down, reached out, and tapped on his exposed fibula with the barrel of my .357 Magnum. He screamed like a wounded hyena.

I looked over at Luke. He grinned and spat a huge stream of brown tobacco juice. He was obviously okay with my interrogation techniques.

"Want to try again, shit for brains?"

"All right . . . Jesus! Just give me a goddamned second."

"Second's up," I said, moving the barrel of my revolver towards his exposed and bloody leg bone.

"Okay, okay! The guy who hired me is named Thorny. Some shit like that. I don't know his real name. He called me and told me to grab your cores."

I grabbed his bandana and told him to wrap it around his leg above the wound.

"Tie it tight and then loosen it every ten minutes or so. I wouldn't want you're sorry ass to bleed to death."

"It hurts like hell, mister."

"Yeah, I bet it does. About like me and Luke would be after you'd pumped a few nine millimeters into us."

"No, sir. I was told not to hurt you, unless absolutely necessary. I was just to get the core."

"And where were you going to take the core?"

"Nowhere. I was told to dump the cores in the Methow River and burn the core boxes."

"Okay, Just hang on while I call my cousin," I said, flipping open my cell phone.

"Your cousin? Goddamn it! I need a fuckin' ambulance."

"I'll see if he can bring one with him."

Luke spit another stream, and started laughing.

I called Henry and filled him in. He said Deputy Haines was just south of Winthrop and could be on scene in about twenty minutes. He'd have Haines alert the paramedics in Winthrop.

I hung up and turned to the injured man. "You're in luck, highwayman. The cavalry is on the way."

"Thank God. I'm dying here."

"Don't worry, dickhead. You're not going to die. But, you may wish you would unless I get a few more answers before help arrives," I said, moving my gun closer to his leg.

"Hold on . . . goddamn it, just hold on with the fuckin' gun barrel."

"Okay," I said, lowering my shooter, "I want a few answers. First off, who the hell are you?"

"My name's Ike Moffit."

"And where did you go to college, Ike?"

Luke cracked up, nearly choking on his chaw.

"College? What in *the* hell are you talking about?"

I chuckled. "Relax. I'm just having some fun. No reason this can't be fun, Ike. So, what do you do when you're not stealing core?"

"I run some numbers, do some loan-sharking, help people remember promises they made. That sort of shit."

"I see. So, who were you supposed to call when the job was finished?"

"I'm to call a number and leave a message."

"What number?"

"It's on a piece of paper in my shirt pocket."

"You right-handed or left-handed, amigo?"

"Right."

"Okay, with your left hand, reach up, very slowly, and take the paper out of your pocket. Try anything cute, and I'll do a little tap dance on your fibula."

Ike retrieved the number and handed it to me. It was a Spokane area number.

"Thanks, pardner. Just rest easy. The law and paramedics are on the way."

"Why'd you say you were calling your cousin?"

"I did call my cousin. Just so happens, my cousin is also the sheriff of Okanogan County."

Deputy Haines and the medics arrived a few minutes later. Luke and I explained what happened while the medics loaded Ike into the ambulance.

"We'll have to haul him to Brewster," Haines said, carefully bagging and tagging Ike's 9mm pistol. "It's the closest hospital. When he's able, we'll book him into the county jail in Okanogan. You'll need to come by and give a statement and file formal charges."

"No, charges, deputy," I said. "He wasn't out to hurt anybody. He just wanted the core. I think I know who put him up to it, but there's no way we'll be able to prove it. Plus, the poor bastard will probably limp the rest of his life."

"Well, if he's a convicted felon, which I'd bet he is, with a handgun, he'll be going away."

I smiled at Deputy Haines. "I think I can live with that."

Nick Wetzel and the night crew were headed up to the drill when they drove up on us.

"Damn, Trace," Nick said, looking at Ike on the gurney, "what in tarnation happened?"

"Luke here got hungry," I replied. "I tried to get him some road-kill."

"What?" Nick said, grinning from ear to ear.

"Dickhead in the ambulance tried to hijack our core," I replied, pointing towards Ike.

"Did you shoot him?" Nick asked, looking at Ike's bloody leg.

"No, but I ran over him pretty good." I replied, with a chuckle. "Can you give Luke a lift back to the rig? Fill Red in, and tell everybody to be on their toes."

"Will do, Trace. Do you need any help getting back to town?"

"No, I'll follow the deputy. I'm good to go. Thanks."

I pulled into Bob Malott's yard and told him about the attempted hi-jacking. We stored the core boxes in the warehouse I'd rented and locked it up. Afterwards, I checked in with my cousin.

"Sheriff, Trace here. Have you spoken to Deputy Haines?"

"Yep, he gave me a rundown on what happened. Are you okay?"

"Yeah, nary a scratch."

"Haines said you don't want to press charges?"

"No. Poor old Ike's just a flunky in this deal. I think I know who put him up to this, but we'll never be able to prove it."

"You think it's Cyrus?"

"No one else. He knows we're operating on a shoestring. I think his plan is to run us short of cash by making us re-drill holes. If we went broke drilling, he could step up with the cash to save the project."

"The Virus for a white knight. Damnation," Henry said, laughing. "So, where do you go from here?"

"We keep drilling, split and assay the cores, and head back to Vancouver with the results."

"Uh-huh. Well, as a precaution, I'm going to have Deputy Haines stop by the rig from time to time. Sort of show the badge, like we discussed."

"Thanks, Henry. I appreciate it."

Coring on the second and third holes went off without a hitch. We cored nearly forty feet of strongly mineralized vein in each hole. Back in Winthrop, with the help of some of Bob's crew, we got all the cores split and shipped to Mineral Valley Labs, in Coeur d'Alene, Idaho.

It took about two weeks for the lab to report the assays. The cores averaged about seven-tenths of an-ounce gold per ton, One and a half percent copper and eight percent uranium. One hell of a vein.

I spent about a week putting together a first-class Power-Point presentation. Will and Wally worked the phones, setting up meetings in Vancouver with investors and brokers. We planned to do a round of dog and pony shows to launch our private placement.

For this round of financing, Montana Creek Mining Corp. would sell one million treasury shares of stock for fifty cents per share. Each share would have a three-year warrant attached for the purchase of an additional share, at seventy-five cents.

If the private offering sold out, the company would receive half a million bucks, less fees and commissions. The warrants could bring in an additional $750,000.

Now all I had to do was convince a bunch of very savvy investors that we'd hit the mother lode.

Chapter 7

Will and I met Wally at the Harbor View Hotel in Vancouver. Wally procured one of their large meeting rooms and invited about fifty brokers and analysts, plus a hundred investors, to attend our presentation.

At 9:00 sharp the next day, we kicked off the dog and pony show. I started running through and explaining each PowerPoint slide. When I clicked on the slide with the core assay results, the room went strangely quiet. It took a few moments for the mining analysts to realize they were looking at Athabasca Basin-type uranium grades. Then their cell phones lit up the room.

I noticed a tall, white-haired, older, but hard-looking-individual sitting toward the back of the audience. I looked over at Wally on the side of the stage and cut my eyes in the direction of the investor.

By noon, I finished the presentation, and we invited the participants to enjoy a light buffet. While the waiters set up the food, I located Wally and Will.

"What'd you think, fellows?" I asked.

"Good job, Trace," Wally replied. "I know most of the brokers and analysts, and I could tell they were eating it up with a spoon. I have copies of the private-placement documents to all the brokerage houses. I think we'll be oversubscribed."

"Either of you notice the older, white-haired, gent sitting near the rear?"

Will nodded. "Yes, I noticed him, but I don't know him."

Wally laughed. "Fellows, you just gave a presentation to the Virus himself."

"No shit. That's Cyrus?" I asked.

"In the flesh," Wally replied.

"Excuse me for a second, fellows," I said, heading off in Cyrus's direction. "I want to meet the gentleman."

I worked my way through the crowd, shaking hands and thanking the participants for coming.

"Mr. McSweeny?" I asked.

"Nice pitch, Mr. Brandon," Cyrus replied, extending his hand.

His hand was hard and dry as granite.

"Thank you, sir," I replied, holding his grip until he loosened it.

"If the tonnage is there, you're sitting on a world-class uranium deposit. Not to mention the gold and copper values."

"Thank you, Mr. McSweeny."

"Please, call me Cyrus."

"Okay, Cyrus, I'm Trace. Are you interested in participating in the private share placement?"

"Could be, Trace. I'm always looking for good mining investments."

"Sorry about Ike, his leg and all," I said.

Cyrus looked at me. "Sorry, I don't believe I know anyone by that name."

I could tell by the flash in his eyes that, I'd hit a nerve.

"Oh, he is, or was, kind of an amateur rock hound. Had a big interest in our core. Said he was a friend of Thorny's."

"I see," Cyrus replied, shaking his head. "Sorry, doesn't ring any bells."

"Well, it was nice to meet you Cyrus. I want you to know I appreciate your interest in Montana Creek Mining."

"Thank you, Trace. I'll probably buy a few shares in your offering, so I can follow your progress. A little equity keeps me interested."

"Very good, sir. I don't think you'll be disappointed."

"I seldom am, Mr. Brandon," Cyrus said, patting me on my shoulder.

Cyrus left the conference room and headed to the hotel bar to meet Bill Thornton.

"Well, Thorny, Brandon gave a hell of a presentation," Cyrus said, taking a sip of his Crown Royal and water. "And he let me know he'd taken care of Ike."

"Damn kid's a player all right, and he's latched on to a once-in-a-lifetime property," Thorny replied.

"Appears so. Who's the lead underwriter for their placement?"

"Vancouver Pacific Securities."

"Thorny, get on the phone with our broker at Vancouver Pacific and tell him Twisp River Resources will subscribe to two hundred fifty thousand shares of Montana Creek's private placement."

"Yes, sir," Thorny replied. "We may be hard pressed to get the two hundred fifty thousand. Judging from the reaction of the brokers at the presentation, I suspect the offering will be oversubscribed."

"I have a good relationship with the principals over at Vancouver Pacific. They'll get us the two fifty. I'll start buying shares in the open market through our offshore account. If I can pick up another two fifty in the market, we'll have half a million shares. Well, below the ten percent reporting level, but enough to flex some muscle."

Back in our hotel suite, Wally briefed Will and me on sales of the private-placement shares.

"Vancouver Pacific Securities received subscriptions for five hundred thousand shares right after the presentation," Wally reported. "Northern Equities placed two hundred and fifty thousand shares, and Baystreet Securities and Commonwealth placed the balance. Boys, we're totally subscribed."

"Nothing like eight percent uranium grades in a hot market to spark a feeding frenzy," Will said, rubbing his hands together.

"Damn, fellows. This calls for a celebration," I said. "Let's have supper and a night on the town."

We hit Vancouver's Chinatown like MacArthur hit Inchon.

The next morning, with near-terminal hangovers, Will and I headed back to Ellensburg. When Wally recovered, he'd see to depositing the net proceeds from the share sales into Montana Creek Mining's bank account.

Wally called my office a few days later.

"Trace, just wanted to let you know we're trading around twenty thousand shares per day. Not too bad with only a million shares in the float. And were hanging in around sixty cents per share."

"Anyone in particular buying a lot of shares?" I asked, thinking about the Virus.

"Hard to tell, Trace, but Cayman Island Securities is a buyer. No large blocks, but steady buying, especially on dips. The shares are held in street name, so no way tell who they're buying for."

"Better get an updated shareholder list from the transfer agent every couple of months. I don't want any surprises."

"One other thing did catch my attention, Trace. The largest subscriber to our private placement was a company called, Twisp River Resources."

"How much did they take down?"

"About half of what we allocated to Vancouver Pacific. Two hundred fifty thousand shares."

"Do you know anything about them?"

"Not much. So, I pulled their corporate records up online. They're a small privately held mineral-exploration company based in Vancouver. But, get this, according to their filings, all their outstanding shares are owned by an outfit called Carib International, Corp. Want to guess where Carib is based?"

"Caymans?"

"Good guess."

"So, if the buying through Cayman Island Securities is related to Twisp River's buying, they're building a serious position in our shares."

"Seems to fit the information we have," Wally replied. "The sixty-four thousand dollar question is, what's their endgame?"

"Maybe they just like the Sullivan Mine, or maybe they're looking for a seat on our board."

"Yeah, or maybe they have something else in mind down the road."

"Hostile takeover? Ain't happening, Wally. Not with me holding three and a half million shares, and you and Will with a half million each."

"Agreed, Trace. But as we do additional financings, our ownership will get diluted. Plus, I'm a little worried about Richard Rosenburg. I've heard some talk on the street. Could be he's in a little financial trouble, and he holds the other half million founders' shares."

"The public market can be a damned rough place," I whispered, to myself.

"What'd you say?" Wally asked.

"Nothing, just something someone once mentioned in passing."

"Well, I'll keep an eye on the trading and Richard, and keep you boys posted. Just keep the drills turning to the right."

I knew Wally was correct. There was nothing to be done about Twist River or the buying coming out of the Caymans. But Rosenburg's founders' shares could be a big problem. If he was bleeding money, the Virus would smell it like a damned great white.

I worked up a second round of core drilling. We'd drill three more holes from the original drill sites, but at sixty-degree angles. The steeper angle would allow us to intersect the vein at a much deeper depth and, if successful, would increase our indicated reserves greatly.

I also planned three more drill locations, one thousand feet apart along the trend, or strike, of the vein. We'd also drill two holes from each of the new locations, again, at forty-five and sixty degrees.

The program would give us a total twelve holes, and go a long ways toward developing additional reserves. I also knew, if the core results continued to be positive, Montana Creek Mining shares were fixin' to take off.

*****

"The kid has permitted nine new holes at the Sullivan," Thorny said, handing Cyrus a cup of coffee.

"Who the hell trained this guy?" Cyrus asked, sipping the very hot black coffee.

"Best I can tell, he worked about eight years with Continental Minerals, down in Denver. Doing mainly uranium exploration."

"So he's no rookie, at least in mineral exploration. We'll see how he does in the public sector. What's our ownership position in Montana Creek Mining?"

"About seven percent."

"Okay, I think it's time we shake their tree a bit. I want to try and get one of our people on Montana Creek's board. It can't be me, I have a damned felony conviction. And you, well, you're a bit too close to me."

"What about Malcolm Trueblood? He's president of Twisp River Resources, has an MBA, and is clean as the pope's underwear."

Cyrus laughed. "Good choice, Thorny. He's done a good job with Twisp, and he's smart and knows the public markets. Have Malcolm contact Montana Creek's board and see how they react."

I'd just hung up from talking to Red. He and his crews were drilling the first of the sixty-degree holes. The phone rang, and I picked it up, thinking Red had forgotten to tell me something.

"Yes, sir. Forget something?" I said, with a chuckle.

"No, I don't believe so, Mr. Brandon. This is Malcolm Trueblood with Twisp River Resources in Vancouver, Canada."

"Sorry, Mr. Trueblood. I thought you were my driller calling back."

"Oh, are you drilling again?"

"Yes, sir. We've started a second round. Just spudding in our fourth hole, as we speak."

"Well, as a shareholder, I am of course pleased to hear the news."

"There'll be a press release at close of trading today. So, what can I do for you, Mr. Trueblood?"

"Excellent, Trace. May I call you Trace?"

"Surely."

"Well, Trace, as you no doubt know, Twisp River bought two hundred and fifty thousand shares of your private placement, and our holding company has acquired a similar number of shares in the open market."

"By holding company, I take it you mean Carib International?"

"My compliments, Trace. I see you've done your homework."

"Well, we like to know who are shareholders are. Especially our larger shareholders."

"Which brings me to the purpose of my call, Trace. Twisp and Carib now own a bit more than seven percent of Montana Creek Mining. We feel very strongly we should have some representation on your board of directors."

"I see. And who would you propose we add to our board?"

"If it's not too presumptuous, I would like to nominate myself."

"What's your background, Malcolm?" I asked, thinking, yeah, it *is* pretty damned presumptuous.

"MBA from Stanford, fifteen years with GoldEx in Vancouver, and the last five years as CEO of Twisp River Resources. I'm widowed. My wife was killed in an auto accident some years ago. We had no children. Other than work, my main passion is flying. I hold a number of ratings and have several thousand hours of flight time."

"I am also well connected with the securities and financial markets in Vancouver and Toronto. I am assuming you will be moving off the Vancouver Stock Exchange and onto the Toronto Exchange as soon as you meet the listing requirements?"

"Sorry to hear about your wife, Malcolm," I replied, ignoring his assumption.

"Thank you. It was a long time ago, but I still miss her."

"I can imagine. Listen, your experience is top shelf. But to be frank, we haven't discussed bringing on any new directors at this time. I will, however, discuss your proposal with the other board members."

"Thank you, Trace. Please be assured we have nothing but the best interests of Montana Creek Mining at heart. I'll look forward to hearing from you."

"I'm glad to hear it, Malcolm," I said. "I'll get back to you."

I managed to get Will and Wally on a conference call and briefed them on my conversation with Malcolm.

"He hasn't got the shares to elect him to the board," Wally said. "Even if he managed to get enough votes to call a special shareholders' meeting, we've more than enough votes among us to keep him off the board."

"Of course, the flip side," Will added, "is the fact Twisp River and Carib International, do own seven percent of our company. A fact not to be taken too lightly."

"Duly noted, Will," I said. "Here's my suggestion, fellows. At some point Montana Creek Mining will qualify for listing on the Toronto Stock Exchange. And at that point we'll need a majority of independent directors. Let's turn Malcolm down for now, but suggest the possibility of a directorship down the road."

Will and Wally both agreed.

"In the interim," I said, "we need to find out a hell of a lot more about Twisp River Resources. And more importantly, find out who controls Carib International."

"I can put the word out around Vancouver," Wally replied. "I'll find out all there is to know about Twisp River. Carib International, however, is a horse of a different color. A privately held Cayman Island Corporation will be tough. However, I may know someone on the island who could help. It will cost a few bucks for her time, but she gets results."

"She?" Will asked.

"Yes, her name is Dominic Rinquet," Wally replied. "She's a French-Canadian ex-pat living in George Town on Grand Cayman. She does corporate development work and knows everybody on the island. And did I mention she's a knock-out?"

"Even better. Put her on it, Wally," I said. "I would really like to know who the hell we're dealing with."

"You got it," Wally replied.

"Okay, fellows," I said, "I'll call Trueblood in the morning and give him the bad news. Afterwards, I'll head back up to the mine and check on the coring."

The next morning I packed my gear in the Bronco and then called Trueblood.

"Malcolm, Trace Brandon here."

"Good morning, Trace."

"Listen, Malcolm, I did talk to the other two directors, and we all feel you're highly qualified to sit on our board. However, for now, we've decided to keep the board as is."

"I see. Well, I am disappointed, Trace."

"Malcolm, we feel it would be more appropriate to bring on independent directors, such as yourself, once we've qualified for a listing on a major exchange. We would like to re-consider your offer a little further down the road."

"I understand, Trace. And, yes, you will need a majority of independent directors on your board for a major exchange listing. Well, good luck with the drilling, and I look forward to renewing this conversation at a later date."

"Thanks, Malcolm. We'll be putting out news releases to keep all the shareholders up to speed. Thanks again you for your support."

I arrived at the drill site a little after lunch. The high-country air now contained a hint of fall. It wouldn't be too long before the snows came.

"Howdy, Red," I said, with a wave. "How's it going?"

"Good, Trace. We're three hundred fifty feet down on a sixty-degree angle. We'll start coring at three ninety-five. According to your cross sections, we should hit the vein around four hundred feet. You're just in time."

Bill Thornton and Cyrus McSweeny sat in the Columbia Resources board-room in Spokane. Malcolm Trueblood was on the speaker-phone.

"Mr. McSweeny, I didn't have much luck with Brandon, or his board members."

"Well, fellows," Cyrus replied, "we had to start somewhere. At least we've planted the seed, and it looks like we'll have a shot at getting you on the board when they go for a Toronto listing. Here's how I would like this to play out, until then. First, Malcolm, I want Twisp River to continue accumulating shares in the open market. Carib International will do likewise. Up to ten percent each, if we can get it. As Twisp is one hundred percent owned by Carib, we may have to report our joint ownership if it exceeds ten percent. I'll run it by our legal eagles."

"In any case, we'll shoot for just under twenty percent ownership of Montana Creek Mining between our two entities. If the cores continue to be high grade, we hold our positions. I suspect at some point one of the big mining companies will propose a joint venture or will tender for control of Montana Creek Mining."

"If, on the other hand, the ore grades drop a bit, we can either dump our shares or short the stock. In either case, we profit."

"What we really need, Cyrus," Thorny added, "is someone on the inside. Someone to tell us how the cores and assays look before it's public knowledge."

"I believe that's called inside information," Malcolm replied, coldly.

"If you have a problem with the concept, Malcolm," Cyrus said, "now would be the time to bow out."

Malcolm hesitated, knowing he was about to cross the line.

"No, sir. No problem. I came on your team because I knew you played hard-ball. I am merely pointing out a possible legal issue."

"Duly noted, Malcolm," Cyrus replied. "Now, if there are no further issues, does anyone have an idea on how we could get on the inside?"

"We could bribe one of the driller's helpers, or better yet, someone at the lab," Thorny suggested.

"I like someone at the lab," Malcolm said. "They would have access to the assay data, not just a look at the core. And they are a bit removed, less likely to be suspected."

"I agree," Cyrus said. "Thorny, find out which lab is running their assays. It'll be in their Vancouver Stock Exchange filings. Hell, it's probably listed on their website along with the assay results. Check out the lab employees. Find out who's got a mistress, is behind on child support, is an alcoholic or on drugs. You know the drill. Find somebody with a weakness we can exploit, and hammer them."

Red hit the vein at 403 feet.

"She's cutting smooth and easy, Trace," Red said, adjusting the pull-down weight on the drill string.

"Steady as she goes, Red," I replied. "I need as close to one hundred percent recovery as you can get."

"Third run coming up," Red yelled. "This one should be all ore."

And it was. Five feet of dark, black pitchblende banded with brassy chalcopyrite copper. Solid pay rock.

"Holy moly, Red," I yelled, looking at the high-grade ore, "it's the mother lode."

"And a deadly lode at that," Red replied, looking down at the pitchblende ore.

I looked up at Red and nodded. "All in all, we cut fifty-one feet of mineralized vein, nearly ten feet thicker than the first cores. Of course, that's apparent thickness. I'll have to calculate the true thickness, but it's still damn good."

I pulled out my pocket calculator and ran some numbers. Length times width, times thickness, times tons per cubic yard, times 8 percent uranium. It was going to be a very, very, big number.

Chapter 8

The assay results from core hole number three were published on our website, and the price of our shares rose to a dollar and a half.

At 9:00 a.m., Tuesday morning, I was back in my office in E-Burg, working on ore reserve 'what-if's' when the phone rang.

"Montana Creek Mining, Trace speaking."

"Trace, this is James Lee with International Uranium Corp., in Sydney, Australia."

"Damn, must be awfully late at night down under, sir."

"You're right, mate. But I am in Los Angeles for meetings. So, no worries."

"Okay, glad to hear it," I said, with a chuckle. "What can I do for you, sir?"

"Well, Trace, we're hearing a lot about your uranium discovery in North Central Washington. I'd like to come up, meet you, and, if possible, have a look at the operation. And of course, the cores."

"Your timing is perfect. No snow yet, and we're drilling away."

"Good, I hate snow," James said, with a laugh.

"Okay, book a flight into Spokane, let me know when you'll arrive and I'll pick you up. It's about a three-hour run to the mine."

"Bloody good, mate. I look forward to meeting up. How's the beer up your way?"

"We have a very good local micro-brewery. They brew a beer I think you'll like. It's called Tumbleweed Ale."

Cyrus and Thorny met at the Mallard Lounge in the historic Ponderosa Hotel in downtown Spokane. They sat at the bar under an inlaid glass ceiling that depicted a flock of Mallards, and ordered cocktails.

"Cyrus, they're using Mineral Valley Labs over in Coeur d'Alene for their assays. I had an old PI buddy do some checking, and I think we found the perfect insider."

"Go on," Cyrus replied, taking a healthy pull on his Crown and water.

"Her name is Mary Johnson, a single mom. Husband's whereabouts unknown. She has an eleven-year-old daughter with brain cancer. It takes every dime she can earn, plus her insurance to keep the kid in treatment."

"Perfect. We get to help a kid with cancer, and we'll get the info we need. Kind of a win-win, I'd say," Cyrus declared, with a grin.

"Yes, sir."

"Have you approached her?"

"Yes. I had my PI friend make the contact. He told her all he needed were copies of the assay results, as soon as they were available. He told her one of his clients owned shares in Montana Creek Mining, and just wanted to be sure the assays published by Montana Creek Mining matched the actual lab assays."

"Nice touch."

"Yeah, makes it seem quite harmless. Simply an investor trying to protect his investment from all the crooks out there."

Cyrus laughed. "Hell, I love it. And?"

"And, for ten grand, she's on board."

"Excellent. Each time Brandon gets core assays, it'll take him a couple of days to prepare a news release for the Vancouver Stock Exchange. We, on the other hand, only need a couple of minutes to evaluate the results. By the time the assays are public, we'll have already bought or sold short."

"It's all about information, isn't it, sir?"

"Information and timing, Thorny."

I drove over to the Spokane airport to meet with James Lee. I knew of his company, but did some online research to get fully up to speed.

I spotted him easily as I entered the airport lobby. He was wearing khakis, with a hand lens around his neck and a backpack. The universal geological garb.

"Mr. Lee, I presume?" I said, extending my hand. "I'm Trace Brandon, Montana Creek Mining."

"Hi, Trace," Lee replied, shaking my hand with a firm grip. "Good to meet you, and thanks for picking me up."

International Uranium Corporation's website listed Lee's age at fifty-two, but he didn't look it. He was about my height, around six feet, and I guessed about 180 pounds. Lee wore his salt-and-pepper hair short and was well tanned from the Australian sun.

"So, Trace, I see you've just released the assays from your third core hole?"

"Yes, sir, and they're the best to date."

"Please call me, Jim."

"Okay, Jim. Thanks."

"Best so far, eh?"

"Yep. About the same grades, but the vein appears to be thickening up at depth."

"Calculated any tonnages yet?"

"With just the three holes, it's pretty early. But if the vein and grades continue for, say, half a mile, we're well into the millions of tons of ore."

"And at eight or so percent uranium per ton, you could be upwards of half a billion pounds of uranium," Jim said, with a whistle.

"Yeah, it could be a whopper. And don't forget the gold and copper values. The uranium's going to be the cream."

"So, Trace, what are your plans to finance this beast?"

"Well, we'll probably do another private placement when the stock price gets around two dollars. And raise enough capital to keep us drilling out reserves."

"Any thoughts toward a possible joint venture?"

"Right now, we're more inclined to keep drilling in-house."

"That's a bit risky, isn't it? What if the vein pinches out or the grade drops. You'll be risking one hundred percent of your capital. Might be wiser to share the risk and the return."

"True enough. But from what we've seen so far, it appears to be worth the risk."

"What's your control position at the moment, Trace?"

"I own three and a half million shares. Will Coffee, my attorney and a director, owns half a million shares, and our other director, Walter Wilkins, owns half a million shares."

"So, out of seven million, issued shares, your group controls four and a half million shares."

"Correct. Fully diluted, the directors will have about fifty-six percent control."

Jim crunched the numbers on his pocket calculator.

"Exactly right."

"And," I added, "with the additional seven hundred and fifty thousand cash from the warrants, we'll be able to keep the drills turning to the right."

I could see a bit of disappointment in Jim's eyes. Even fully diluted, International Uranium Corp. had no chance of obtaining control through a hostile takeover.

I'd reserved two rooms at the W in Winthrop before I left E-Burg. We stowed some of our gear, grabbed a quick lunch, and headed up to the Sullivan Mine.

Red and the day shift were coring on the fourth hole when we arrived. Jim and I walked over to the rig.

"Red," I yelled, above the rig noise, "this is Jim Lee with International Uranium Corp., down in Australia."

"Nice to meet you," Red shouted back. "You came a hell of a long way to look at some damned rocks."

"Indeed I have," Jim replied, glancing down at the neat rows of core.

I laid out some cross-sections and showed Jim where this hole had intersected the vein.

"This is the first of two holes at this location. We're at a forty-five degree angle on this one. We'll drill at sixty degrees on the second hole."

Jim picked up a small section of very high-grade ore and inspected it with his ten-power hand lens.

"Damn, Trace," Jim said, turning the core over and over in his hand, "it's the best-looking uranium ore I've ever seen. And I've seen some damned good ore."

"Yeah, it's amazing. The old-timers here were after the gold and copper. The uranium was probably just a headache for them."

"Yeah, likely in more ways than one. With this kind of grade, you wouldn't want to be exposed underground for too long."

I showed Jim our claim layout and took him part way into the original adit.

"We'll have to dewater the second level at some point," I said as we came up to the area of the flooded winze. "I took a pretty cold dip, right about here."

"A winze?"

"Yeah, connects with level two."

"Jesus, you were lucky to get out."

I laughed. "Yep, I looked just like Indiana Jones, but without the vine."

We spent the rest of the day watching the coring operation. I could tell Jim was more than just a little interested. Just before shift change, we headed back to the W.

"Cold beer, Jim?"

"Grab us a table and order me a, what was it?, Tumble Down . . . ?"

"Tumbleweed Ale."

"Make it a big one. I'll be down in a second. Just need to check in with my office. Should be business hours tomorrow, about now."

I was sipping on my Ale and perusing the menu when Jim came in and sat down.

"So, this is the Tumbleweed, eh?," Jim said, taking a frothy gulp. "Damn, mate, that's good brew. And we Aussies know a thing or two about beer."

"I thought you'd like it. Besides the Ale, how'd you like the mine?"

"I won't bullshit you, Trace. I think the Sullivan Mine could be a world-class deposit, and we'd love to work out a deal to be Montana Creek Mining's partner. This mine's going to attract a lot of interest from other majors, Trace. But I think, if you'll check around, you find all of our partners are glad they teamed with International Uranium Corp."

"I did a fair amount of research on your company, and I've got to admit I liked what I saw. Let me throw this out to you. We'd prefer selling a minority interest in Montana Creek Mining, rather than participating in a joint venture. Along with purchasing a minority interest, we'd like your technical help in bringing the project to production.

"What kind of interest are we talking about?"

"No more than twenty percent, Jim. Also, as the additional shares would dilute our control to less than fifty percent, I would need a standstill agreement, whereby I could vote IUC's shares in the event of a hostile takeover attempt.

"I see. What kind of price per share have you got in mind, Trace?"

"It would have to be at a premium to the share price at the time of the sale. So, it'll likely be north of two dollars per share."

"I know we'd like a bigger piece, Trace, but let me run it by my board. I'll let you know something in a week or so."

"Agreed," I said, clinking my beer mug with Jim's.

The next afternoon, I dropped Jim off at the Spokane airport and headed back to my office. I called Will and asked him to come over. When he arrived, we called Wally and put him on the speaker-phone.

I briefed them on my meeting with Jim Lee.

"Okay, fellows, here are my thoughts on selling a minority interest in Montana Creek Mining to IUC. First, it further validates our discovery. Having a major company take a position in Montana Creek Mining will increase the appetite of other big companies to participate in future offerings, or sale of the company."

"Secondly, it will provide us with working capital to advance the project and enhance our share price. And lastly, the shares will be held by a major company rather than by short-term investors and promoters, in Vancouver."

"If IUC comes back with an offer, as you've just outlined, I'm on board," Wally said.

"Ditto for me," Will added.

"We're going to have several additional suitors," Wally said. "Canadian Uranium Group and the French company, MinUranCo, have both contacted me. You're going to have a lot of company over the winter."

"Well, there's nothing like a little competition to sweeten the pot," I replied.

"I've got some other news as well," Wally continued. "My contact in the Caymans, Dominic Rinquet, was able to dig up some information on Carib International. You'll never guess who owns it."

"Cyrus the Virus?" I replied.

"How did you know?" Wally asked, slightly stunned.

"Just a nagging hunch, I've had. It's all starting to fall into place, fellows. Ike Moffit tries to steal our core. Ike works for Thornton, who's Cyrus's right-hand man. Twisp River takes down a big chunk of our private placement, and they're owned by Carib, and Cyrus owns Carib. It's classic Cyrus the Virus."

"Well it could be trouble down the road," Wally noted.

"What's on your mind, Wally?" I asked.

"Just this, fellows. Right now our cash position is good. The warrants are getting exercised, giving us another infusion of cash."

"Seven hundred-fifty thousand," Will interjected.

"Exactly," Wally replied. "So in the short term we're okay. But farther down the road we're going to have to raise additional capital. Which means additional dilution."

"Which means the Virus could accumulate even more of our shares," I added.

"Exactly," both Wally and Will replied, simultaneously.

"Okay, what are our options?" I asked.

"Even if Cyrus and company could manage to get up to twenty percent control, they would have to get additional votes from other shareholders to cause us much of a problem," Will replied. "And right now I don't see that happening. I think we're okay as long as the ore grades remain positive."

"Agreed. As long as our drilling keeps churning out good results and we keep adding to our reserves, the share price will stay strong," I replied. "And we'll have a bunch of happy shareholders."

Bill Thornton received an e-mail from Mary Johnson's home computer. New assays were attached. He called Cyrus on his landline.

"Cyrus, Thorny. Got a sec?"

"Always, Thorny. What's up?"

"Just got some assays from our friend at the lab."

"And?"

"Well, they're damned good. No indication the grades are dropping off."

"Good and bad, Thorny. Kind of like seeing your mother-in-law drive off a cliff in your new Maserati."

"Sir?"

Cyrus laughed. "Good news is, as shareholders, we want a damned good mine. Makes our shares worth a lot. Bad news is, it'll be harder to acquire more shares in any upcoming offerings."

"Any ideas, sir?"

"What have you been able to find out about the other shell founder, Rosenburg?"

"Word on the street is, he's in trouble. Turns out Mr. Rosenburg is a big-time Las Vegas gambler. Word is he's into the Comstock Casino for about a mil."

"The Comstock, eh? The Pantelli family out of New Orleans are the dough behind the casino. Some very tough fellows. I met one of the brothers, Al Pantelli, in the pen. I'll give him a call and see what kind of trouble Rosenburg's in. Might be an opening for us? A way to pick up another half million shares?"

Wally set up field trips for Canadian Uranium Group and MinUranCo, and I did my standard dog and pony show, right down to the Tumbleweed Ale, at the W. Both groups did their best not to drool all over themselves when they looked at the cores.

I told them we were looking for a proposal from a major to acquire around 20 percent of the company. Both said they'd prefer a Joint Venture, but I told them we had no interest in a JV. Each party said they'd review my proposal with their respective boards, and get back to me.

Winter kicked in, and it was tough going at the mine. Costs for drill camp supplies and road clearing were getting pretty high. But we were on the last drill location with just two holes left. I called Red and discussed the situation with him. He said they'd be able to finish in about four or five days.

The share price was holding steady in the two buck range, and we still had a fair amount of cash in the bank. All in all, a hell of a good year, and it was about to get even more interesting.

Chapter 9

I was looking over assay results on a very cold and overcast afternoon when my office phone rang.

"Trace, Cyrus McSweeny."

"Cyrus, long-time no hear."

"Yes, it's been a while. But I've been closely following your progress. Well done, lad."

"Well, we've been lucky, Cyrus. We managed to get the drilling done before the heavy snows hit."

"Winters in the upper Methow can be damned tough."

"Yes, sir. Hell, it's pretty damned cold right here in Ellensburg."

"Well, maybe I can do something about that, Trace."

"How so?"

"As you know from your inquiries, I own Carib International."

"My inquiries?"

"Don't be modest, Trace. Dominic is quite effective. But when someone is checking me out, I usually get wind of it."

"I see. We'll it's nothing personal, Cyrus. Just business."

Cyrus laughed. "That's supposed to be my line."

"You were saying, sir?"

"Ah, yes. I would like to invite you to come down to Grand Cayman for a long weekend as my guest. It would give us a chance to get to know one another, and to discuss your future plans for Montana Creek Mining. As one of your largest independent shareholders, I think it would be time well spent for both of us."

I looked out my frozen window at the blowing snow. "Can I bring a friend?"

"Of course. What's his, or her, name?"

"Tina Hart."

"Excellent. Just call me back on this cell number, and I'll make all the arrangements."

Immediately after I hung up with Cyrus, I called Tina. To say she was excited would be the proverbial understatement. We worked out our schedules, and I called Cyrus back. In ten days, we'd be in George Town, Grand Cayman. Guests of Cyrus the Virus.

Later, I called Will and Wally and filled them in. Will wasn't too keen on the idea. But Wally loved it.

"It's going to be a two-way pump, Trace," Wally said, with a laugh. "Just get all the info you can about his plans without giving away too much about ours."

"Exactly," I agreed.

"Also," Wally continued, "you should meet with Dominic and give her a heads-up about Cyrus. Tell her he knows she's been looking into Carib International."

"Will do, Wally."

"Too bad you're taking Tina. Dominic is single, uninhibited, and really ugly."

"What?" I said, laughing.

"Just kidding. She's a ten and a half."

"Well, I'll give her your best."

Wally laughed. "On your best day, you couldn't give her my best."

"Uh-huh. I'll keep you posted."

It was snowing hard in Spokane when Cyrus called Al Pantelli's New Orleans office. Al's secretary put him through.

"Al, it's Cyrus McSweeny, up in Spokane."

"Cyrus, you're not back in the can, are you?" Al asked, with a rumbling laugh.

"No. I'm clear and clean."

"Good to hear it, my friend. So what can I do for you?"

"It may be what I can do for you. What do you know about a Canadian promoter named Rosenburg? Word on the street in Vancouver is he's into the Comstock for some serious dough?"

"You heard right. The little creep plays craps like he's jerking off. He's in to us for a mil."

"Is it getting serious on your end?"

"Cyrus, what'd you think? It's a million fuckin' dollars."

"How much time has he got?"

"Not very goddamned much. You got something in mind?"

"What would you take, cash money, to assign me his gambling debt?"

"This jerk got something you want?"

"Let's just say he's screwing up a deal I'm in. I'm going to make him an offer he can't refuse."

"Corleone style, eh?"

"Something like that."

"Okay, we'll knock it down twenty percent for a fast, all-cash, buy-out. You in or out?"

"I'm in, Al. Draw up an assignment of his debt, and I'll have my associate, Bill Thornton in New Orleans, in forty-eight hours."

"With the cash?" Al asked.

"Eight hundred thousand.""Always a pleasure, Cyrus. Listen, if it should get to the point where you need some outside help to solve your little problem, well . . . we're in the problem-solving business."

Forty-nine hours later, Bill Thornton left Al Pantelli's office with a document assigning Richard Rosenburg's gambling debt to Cyrus. He called Cyrus from the New Orleans airport.

"Did everything go okay?" Cyrus asked.

"Yeah, no problems, Cyrus," Thorny replied. "But Mr. Pantelli is very interested in your interest in Rosenburg."

"I'll bet."

"Cyrus, I'm a little concerned about this deal."

"How so, Thorny?"

"Well, we're out eight hundred thousand for a million-dollar note. On the face of it, a damned good deal. But how do we collect the mil from Rosenburg?"

"We get his five hundred thousand shares of Montana Creek Mining in return for the note. The share price is steady at two bucks. So we'll make our eight hundred K back, plus two hundred thousand-profit."

"If we sell the shares."

"Correct. Which we are not going to do, at least not yet."

"What if Rosenburg won't assign us his shares?"

"Well, Thorny, you're going to make him an offer he can't refuse."

"How tough do I get?"

"Well, you can't kill the bastard, but short of that, whatever it takes. Understood?"

"Yes, sir."

"I'll have the lawyers draw up a stock-power agreement for Rosenburg to sign. He assigns Carib International his shares, and we cancel his debt. Paid in full."

"I'll be in your office in the morning."

"Good. I'm leaving for the Caymans in a couple of days, and I want you to wrap Rosenburg up, while I'm offshore."

"Understood. I'll see you in the morning, Cyrus."

Red and his crew finished plugging the final drill hole for this phase of drilling. I figured we wouldn't resume drilling until early spring. I finished putting together a summary of the drilling and core results for the Vancouver Stock Exchange. And squared things away so I could leave for the Caymans.

There was a knock on my door, and Tina stepped into my office.

"Trace, I've got some bad news. My mom's in the hospital over in Seattle. She's had a stroke, a pretty bad one, and I've got to go. I won't be able to make the trip to the Caymans. I am so sorry."

"Hey, kiddo," I said, giving her a hug, "there'll be lots of trips down the road. You just take care of your mother."

"You sure you're not mad?"

"No, I'm not mad. Listen, we can go to the Caymans anytime you want. And we won't have to listen to Cyrus the Virus."

"The Virus?"

I laughed. "Just a nickname for one of our larger shareholders."

"Thanks, Trace," Tina said, wiping her eyes. "I'm driving to Seattle today. So I'll see you when you get back?"

"You better believe it," I said, giving her a hug and a kiss.

I e-mailed Cyrus and told him I'd be coming to the Caymans solo. Then I called Wally and Will and put them on the speaker.

"Fellows, I am driving to Spokane tomorrow, spending the night, and then flying out early the next day to Grand Cayman. Tina's not going with me. Her mom's had a stroke and is in the hospital over in Seattle."

"Sorry to hear about her mom, Trace," Will said.

"Me too, Trace," Wally added. "Listen, Trace, let me give you Dominic's contact info."

Will whistled softly.

"Will, I'm not trying to set him up. Trace needs to meet Dominic and give her a heads-up about Cyrus. Cyrus knows she was snooping around, and it could be dangerous for her. I'd feel awful if something happened to her."

"It's a good idea, Wally," I said. "E-mail me her contact information and copy her so she knows I'll be contacting her." I paused a half-beat. "Is she really a ten and a half?"

"I knew it," Will said, with a laugh.

"Affirmative," Wally replied, "and more."

Bill Thornton flew from Spokane to Vancouver with blank stock powers and a share-transfer agreement. He'd set a meeting for 10:00 a.m. at Rosenburg's home.

Rosenburg's house was an older Tudor-style home on a quaint tree-lined street in North Vancouver. A vintage-green Jaguar sat in the circular driveway. Thorny walked up and knocked on the ornate wooden door.

The man who answered the door stood about six feet two. Rosenburg looked like what he was, an athlete gone soft. He was at least forty pounds overweight, and too much booze had left a road map of broken capillaries on his face.

"Mr. Rosenburg, I'm Bill Thornton," Thorny said, stepping into the massive foyer.

"You represent the Comstock?"

"I'm associated with the family that controls the casino."

"The Pantellis? Are you in the muscle end?"

"No, I'm more of an intermediary."

"You look like muscle to me."

"Actually, I look like my father. Can we get past this?"

Rosenburg nodded. "Sure, come in to my study and have a seat. Can I get you a drink? Coffee? My wife's in Europe, but I can fix you just about anything you may care for."

"No, nothing. Thank you."

"I'm at your service, Mr. Thornton."

"I'll get right to the point, sir. Your gambling debt to the Comstock is way overdue. My job is to settle this debt."

"I just need a little more time."

"You have no more time, sir."

"Well, I can't just write you a check for a million fucking dollars."

"It's a million fifty thousand," Thorny replied, thinking he'd make a couple of bucks on the side.

"What?"

"The casino charges interest on overdue balances, just like your credit card."

"That's outrageous!"

"No sir, what's outrageous is owing a million bucks to a family like the Pantellis."

Rosenburg dropped his shoulders and nodded his head. "Yes, you are quite right about that. Do you have any suggestions on how we might solve this situation?"

"Do you have any assets you could transfer to cover the debt?"

"The house is in my wife's name, but I do have some shares in a publicly trading mining company."

Jackpot, Thorny thought. "What do the shares trade for?"

"Two dollars a share. But if I sell them all at once, to pay you, it'll drive the share price down. Also, I'd be looking at a hell of a capital gains tax bill. Would you be willing to take the shares in kind?"

"How many shares do you have?"

"Five hundred thousand. The company has a hell of a uranium and gold mine down in Washington State."

"Really? And could you write me a personal check for the fifty-K of interest?"

"Yes, I could manage that."

"Let me make a quick call," Thornton said, getting up from his chair and heading toward the foyer."

Thorny spent a couple of minutes pretending to call the Pantellis and then walked back into Rosenburg's study.

"Are the shares here?"

"Yes, in my desk safe."

"Okay, we've got a deal. I think I have a blank stock-power agreement in my briefcase.

Rosenburg looked taken aback. "You brought a stock power with you?"

"Don't look so shocked, Mr. Rosenburg. This isn't my first rodeo. I came prepared for any contingency."

Rosenburg looked up from opening his desk safe. "Really? Did you come prepared for *this* contingency?"

Rosenburg pulled a snub-nosed .38 from his safe and pointed it at Thorny's chest.

"This isn't my first rodeo either, Mr. Thornton."

"You'll never get away with this. The Pantelli family will take you off the board along with your entire family."

"I don't think so. I can cut the same deal directly with the Pantellis. Probably even get them to discount the debt, and I sure as hell won't pay any *vig.*"

"People know I'm here. Someone may have seen me come in. And I don't have a weapon."

"You will have. It's going to look like you came in, tried to rob me, and I shot you in self-defense."

Before Thorny could reply, Rosenburg pumped three hollow points into his chest. Thorny was dead before he hit the floor. Rosenburg stepped from behind his desk, slipped a wicked-looking open stiletto into Thorny's hand, and dialed 911.

Chapter 10

I stepped off the plane at George Town, Grand Cayman Island, and stepped into paradise. The warm, humid sea breeze sure beat the cutting cold wind I'd left behind. Clearing customs, I saw Cyrus in the small crowd waiting to meet passengers. He looked right at home in cream-colored slacks and a light-blue silk shirt.

"Trace," Cyrus yelled, waving his hand.

I grabbed my luggage and headed in his direction.

"Cyrus, thank you for picking me up," I said, shaking his hand.

"My pleasure, Trace. Sorry to hear about Tina's mother. I was looking forward to meeting Tina."

"Thanks, Cyrus."

"I keep a townhouse here, but I've booked you a suite at the Colonial. The Hollywood boys have used the hotel in lots of movies. Just beware of hookers at the bar," Cyrus said, with a laugh.

"I remember some of the movies. And don't worry. I'll be careful . . . but not too careful."

"Fair enough. I'll drop you at the hotel. Take a swim, relax a bit, and I'll meet you there for dinner. Jack's Grill, in the hotel, around seven?"

"Perfect."

"See you then."

Cyrus dropped me off at the hotel. I checked in and then hit the pool for few laps. Rejuvenated, I plopped in a lounge chair and called Dominic.

"Dominic? Trace Brandon. Did Wally get hold of you?"

"Yes, Trace. Do you want to meet?" she asked, her French accent adding to her allure.

"Can you come over to the Colonial?"

"Give me about fifteen minutes."

"Okay, I'll be at the pool. I'm about six feet with dark hair, navy swimsuit, and Central Washington University tee shirt. Bring your swim-suit if you want to take a dip."

Twenty minutes later, I spotted her. Wally's rating was a tad low. I put her closer to a twelve. Dark complexion, shoulder-length, jet-black hair, sapphire-blue eyes, and a body like a centerfold. She looked in my direction, and I waved her over.

"Trace?" she asked, extending her hand.

"Dominic, very glad to meet you," I replied, shaking her firm hand.

"So, Trace, you're meeting with Cyrus?"

"Well, when he called and invited me to come down here for a meeting, it was about twenty degrees in Ellensburg with blowing snow. Coupled with the fact that Cyrus is a large shareholder in Montana Creek Mining, the decision wasn't too tough," I said, with a laugh.

Dominic laughed. "Very understandable. I hate snow too. Have you met Cyrus before?"

"Yes, he came to a presentation I made in Vancouver. We spoke for a few minutes. He's quite a character."

"Yes, he can be all charm and wit, but don't underestimate him, Trace. He's hard as nails and gives no quarter."

"I know. He's already had a couple of his miscreants try and foul up our drilling operation. And as you found out, he's acquiring our shares both here, and in Vancouver."

My cell phone rang. "Speak of the devil. Excuse me just a sec."

"Trace, Cyrus."

"Yes, sir, what can I do for you?"

"Listen, Trace. I'm bringing a date with me to dinner. Do you want me to have her bring a friend for you?"

"Hold just a sec, Cyrus," I replied, cupping the phone. "Dominic, care to have dinner with me, Cyrus, and his date? Jack's around seven."

"Love to. It should be quite interesting."

"Cyrus, I've got a date. We'll meet you at seven."

"Tell Dominic I look forward to her company," Cyrus said, with a chuckle.

"Why am I not surprised you'd figure it out?" I said.

"It's a small island, Trace. See you tonight."

Dominic and I swam, had a drink with an umbrella in it, and got to know each other a bit. Around five she left to get ready for dinner.

At seven sharp we all met at Jack's Grill.

"Dominic, Trace, I'd like you to meet Lisa Miller. She's from Savannah, Georgia. Graduated from the University of Georgia and is a former Miss Georgia. Lisa manages the day-to-day operations of Carib International. Of course, you may already know that." Cyrus said, smiling at Dominic.

"Nice to meet y'all," Lisa said, her southern drawl like warm butter.

She looked to be in her early forties, but still a beauty.

Cyrus had reservations, and we were seated ahead of a large crowd waiting for tables.

From our table, in a VIP reserved area, we had a breathtaking view of Seven Mile Beach.

We all ordered drinks, and Cyrus ordered a starter of broiled scallops for the table.

"I think you'll find the food here excellent," Cyrus said, between bites of seared, curried scallops. "Jack's has become one of the most popular restaurants on the island. If you're not a friend of the management, so to speak, it's damned hard to get a reservation."

Dominic and I ordered the red snapper with cous-cous. Lisa went with the wahoo, and Cyrus chose lobster. Several bottles of two-year-old, and very expensive, Sauvignon Blanc complemented the seafood and the conversation.

"So, Trace, my compliments on your acquisition of the Sullivan Mine, going public, and a rising share price," Cyrus said, raising his wine-glass in a toast. "I'm glad my vigilance of new mining claims allowed me the good fortune to participate in your venture."

"Thank you, Cyrus," I replied. "We appreciate Twisp River taking down a good portion of our private placement, and Carib's continued investment in our shares."

Cyrus smiled and nodded at Dominic. "Actually, I'm quite happy Dominic was able to provide you with information on my ownership of Carib International. Without which, I doubt we'd all be together here tonight."

Dominic smiled at the polite jab. "Corporate research is my speciality, Cyrus."

"Touché," Cyrus replied, winking at Dominic. "Dessert anyone? The vanilla bean créme-brûlée is top of the line."

As we were leaving Jack's, Cyrus invited Dominic and me to join him and Lisa tomorrow for a cruise and lunch on his boat.

"Tomorrow at eleven, Blue Water Yacht Club. Dominic knows the way," Cyrus said. "I'm moored at slip number thirty-five. She's a black-and-white, forty-four-foot Atlantic."

'I'm good to go," I said. "How about you, Dominic?"

"I think I can clear my schedule," Dominic replied. "I'll pick you up in front of your hotel at ten forty-five."

"Excellent. We'll look forward to seeing you both," Cyrus said, "and thank you for a lovely evening."

Dominic and I watched as Cyrus escorted Lisa out of the hotel.

"Well, that wasn't too bad," I said, with a smile.

"No, it was fine," Dominic replied. "Cyrus even picked up the tab."

"Yep, he's a major piece of work," I said, with a laugh. "Could I interest you in a night-cap?"

"I would, Trace, but I'm going to have a busy morning if I'm to make our lunch date."

"No problem. I'm full of wine and great food, and I'm pooped. I'll see you tomorrow at ten forty-five," I said, giving her a good-night kiss on the cheek.

"Tomorrow it is. Sleep well. I enjoyed your company, Trace. See you in the morning."

The next morning Dominic picked me up. and we drove a short distance down Seven Mile Beach to the yacht club. We parked her car and walked down the docks until we found Cyrus's slip. His boat was named the *TaxEvader,* and she looked sleek and fast.

"Welcome aboard," Cyrus called out. "We're just about to shove off."

Dominic and I hustled aboard.

"I love the name," I said, grinning broadly.

"Yeah, me too," Cyrus said, squeezing my shoulder. "I thought it up while I was making license plates in Oregon."

"Income tax evasion?"

"You got it. I had a crooked accountant," Cyrus said, with a laugh. "Can you believe it? The SOB cooks the books, and I go to jail."

"What happened to the accountant?"

"Sky diving accident," Cyrus replied, with a wry grin. "Chute didn't open. Guess he couldn't pack a parachute any better than he could keep books."

I helped Lisa cast off the lines, and Cyrus piloted us out of the marina. Dominic and Lisa went below to prepare a light lunch. I went up on the bridge with Cyrus.

"It's a hell of a nice boat, Cyrus."

"Thank you. She's one of a kind. A custom-built Atlantic. Forty-four feet with twin three-hundred-eighty-horsepower engines. She'll do thirty knots, flat out."

"Impressive."

"I'll take her out a bit and drop anchor. We'll have a hell of a view of the island while we eat lunch."

Cyrus found a good spot and, dropped anchor and the girls laid out lunch. We were enjoying conch fritters and cold beer when Cyrus's cell phone went off.

"Excuse me just a second. It's Malcolm with Twisp River."

Cyrus listened but asked few questions. I could see his demeanor change during the call.

"I'm sorry all, but I'm going to have to head back in after you finish your lunch," Cyrus said, closing his flip phone. "There's been an accident. Bill Thornton, my long-time associate and close friend, has been killed. I'm going to have to get back to Spokane as soon as possible."

"What happened, Cyrus?" I asked.

"Well, I may as well tell you, 'cause you're going to find out in any case. Richard Rosenburg, one of the founders of the Vancouver shell you merged with, shot and killed Thorny."

"Why would he kill Mr. Thornton?"

"I don't have all the details, Trace. But, I'll get to the bottom of it when I get back to Spokane."

With Cyrus leaving, there was little point in me sticking around. Although, if Dominic would've asked, I'd have stayed on. We'd developed a very good chemistry in only a few days. I sensed if I stuck around, we would find ourselves in a relationship. Discretion being the better part of valor, I packed up, said good-bye to Dominic, and flew back to frozen Spokane.

On the long flight home, I pondered why Rosenburg would've killed Thornton. In my gut, I knew it had to be connected to the shares he owned in Montana Creek Mining.

Chapter 11

Richard Rosenburg was a long-time donator to the Vancouver Police Department and a close friend of the chief constable. His testimony and the physical evidence at the crime scene supported his claim of self-defense in the shooting death of William Thornton. No indictment was issued.

After the heat simmered down, Rosenburg called Al Pantelli in New Orleans.

"Mr. Pantelli, this is Richard Rosenburg in Vancouver, Canada. I would like to talk to you, if you have a minute?"

"Goddamn, Rosy, you sure took care of Thornton."

"He tried to steal some stock certificates from me, and pulled a knife. I had little choice."

"Uh-huh. Well, it's water under the freakin' bridge. So, what can I do for you?"

"It concerns my debt to the Comstock Casino, Mr. Pantelli."

"Rosy, I assigned your debt to a third party, one of whom you've already drilled."

"What? Who?"

"I assigned it to a Cayman corporation called Carib International."

"I see," Rosenburg said, nervously as he grabbed for a pen and paper. "Carib International?"

"Correct."

"So you and I are square?"

"As a four-by-four. Makes me wonder, though, why Thorny tried to steal your cert's. Hell, he could have filed a lien on any of your property and gotten the shares legally. He didn't have to heist them."

"Well, maybe he wasn't too smart."

"I guess not. He's dead."

"I appreciate the heads-up, Mr. Pantelli."

"It wasn't a heads-up. It's just how it is. One other thing, Rosy. Stay out of our casino. Next time you get behind, will be the last time you get behind. *Capisce?*"

"Understood, Mr. Pantelli," Rosenburg replied, hanging up.

Rosenburg put both elbows on his desk, interlocked his fingers, and rested his chin on his thumbs. This could be a damned dangerous situation, he thought. Or, it could be a hell of an opportunity.

When I got back to my office, my first call was to Tina.

"Tina, it's Trace. How's your mom doing?"

"Better, Trace, but it's going to be a long haul. How was your trip?"

"It got cut short. One of Cyrus's associates was killed in Vancouver, and he had to get back. So I didn't get much on-island time, but what I did see, I liked. When we get a break, and your mom's better, I'll take you down there."

"Sounds good, Trace, and I'm sorry about Mr. McSweeny's friend, but I'm very glad you're back."

"Let me get caught up a tad, and we'll spend some time together."

"You've got a date, cowboy."

My second call was to Wally, in Vancouver. I wanted his take on what went down with Thornton.

"Well, Trace, Rosenburg told me this Thornton character pulled a knife and tried to steal his Montana Creek Mining shares. Richard kept a revolver in his safe and pulled it out instead of the stock cert's. He shot Mr. Thornton three times in the chest. Point-blank range."

"Damn, what in *the* hell is going on?"

"Good question. Listen, the name Thornton seems familiar to me. Do we know somebody by that name?"

"Remember Ike, the core rustler?"

"Yes."

"Well, Ike told me he'd been hired by someone called 'Thorny'."

"I'm surprised that idiot told you anything."

"Yeah, well, I had to use enhanced interrogation techniques."

"What?" Wally said, stifling a laugh. "What did you do to him? Or maybe I don't want to know."

"Nothing much really. My techniques are a few levels below water-boarding."

"Uh-huh. So, if Thorny and Thornton are one and the same, then this leads back to Cyrus?"

"Could be."

"Stealing the shares for Carib wouldn't have worked. The shares would have to be transferred legally. New cert's issued from the transfer agent, all the normal paperwork."

"Maybe Cyrus has something on Rosenburg and was trying to get the shares legally?"

"Well, there were some rumors on the street about Rosenburg being into a Vegas casino for some serious money. Could be there's a connection?"

"Possible. At least the shares are still in Rosenburg's hands. Maybe we should see if we can buy him out. Before someone else comes after him or he dumps the shares."

"My thoughts exactly. And we better move fast, before the Virus whacks him for killing his buddy, Thornton."

Chapter 12

A couple days later I got a call from Jim Lee at International Uranium Corp.

"Trace, Jim Lee with IUC. Got a minute?"

"Yes, sir. How are you?"

"Good, Trace. I'm in Toronto meeting with fund managers and wanted to get back to you on acquiring a minority interest in Montana Creek Mining."

"What did your board think?"

"Oh, they're like me. They'd like a bigger stake. But I convinced them this is all that's available at the present time. The situation hasn't changed, I assume?"

"No, we'll sell up to a twenty percent interest. I've already cleared it with my board."

"Okay, Trace. We're willing to take twenty percent of Montana Creek Mining at a twenty percent premium to the share price. Based on a thirty-day price average prior to the closing date. We'll also agree to provide all the technical support you'll need. We would like a first right of refusal to meet or beat any offers, should you decide to sell additional interests in Montana Creek. And I would like a seat on your board."

"Sounds doable, Jim. I'll brief my board, and we'll look forward to receiving a formal proposal."

"I'll FedEx it to you today. I'll be in Vancouver later in the week. Would it be convenient to meet on Thursday?"

"Perfect, we can meet at Walter Wilkins's office. Wally's one of our directors and a Vancouver attorney. I'll bring Will

Coffee, our other director, and we can approve the deal in Vancouver."

"Sounds good. My board has already approved the deal in principal, and I'll be able to sign for IUC."

"Okay, I'll e-mail you Wally's coordinates after we hang up. I look forward to seeing you in Vancouver, and to a long and profitable partnership."

"Same here, Trace."

I set up a conference call with Wally and Will and filled them in.

"Boys, this is a hell of a deal for us," I said. "We get a major mining company for a partner, technical expertise to production, and a cash infusion of about three and a half million bucks."

"Should be enough cash to carry us through the drilling," Will replied.

"I'm damned glad you got the standstill agreement, Trace," Wally added. "This deal with IUC is going to whet a lot of appetites for a piece of Montana Creek Mining. Being able to vote their shares will keep us out of a hostile takeover attempt."

"Yes, absent any further dilution, it will," I replied. "However, fellows, at some point we're going to be approached to sell the balance of the company. Either to IUC or another major company."

"You've just summed up our exit strategy, Trace," Will said.

"Agreed," Wally replied.

"I'm glad you guys agree. It's the only way for the three of us to cash out and leave the company, and our shareholders, in good stead."

Cyrus was not subject to a standstill agreement. He hit speed dial and called Malcolm.

"Malcolm, Cyrus here."

"Yes, Cyrus, how are you, and what can I do for you?"

"I'm fine. I've taken care of Thorny's family, and now I'm ready to take care of that miserable son of a bitch, Rosenburg."

"What've you got in mind?"

"Getting his Montana Creek Mining shares, is what I've got in mind. I'm out eight hundred grand I paid the Pantellis, Thorny's dead, and I want some payback."

"Well, he still owes the million-dollar debt Pantelli assigned to you. I can make contact with him and tell him we're taking legal action to collect. I'll make it plain we'd like his Montana Creek Mining shares as payment in full."

"Okay, but the gloves are off. You let that SOB know if he doesn't cooperate, it'll go hard on him."

"I'll get the message across, sir."

"You do that, and get back to me."

Rosenburg was working the phones too, calling the best stock promoters in Vancouver. He was looking for a home for his half million shares of Montana Creek Mining, and he really didn't give a shit who bought them.

He'd just hung up from pitching his deal to a notorious pump and dump promoter when he got an incoming call.

"Rosy, it's Al Pantelli. I wanna throw something out to you."

"Okay, I'm listening."

"My family wants to buy your shares of Montana Creek Mining."

"I'm still listening."

"We'll pay you two dollars a share, and I'll work out something with the Carib people. You'll be in the clear and have a million bucks in your pocket."

"What kind of deal with Carib?"

"You let me worry about that."

"How about two-fifty a share? I think this company's mine is the real deal."

"How about we break your freakin' legs and buy your note back from Carib? You get my drift, Rosy?"

"You make a very convincing proposal, Al. How could I refuse?"

"Smart move, Rosy. Catch a plane and be down here tomorrow with the stock cert's and signature-guaranteed stock powers. *Capisce*?"

*****

Will and I flew to Vancouver to meet James Lee at Wally's law office. We took a cab from the airport to Wally's office in the Hastings Building in downtown Vancouver. Wally's office was on the twentieth floor.

"Trace, Will, good to see you fellows," Wally said, shaking our hands. "Jim's already here. He's in the conference room."

The three of us went into Wally's conference room. The view of the harbor and the mountains above North Vancouver was spectacular. Wally had done quite well for himself in Vancouver.

"Gentlemen, Jim sent me a copy of IUC's proposal, and I've drafted an agreement I believe covers all the terms and conditions," Wally said, handing each of us a copy of the twenty-page document.

It took a couple of hours to work through the agreement. With just a couple of minor changes, we affixed our signatures.

"Really good job on the agreement, Wally," I said, pushing the signed agreement across the table.

"I couldn't agree more," Jim said, putting his gold pen back in his shirt pocket. "It's going to be a pleasure working with you fellows."

"Now that we're partners, I think a little celebration is in order," I said. "How about supper at the Blue Whale Café?"

"Is it a good place?" Jim asked. "I would love some fresh Pacific Northwest seafood."

"Yeah, it's the best in town," Wally replied. "Everybody, bring plenty of money."

"Expensive?" Jim asked.

"Yep, but worth every penny," Wally replied.

"Well, since Jim just ponied up three mil," I said, with a laugh, "I guess Montana Creek will buy."

Wally was right. The food was incredible, the setting perfect. As we got up to leave, Bart Yancey, the two-time Academy Award-winning actor, and some friends were just passing our table. Yancey kindly waved us by. I put my hand out, and we shook hands. I told him I really liked his movies.

Will also extended his hand and blurted out, ... "Food's good."

Yancey grinned. "Glad to hear it."

Outside, I started laughing. "Jesus, Will, that's probably the only time you'll ever meet Bart Yancey, and all you could say was, 'the food's good'."

"Sorry, fellows. He's my hero, and I sort of froze up."

Cyrus got the call early Saturday morning. He was enjoying a cup of coffee and watching his girlfriend, Sally Friesen, scramble some eggs while wearing nothing but a pair of black silk panties.

"Cyrus, Malcolm. Sorry to bother you on a Saturday, but this can't wait."

"No problem, Mal. I'm in a very good mood this morning. What can I do for you?"

"It's Rosenburg."

Cyrus put his coffee cup on the table, his hand trembling just bit.

"What's that bastard done now?"

"Well, I called him, as we discussed, but before I could finish my pitch, he told me he no longer owned the shares."

"What! What in the hell did he do with them?"

"He sold them to the Pantelli family."

Cyrus took a deep breath. "Jesus Christ, I can't believe it."

"Do you have a relationship with the Pantellis?"

"I thought I did."

"Rosenburg also told me the Pantellis said they would take care of his debt to Carib International."

"He did, did he?"

"Yes, sir, that's what he said."

"Well, I'm still holding the paper on Rosenburg. I'll call the Pantellis and find out what in the hell is going on."

I met Will for lunch at the First Inn. He said he had some good news.

"Trace have you seen our share price?"

"Yep, it's been climbing steadily since we announced the final core assay results."

"Yeah, the deal with IUC didn't hurt either. Wally says he's getting calls from all the major uranium and gold companies. They all want a piece."

"*Laissez les bons temps rouler*," I said. "Let the good times roll."

"Okay, Mr. Good Times, how about buying me a burger and a beer?"

"You're on," I said, catching the waitress's eye.

"Have you seen the latest charts on the projected price of uranium?"

"It's around sixteen dollars a pound, up from around ten. Looks like it may hit twenty early next year."

"Man, the numbers just keep looking better and better," I replied, taking a swig of cold beer.

"Trace, as you know, the metals markets are cyclical. We damn sure want to be selling the property into a rising metals market."

"Couldn't agree more, Will. But, I think we've got a three or four-year window. The problem is, once the price gets up, more mines start coming on stream. Uranium production goes up, and the price backs off."

Will nodded between bites of his burger. "The other thing I worry about, is another Three Mile Island. That little cluster-fuck killed the uranium market for damn near twenty years."

"I agree. It's a potential fly in the buttermilk. I've been talking with Jim, and now that Montana Creek is cashed up, we may want to initiate at least a limited winter-drilling program. Cut enough core to keep building reserves and keep investor interest up. And thereby our share price."

"I think it would be a wise decision. If we can get the share price up in the four-dollar range, we could apply for a Toronto Stock Exchange listing. Move up to the big board."

"Yeah, it's pretty sporty trading in Vancouver. Let's kick it around with Wally and our new partner, and come up with a game plan."

"Sporty. Hell, it's the god-damned Wild West," Will said, with a chuckle.

Cyrus called Al Pantelli and set up a meeting at the Comstock Casino in Vegas. When he landed at McCarron International Airport, a Comstock limo was waiting.

Al Pantelli waited for Cyrus in the conference room of his casino office. He was seated in one of the overstuffed chairs, his feet propped on the $20,000 dollar reclaimed teak conference table. A glass of Jack Daniels rested on a coaster. He rose as Cyrus entered the room.

"Cyrus, good to see you. No hard feelings on the freakin' stock, I hope? As they say in the movies, it wasn't personal, just business."

Cyrus, shook Al's massive hand and looked him hard in the eye. "No, Al, no hard feelings. It was a smart move." Cyrus walked over to the conference room bar and poured two inches of Crown into a glass of ice. "But I do have a business proposition for you."

Al sipped his bourbon and motioned for Cyrus to sit down. "I'm all ears, my friend."

"Well, Al, as you probably guessed, I'm a player in Montana Creek Mining. I've been buying shares in the open market and took down a chunk of their private placement."

"I see," Al replied, absent-mindedly rotating his three-carat-diamond pinky ring with his thumb.

"I tried to get one of my people on their board, but didn't have the votes to force the issue. But I'm getting close."

"I'm listening."

"With your five hundred thousand shares, I would be in a strong position to force the issue."

"Cyrus, I'm not interested in selling my shares, at least not yet."

"I don't really need your shares, Al. All I need is your proxy to vote your shares. In return for which I would pay you two hundred thousand dollars from the money Rosenburg owes me. With the eight hundred grand I've already paid you, you'd have the million Rosenburg originally owed you. Plus you'd still have the shares, which at today's price is another mil plus."

"How long do you need the voting proxy?"

"I'd like five years."

Al took a deep pull on his bourbon. "Three years."

"Agreed, provided your crew collects my mil from Rosenburg. You know, Al, that son of a bitch killed one of my oldest friends."

"You've got a deal, Cyrus, and don't worry about the dough. They say you can't get blood out of a turnip. Well, my people can. As for Rosy, well, after we get the dough, we probably won't see Rosy no more."

After discussing a winter campaign with Jim Lee and Wally, Will and I drove up to Oroville to discuss the project with Red Blackstone.

"What do you think, Red?" I asked, after laying out our drilling proposal.

"It'll cost more," Red replied. "You've got to have heated areas. Resupplying is tougher. Things break when it gets real cold. And it gets colder than a defrocked cardinal's heart in those mountains."

I laughed. "That cold, huh?"

"Want to take a crack at it?" Will asked, smiling at the cardinal comment.

"Sure, it beats sitting around waiting for spring," Red replied. "We'll still have to run two shifts. We can't let the equipment sit out there at night and freeze up."

"We'll leave it to you, Red," I said. "Come up with a cost estimate. In the meantime, we'll start the permitting process. Shouldn't be too tough. The Forest Service prefers winter work. Less risk of forest fires."

"I'll have something for you in a day or two, fellows," Red replied.

"Sounds good," I said. "We'll swing through Winthrop on our way back to Ellensburg and give Bob Malott a heads-up.

He'll have to build a few more locations and open up the roads. I think he'll be glad for the work. His business gets pretty slow in the winter months."

My assumption was correct. Bob was very happy to get the work. He'd been carrying most of his crew out of his hip pocket just to help them through the winter. In a couple of weeks we'd be turning to the right.

Al Pantelli summoned his deadliest assassin, Peter Manetti, aka, the Chemist. Manetti stood five feet eight and weighed about one hundred fifty pounds. He had graying hair, cut short, a pallid complexion, and rather unexpressive pale-blue eyes. Dr. Manetti looked more like the frumpy college professor he'd once been, than a stone-cold killer. His weapon of choice was any of a number of chemical compounds, all of which killed in rather unpleasant fashions.

"Peter, I've got a job for you," Al said. "Take a seat, and I'll fill you in."

It took about fifteen minutes for Al to brief his assassin.

"I'll call Rosenburg and tell him he has to come up with the mil. He's to deliver the money to you, in cash. After you get the money, take a few days and plan a hit on this SOB. And Peter, this prick killed a friend of a friend. No quick exit for him. *Capisce?*"

A couple of hours after his meeting with the Chemist, Al Pantelli picked up the phone in his penthouse suite, and dialed Richard Rosenburg's number.

"Rosy, it's Al Pantelli. I need to speak with you for a sec."

"Sure, Mr. Pantelli. What's on your mind?"

"As you know, my casino assigned your IOU to Carib International. And they want their money."

"What? Wait a fucking minute. You said you'd take care of Carib."

"You'd better watch your mouth when you're talking to me, you out-of-shape piece of shit."

"Sorry, Mr. Pantelli, but I thought we had a deal."

"I tried to negotiate a deal with Carib, but they're mixed up with a goddamned Colombian cartel. I couldn't make a deal," Pantelli replied, the lie coming as easily as a Hail Mary. "Listen, Rosy, these are some very rough bottom dwellers. Even the Outfit doesn't mess with these bastards. They're crazy. You can't do business with them."

"Jesus, I've lost my shares, and now I'll lose my money too."

"Damn it, Rosy. You owed us a million bucks. The money you got from us will cover your debt. You're even, off the hook. And you got to pop Thornton as a bonus."

"It was self-defense."

"I'm sure it was. In any case, my associate, Mr. Manetti, will be in Vancouver day after tomorrow to pick up the money. Have the million ready, in cash. Once he calls me, confirming receipt, I'll contact Carib and set up a payoff meet. I'll get your note canceled, and you'll be clear. *Capisce?*"

Cyrus was in his Spokane office, going over Twisp River Resources and Carib's current ownership position in Montana Creek Mining. With Al's proxy he controlled about 17 percent of the outstanding shares. More than enough to demand a seat on their board. Smiling, he flipped open his cell phone and made the call.

"Trace, Cyrus McSweeny. Sorry your Cayman trip got cut short."

"No problem, Cyrus. I was very sorry to hear about Mr. Thornton. Did he also go by Thorny?"

"Yes, it was his nickname. He was a very good man and a good friend to me over the years. He handled my business interests while I was locked up. Didn't steal a damn dime."

"A hard man to replace," I replied, my suspicions about Thorny and Ike confirmed.

"Exactly. Listen, Trace, I called to talk to you about getting Malcolm on your board. My companies now control a little over seventeen percent of your shares. More than enough to warrant a seat on your board."

"Are you sure about the percentage, Cyrus? I just looked at a shareholders list, and it looks like you should be around fourteen percent. Assuming the buying through Cayman Island Securities is all for Carib International's account."

"Your numbers are correct, as far as they go. But, I also hold a proxy to vote five hundred thousand shares previously issued to Richard Rosenburg."

I took a deep breath. "How the hell did you manage that?"

Cyrus laughed. "Rosenburg owed a mil to a Vegas casino. He settled the debt with his five hundred thousand shares of Montana Creek Mining. I simply made a deal with the casino principals to vote their shares for the next three years."

"Damn, Cyrus. You don't miss a trick, do you?"

"Not many. By the way, I've seen your recent filings and noted that you put IUC's Jim Lee on your board. I believe IUC now owns a twenty percent interest in Montana Creek Mining."

"Yes, Jim's now on the board."

"Well, there you go, Trace. My interest is close to theirs, and I expect board representation."

"Valid argument, Cyrus. Let me run it by my board, and I'll get back to you."

"Fine, Trace. I'll wait to hear from you."

I hung up and got all our directors on a conference call.

"Well, I guess we don't have to worry about Rosenburg's shares any longer," Wally said. "Cyrus is right, of course. He owns or controls enough shares to seek board representation, and we've set a precedent by putting Jim on the board."

"I agree, Trace," Will concurred.

"Is there some reason why we wouldn't want to bring Cyrus or his representative on the board?" Jim asked.

"It won't be Cyrus," I replied. "He's got a federal felony charge for tax evasion. It'll be Malcolm Trueblood, CEO of Twisp River Resources."

"What's his background?" Jim asked.

"MBA from Stanford, fifteen years with GoldEx, and last five years with Twisp," I replied.

Jim whistled. "Pretty impressive. So what's the bad news?"

"His association with Cyrus," Wally said. "Cyrus is a notorious stock promoter, pump and dumper, and big-time short seller. Hell, he's been known to short his own deals."

"I see," Jim replied. "Not a group we'd really like on the inside."

"Not my first choice," I replied.

"Well, if we don't bring Malcolm on, we'll likely face a legal action, which we'll lose, and which could have a negative effect on our share price," Wally added.

"Agreed," I replied. "Well, Malcolm's only one vote on our board, he's got a hell of a resume, and he does represent almost twenty percent of our outstanding shares. I vote we bring him on, emphasize his resume to the investment community, and make the best of it. All in favor, say aye."

With no real alternative, the measure carried unanimously.

"I'll call Malcolm and let him know he's been appointed to the board," I said. "The shareholders can ratify it at the next annual meeting."

Peter Manetti disembarked from his Continental flight and cleared customs, using a bogus passport in the name of Joseph Baglio. He rented a car, drove to the ferry landing in downtown Vancouver, and crossed the harbor to North Vancouver. Fifteen minutes later he knocked on Rosenburg's front door.

Rosenburg answered the door and instinctively stepped back a half-step when he got a look at the Chemist.

"Mr. Rosenburg, I'm Peter Manetti. I believe Mr. Pantelli contacted you?"

"Yes, please come in. I've got your package in my den. Please follow me."

"No. I was instructed to take delivery in the foyer. I understand the last transaction completed in your den didn't turn out so well for one of the participants."

Anger flickered in Rosenburg's eyes.

"Is there a problem, Mr. Rosenburg?"

"No, no problem. Please wait here, and I'll get the package."

Rosenburg returned with a briefcase and opened it for Manetti's inspection.

"Want to count it?"

"No, I'm sure it's all there," Manetti replied, closing the briefcase and turning toward the door. "I doubt you're dumb enough to short the Pantelli family."

Peter returned to the Hotel Victoria, counted the money, just in case Rosenburg was dumb enough, and called Al Pantelli.

"Mr. Pantelli, I've got the package, and it's complete."

"Okay, I'll send the casino's jet up tonight to pick up the package. Meet the plane at the corporate terminal and give the package to the pilot. When you've completed all your business, take a commercial flight back to Vegas."

"Understood. I should have this wrapped up in a couple of days."

"Perfect. I'll have the jet up there in about three hours."

Manetti met the jet, handed the briefcase to the pilot, and returned to the Hotel Victoria to prep the delivery system for the nerve agent.

After our impromptu board meeting, I called Cyrus.

"Cyrus, Trace Brandon. Just wanted to let you know. I've contacted the other board members, and we've voted on adding Malcolm to our board."

"And?"

"The resolution passed unanimously. Malcolm Trueblood is now a director of Montana Creek Mining Corporation."

"Thank you, Trace. I appreciate it, and I think it is fair. After all, I do have a hell of a stake in your company."

"You mean, our company, don't you?"

Cyrus chuckled. "Yes, our company. Don't worry, Trace. We both have the same long-term goal."

"Which is?"

"Whatever best benefits the shareholders of the company."

"Glad you feel that way. Do you want to notify Malcolm, or should I call him?"

"I am scheduled to call him this morning on another matter. I'll tell him you'll be calling him. I believe his appointment should come from the chairman of the board."

Peter Manetti didn't get the moniker of "the Chemist" by accident. In another life, he'd earned a PhD in chemistry from LSU. After the death of his wife, Julie, from an especially virulent form of colon cancer, he'd grown increasingly bitter and hateful. Molecule by molecule his soul, like his wife's cancer, metastasized into pure evil.

For this job, Manetti brought an organophosphate pesticide he'd upgraded to military toxicity. Originally marketed to the public in the 1950's under the name OPP-D, the compound had killed nearly as many farmers as bugs. Realizing its potential value as a chemical weapon, the government had seized most of the commercial supply and turned it over to the military, who, with taxpayer dollars, refined the compound into one of the deadliest nerve agents known to man, VX Agent. Manetti had neglected to turn in the two gallons of OPP-D he'd been experimenting with.

VX could be applied as a liquid or aerosol. Odorless, tasteless, with just a slightly oily feel, it could kill from either skin contact or inhalation. Death from VX was especially violent.

For two days Manetti surveilled Rosenburg's movements. At noon on the third day, an opportunity presented itself. He'd followed Rosenburg to a mall parking garage and parked two rows over from Rosenburg's Jag. Manetti pulled on a pair of surgical gloves and took the tubular shoe polish applicator from his overcoat pocket. Very carefully, he unscrewed the cap and examined the angled sponge applicator tip. It appeared clean and dry. Slowly, he twisted the applicator head in a counterclockwise direction. Exactly one-quarter turn armed the device. Manetti replaced the cap and headed for Rosenburg's Jag.

The Jaguar was an older model and lacked an alarm system. Using a long, flat, metal tool, called a 'Slim Jim', that he'd concealed up the sleeve of his overcoat, Manetti popped the door lock in less than five seconds. Taking a last glance around the garage, he slipped behind the wheel. Taking a deep breath, he carefully unscrewed the top of the applicator and gently pressed it to the steering wheel. He laid down a light coating of the agent on the top half of the wheel then carefully capped the applicator. He stepped out of the Jag and closed the door behind him. Only then did he exhale.

On the way back to his car Manetti dropped the Slim Jim in a garbage can. He then drove down to the harbor and parked in a lot near the ferry landing. He bought a round-trip ferry ticket and boarded the next ferry to North Vancouver. About half-way across the bay, he sauntered over to the rail. The shoe polish applicator was cupped in his right hand. Satisfied no one was paying any attention to him, he casually opened his palm and dropped the applicator into the deep harbor. Disposal complete, Manetti rode the ferry back to downtown, retrieved his rental car, and drove to the airport.

Just before lunch, I called Malcolm in Vancouver.

"Malcolm, Trace Brandon with Montana Creek Mining."

"Yes, Trace, Cyrus said to expect a call from you. What can I do for you?"

"The board has approved you as our fifth director."

"I am glad to hear it, Trace. I think we'll all work very well together, and I look forward to the next board meeting."

"Now that you're a director, I'll can tell you one of our primary goals is to achieve a listing on the Toronto Stock Exchange. As you and Walter Wilkins are our two Canadian directors, I would appreciate it if you two would work together towards that end."

"Of course, Trace. I know several of the principals on the exchange. I'll be glad to work with Walter. We'll get you the listing requirements in short order."

"I would like to shoot for a Toronto Stock Exchange, TSX, listing this spring. Between now and then, we need to quantify our reserves and contract for an independent engineering report."

"I have a relationship with a good engineering firm here in Vancouver. They've completed several engineering reports for Twisp River Resources. All of which were well received by regulators."

"Perfect. Please send me their contact info, and I'll start the ball rolling."

Richard Rosenburg returned from the large department store,where he'd purchased a bottle of Midnight Sin perfume for his wife. She was due back from Europe in a couple of days, and it was her favorite.

He started to unlocked the Jag and noticed he'd forgotten to lock the driver's side door. Shaking his head, he placed the gift box on the passenger seat and slid behind the wheel. He put his left hand on the top of the wheel and inserted the ignition key.

"What the hell?" he said, taking his hand from the wheel and rubbing his thumb and index finger together. "Feels like some kind of oil."

Rosenburg suddenly felt nauseous and started to perspire heavily. He felt a severe tightness in his chest. Thinking it must be a heart attack, he reached for his cell phone to call 911. He didn't get past nine. The contraction hit him like a sledgehammer, slamming him violently into the steering wheel. Dropping the phone, he grabbed the wheel with both hands to try and steady up. But this merely doubled his exposure to the nerve agent. The contractions continued as the VX agent attacked all his muscle groups, causing them to go into a state of paralysis. As the muscles in his diaphragm began to shut down, he slowly and agonizingly died of asphyxiation.

Chapter 13

As part of IUC's agreement to lend technical support, Jim Lee assigned a young geologist, Tom Troutman, to help with the winter coring program. Tom would log the core, send splits to the lab for assay, and be the project geologist. I decided to drive up to Winthrop and spend a little time with the new guy.

The mine road was in good shape, thanks to Bob Malott's crew and the constant truck traffic. But, out of habit, I locked the hubs and engaged the four-wheel drive.

I pulled into the drill site and parked the Bronco. Troutman saw me pull up and walked over. He'd been logging cores in the heated core shack Red's crew had constructed for the winter operation. I got out and met him halfway. I knew from talking with Jim, and from Tom's resume, that he was an American and worked mainly in eastern Canada. He was twenty-eight years old, tall and slender, with a scruffy beard all young geologists feel is requisite. He'd earned his BS and MS at the University of Montana, in Missoula.

"Mr. Brandon?"

"Yep, that's me. You must be Troutman?"

"Yes, sir. I figured it had to be you. All the drillers talk about is your Bronco."

I laughed. "Yeah, they appreciate a truly fine piece of machinery, and please call me Trace."

"Thanks, Trace. Most of my friends call me Fish, for the obvious reason."

"Okay, Fish, how's the coring going?"

"Damn good. This is some mighty fine-looking ore, Trace."

"Ain't it though," I said, heading in the direction of the core shack.

"I've seen grades like this in the Athabasca Basin in eastern Canada and in a couple of mines in Africa. But never anything like this in the US."

"This old mine actually started out as a gold and copper mine in the late eighteen hundreds. The uranium was a pain in the ass to them," I said, with a chuckle. "Boy, how things change, huh?"

Fish nodded his head and picked up a section of high-grade ore. "It's a miracle they didn't all die of radiation poisoning."

"I'd bet the rate of cancer was pretty high for the old boys who worked in the mine," I replied.

"Yeah, and back then they wouldn't of had a clue what was making them sick," Fish said, putting the length of core back in its slot. "Truly a deadly lode."

"Yep," I replied. "They couldn't see it, smell it, or taste it, but it attacked them just the same."

I spent a couple of days on site with Fish. He was a damned good geologist, and I was glad to have him on the project.

On my way back to Ellensburg, Wally called me.

"Trace, you're not going to believe this."

"Hell, Wally, Cyrus the Virus has one of his minions on our board. I'd believe damn near anything."

"Yeah, well, believe this—Rosenburg was found dead in a downtown Vancouver parking garage. They think he had some kind of a seizure, but they're doing an autopsy just to be sure."

"Jesus, first he shoots Thornton, then he sells his shares to cover his gambling debt, and a few days later he's dead?"

"Yeah, makes you wonder, doesn't it?"

"Don't it though?"

Al Pantelli picked up the phone in the Presidential Suite of the Comstock Casino and called Cyrus.

"Cyrus, it's Al. I've got the dough Rosy owed you. When can you come down and pick it up?"

"I'll call my pilot and have him get the Lear ready. I'll be there first thing in the morning. How'd it go with the principal?"

"No problems. His account is closed."

"I'll see you tomorrow for a late breakfast. And thanks, Al. I owe you one."

Cyrus hung up and called his pilot and told him to file a flight plan to Vegas and then on to Grand Cayman. He then called Lisa Miller and told her he'd be in George Town late tomorrow evening and asked her to meet him at the airport.

The next morning at 10:00 a.m., Cyrus's Lear-jet landed in Las Vegas. The pilot taxied to the McCarran corporate terminal. Cyrus spotted the Comstock's limo parked and waiting. Forty-five minutes later he was in Al Pantelli's office, which overlooked the main casino floor.

"Eight hundred-K," Al said, handing Cyrus the black briefcase, "I took out the two hundred grand you owed me for the proxy. Please check it."

Cyrus laid the brief-case on a coffee table in front of Al's desk and popped the latches. He riffled several random bundles of hundreds and closed the case.

"That wasn't necessary, Al. I knew it would be correct."

"I like everything neat and tidy," Al replied, moving to his desk chair.

"Any problems in Vancouver?" Cyrus asked.

"No, no problems," Al said, clasping his hands over his stomach and swiveling his chair to check the action on the casino floor.

Cyrus watched him surveying the action.

"How's the casino business?"

"This is the real gold mine," Al said, spreading his hands out in the direction of the casino floor.

"Well, anytime you want to get rid of your Montana Creek Mining shares, just let me know."

Al turned to Cyrus and smiled. "Not just yet, my friend. You just be sure to vote my proxy in our best interests."

"Don't worry, Al. Your best interests are my best interests."

Chapter 14

Red motioned from the drilling rig for Troutman to come over to the rig.

"Something's not right, Fish."

"What's the problem, Red?"

"We should be in vein, but I can tell by the way the bit is cutting. we're still in granite."

"Finish this run, then trip out. Let's be sure."

Red finished the core run and pulled the tubing from inside the core barrel.

"Here she comes," Red said.

The drill helpers emptied the contents of the core liner into a core box.

"Damn—you're right, Red. Nothing but granodiorite."

"What do you want me to do?" Red asked.

"Cut another five feet of core. If we're still in granodiorite, I'll call Trace and get him up here."

An hour later my office phone rang.

"Trace, it's Fish. We've got a problem."

"What's wrong, Fish?"

"The vein is gone. It's either pinched out or been displaced by a fault."

"Holy shit—no vein at all?"

"None. We cored ten feet in granodiorite, where the vein should have been. I had Red pull out of the hole and go back in with the down-hole hammer, and drill until we hit the footwall schist. We grabbed samples every two feet, just to be sure. No vein."

"Okay, move the rig to the next location and start drilling. Drill down to where we would normally start coring. If I'm not there by then, put the rig on standby. I'm on my way."

I called Will and Wally, and e-mailed Jim Lee, and filled them in on the situation. I decided to wait to call Malcolm until I got on-site and reviewed the situation in person. I knew he'd be on the phone to Cyrus the minute we hung up. I packed my gear and headed for the Sullivan Mine.

Cyrus refueled the Lear in Houston, skirted some thunderstorms, and made Grand Cayman by 8:00 p.m. Lisa Miller was waiting in the terminal. Cyrus had longstanding arrangements with Cayman customs officers, and he breezed through with no luggage check.

"Thanks for meeting me, Lisa," Cyrus said, giving her a hug and kiss on the cheek.

"No problem, Cyrus. What's up?"

"I've got eight hundred thousand U.S. in this briefcase that I need to get it into Carib's account. And, I want to strategize a bit on our plan of attack now that Malcolm is on Montana Creek Mining's board."

"Anything else?" Lisa said, with a seductive smile.

"Well, maybe just one or two other items," Cyrus replied, a grin spreading across his face.

Chapter 15

"Chief Constable Rand? This is David Osgood, with the Ministry of Public Safety here in Vancouver."

"Yes, Mr. Osgood. What can I do for you today?"

"It's actually more what I can do for you, sir. We've got a cause of death on Richard Rosenburg, and you're not going to believe it."

"Really? Not your run-of-the-mill heart attack or stroke?"

"Only if you call VX a run-of-the-mill nerve agent."

"Come again?"

"Rosenburg was killed by percutaneous exposure, that is, skin contact, with the nerve agent known as VX."

"How is that possible? I thought only the military had access to VX."

"VX is a derivative of a 1950's pesticide called OPP-D. It's possible not all of the pesticide on the market was collected or destroyed. A good chemist could upgrade the pesticide to a weapons-grade nerve agent."

"Absolutely sure on this?"

"We nearly lost one of our paramedics getting Rosenburg out of his car. Only the fast decontamination of her exposed skin and an injection of Atropine saved her. So, yes, I'm sure."

"I see."

"Whoever killed Rosenburg applied liquid VX to the steering wheel of his Jag. The poor bastard died one horrible death."

"A terrorist hit?"

"I shouldn't think so. They wouldn't waste something as valuable as VX on Rosenburg. They'd just cut his throat."

"Okay, thanks, David. We'll check with RCMP, the military, and I'll contact the FBI down in Washington."

"Good luck, sir. And be careful. This is one of the worst nerve agents on the planet."

Rand shook his head in disbelief. "Better living through chemistry, eh?"

I arrived at the mine-site around noon and immediately checked the core. Red had moved the rig and was drilling down to the projected coring interval. He still had about seventy-five feet to go.

"Well, you're sure as hell right about the vein, Fish," I said, looking at the last core runs. "The vein's either pinched out in this area, or she's been offset by faulting."

"Have you been to the working face at the end of level one?" Fish asked.

"No, we'd need to bridge a winze to get all the way to the back."

"I think we should get a crew up here and get some planking across the winze. We need to get a look at the vein where they stopped mining. If it is faulted off, we may be able to tell the direction of offset."

"Agreed. I'll get Bob Malott to put the timber together and get up here with a crew. In the meantime, we'll see if Red intersects the vein from the new location."

I called Malott and explained what we needed. He said he'd have everything together and be on-site around ten in the morning. I hung up, and Fish and I went up the new drilling location.

"How's it look, Red?" I asked.

"We're in granite but should be at the projected vein intersection in another couple of feet."

Fish and I went over to the sample splitter where the driller's helpers were catching samples. I grabbed a handful of the drill cuttings and showed it to fish.

"Granodiorite," Fish said, looking at the small cuttings with his ten-power hand lens.

Red yelled down from the rig. "We should be in vein now, but it's cutting like granite."

We drilled another twenty-five feet of granodiorite and then hit the footwall schist.

"Damn, she's not here," Fish said.

"No, she's not," I replied, in disgust.

"What do you want to do, Trace?" Fish asked.

"Only one thing to do, Fish. Have the rig stand by while we put together some cross sections and maps. Maybe we'll be able to figure out what's going on after we get to the working face on level one."

Fish nodded and waved his hand at Red. When he got Red's attention, Fish drew his index finger across his throat.

"Shut her down," he yelled.

Paying rig time while a drill stands idle is a worst-case scenario for a project geologist. But in this case, I could see no alternative.

Fish and I went back to our storage warehouse at Malott's yard in Winthrop. We cranked up a couple of space heaters and went to work. While Fish worked on cross sections, I made a call I didn't want to make.

"Malcolm, it's Trace. Got a sec?"

"Sure, Trace, what's up?"

"We've lost the vein. We drilled two holes along the projected strike of the vein. When we hit the vein interval, she wasn't there. Tom Troutman, the IUC geologist, and I are working up cross sections of the drilling to see if we can figure out what's going on."

"Any guesses?"

"Well it's either a pinch out, which could be just a local event, or not. Or a fault has cut the vein and displaced it in some manner. We're going to do some work in the main adit in order to get back to the working face and see if the vein is still in sight. If it's not, we may get some indications from fault striations as to the direction of movement."

"Okay, Trace, I know you're on top of it. Thanks for calling me and please keep me informed as work progresses."

Malcolm hung up and hit Cyrus's number on speed dial.

"This better be good, Malcolm. I'm in the Cayman's and dead center in the middle of a piece of work."

Malcolm could hear a muffled female giggle in the background.

"I just got off the phone with Trace. There's a problem at the Sullivan Mine."

Cyrus focused immediately. "What kind of problem?"

"The last two core holes did not intercept the vein."

"Who knows about this?"

"Just the directors and the drillers."

"Okay, I'm going to make a few calls in the morning. We're going to short the stock. When news of this gets out, the shares price will drop. We'll take some profits now, and if they relocate the vein, we'll know ahead of time, and we'll cover our short position. And Malcolm, not a damn word to anyone, clear?"

"Understood, sir."

Al Pantelli was on his second Bloody Mary of the morning. It'd been a hell of a party last night, and he was paying the price. His cell phone rang and he picked it up.

"Al, Cyrus here. Are you in Vegas or New Orleans?"

"I'm back in the Big Easy. What's up?"

"Listen, Al. There's a problem at Montana Creek's mine in Washington."

"What kind of problem?" Al asked, taking a healthy pull on his Bloody Mary.

"I don't know how much you know about drilling out an orebody."

"Not a hell of a lot, so educate me."

"Well, they're drilling along the trend, called strike, of the vein, and the vein has disappeared."

"What the hell you mean, disappeared?"

"It means it could have petered out, or it could have been cut by a fault and displaced, moved laterally or vertically, or both."

"Which means what the fuck to me?"

"It means, Al, they are going to have to try and find it. And they may or may not. It also means, when word gets out, the share price is going south."

"How many people know about this?"

"Only Montana Creek's board, the drillers, me, and now you."

"So, your man on their board called you with the info?"

"You got it."

"So we're on the inside?" Al asked.

"Totally, at least until Trace puts out an update to the shareholders and regulators."

"I assume you've got a plan to take advantage of this situation?"

"I do, Al. I'm shorting the stock when the market opens tomorrow. I suggest you do likewise."

"How many shares do you think I should sell?"

"Well, you've got half a million shares, Al. You could short against all of them."

"How many shares are you selling short?"

"A million."

"Jesus! Are you god-damned sure about this, Cyrus?"

"Look, the shares are going to tank when the news gets out. You sell short a half million shares at two bucks and buy it back at a lower price, and it could be a much lower price. You could make several hundred grand, and still have your half-million shares."

"Okay, Cyrus, I'm in. But you better keep me posted, and I mean up to the fucking minute posted."

"Don't worry, Al. We're partners."

Fish was pouring over cross sections and fence diagrams of the cores. "Trace, it has to be a fault. The damn vein was nearly thirty-feet thick in the drill hole before we lost it. It can't have totally disappeared in a thousand feet. It's offset somehow."

I looked at Fish's sections and agreed. We needed to get to the working face on level one and see how it looked.

Bob Malott's crew was already on-site and hauling six-by-six mine timbers and military-surplus, perforated steel plate, commonly called PSP, into the mine adit.

"Morning, Trace, Fish," Bob said. "We'll lay the six-by-six's across the winze and then cover it with the PSP. It's about a five-foot-wide span, but the timbers and PSP will be strong enough to take an underground drill across, if needed."

"Perfect. Just let me know when we can get across," I said, turning to Fish. "Let's get geared up."

It took Bob's crew only about an hour to bridge enough of the winze so Fish and I could cross. The working face was about a thousand feet past the winze.

"Here it is, Trace," Fish said, shining his mine lantern on the rock wall where the adit came to an end.

"No sign of the vein, but look at these horsetail striations," I said, pointing to the feathery lineations cut into the rock face. "A fault has cut the vein, and from the looks of the horsetails, I'd say she's been displaced downward and to the southwest."

Fish examined the striations in the rock and checked his compass. "Agreed. It explains why the old-timers stopped advancing this adit. They ran into the same problem as us. They lost the vein."

Fish made a few calculations on his clipboard. "We need to either back the rig off to the southwest or drill a very steep hole from the current location. And we'll have to go deeper."

"I vote for the steeper hole from Red's current drill pad. If we move him farther to the southwest, we'll need to revise our permits and build a new location."

"Agreed—it's worth a shot. If we miss it, we'll just have to re-permit and get after it."

Fish and I exited the mine adit and found Bob and Red waiting for us. I explained the plan of attack based on our findings in the mine.

"Sounds like a plan," Red said. "I'll get the rig ready to start drilling. We'll use the down-hole hammer and catch samples until we hit the vein."

"Okay, Red," I replied, "angle the hole at seventy-five degrees and grab samples every ten feet until you get to three hundred feet. After that, I'll need samples every five feet."

"You got it," Red replied. "I'll get the rig fired up, and we'll be making hole in about fifteen minutes."

"Trace, if you don't need us anymore," Bob said, "I'll send my crew back to town. We'll leave the extra timbers and PSP by the mine entrance, in case it's needed later."

"Perfect," I replied, shaking hands with Bob. "We'll make some hole and see if we can't get back in ore."

Cyrus was on the phone to his broker, Nigel Cunningham, at Cayman Island Securities, as soon as the market opened.

"Nigel, Cyrus McSweeny here."

"Cyrus, good to hear from you. Are you on-island?"

"Yes, just flew in and will be leaving shortly. Listen, Nigel, I want to place a short-sell order against some shares held in Carib International and Twisp River Resources' accounts."

"Okay, Cyrus, what's the company name and symbol?"

"It's Montana Creek Mining Corp. Symbol is MCM.V, on the Vancouver Stock Exchange."

"We've been buying shares on MCM for both accounts. Now you want to go short?"

"You got it. I've got a hunch they're oversold and looking at a correction."

"Uh-huh. How many shares do you want to sell short?"

"A million."

"Damn, Cyrus. My information shows they only have about eight million shares issued and outstanding. You're talking about twelve and a half percent of the company."

"Your information is correct, Nigel. Place the order."

"Do you think I, that is, our firm, should short them as well?"

"You mean a naked short?"

"Naked shorts are illegal, Cyrus, at least in the U.S. But I reckon we could borrow some shares from a Canadian brokerage. If we thought the risk was worth taking."

"If they get hit with a lot of short selling, it's sort of a self-fulfilling prophecy, is it not?"

"Unless the company generates enough buying to squeeze the short sellers. Sometimes all it takes is a significant positive announcement. It can be a risky proposition, Cyrus."

"No balls, no bucks, Nigel. Listen, I think the company is way overpriced at two dollars Canadian. You make your own decision. You've got a bunch of analysts. Crunch the numbers."

"We'll see, Cyrus. In any event, I'll place your short-sell order."

Al Pantelli met his older brother, Crispino, at a small café, in the French Quarter.

"What's the occasion, little brother?" Crispino asked, running his fingers through his curly-black hair.

"Whadda you know about short-selling?"

"I know if you guess wrong, and the market moves against your short position, there's no limit to how much money you can lose."

"You remember the old guy I was in the can with, up in Oregon?"

"Cyrus, something or other?"

"Yeah, Cyrus McSweeny. They call him Cyrus the Virus. He's a major piece of work. Anyway, he was after the Montana Creek Mining shares we got from Rosenburg."

"Yeah, so?"

"So, Cyrus calls me yesterday and says he's going to short the stock. He thinks the company's in trouble. Some bullshit about a vein pinch out at their mine. I'm not too clear on the whole situation. Bottom line, he says we should short the stock and cover it with the shares we got from Rosy."

"You remember what Pop used to tell us, 'If you don't understand the deal, either whack the promoter or get the fuck away from it.' And from what I've heard about this Virus prick, maybe we should vaccinate him."

"Vaccinate him?" Al said, with a chuckle.

"Yeah, inject a little humility in his ass. Look, just play along with the scam but don't short the stock. When we got the shares from Rosy, I had our accountants dig into Montana Creek Mining. They think it's the real deal. Cyrus is looking for an angle to tank the stock, make some dough, then buy back in on the cheap. There might be an opportunity to catch him in a short squeeze. Maybe bail his ass out at a steep discount, or take his shares."

Al laughed, and damned near choked on his beignet. "*Perfezionare, I'amo,* dead solid perfect, brother."

Fish and I hiked up to the rig. Red was at the controls and turned in our direction as we approached the drill.

"She's drilling like a damn gopher," Red shouted, over the compressor noise. "How deep do you think we'll have to go to intersect the offset vein?"

Fish checked his calculations. "If she doesn't flatten out any, we should hit it around seven hundred feet."

"It'll be some time tomorrow morning," Red replied. "Assuming Nick's crew doesn't have any problems on the night shift. You all may as well head to town and get some chow, and shut-eye. If there's any problems, we'll call your cell."

"Okay, Red, sounds like a plan," I said. "See you in the morning."

Early the next morning Fish and I were just finishing breakfast at the W when my cell went off. Caller ID showed it was Wally.

"Hey, Wally," I said. "What has you up at the crack of dawn?"

"The markets just opened, and someone has shorted our stock one million shares."

"Holy crap, Wally. Do you know who's shorting us?" I said, looking over at Fish.

"I'm working on it, but there's only one shareholder I'm worried about."

"Cyrus?"

"Yep, his companies own enough of our shares to cover the short position. And a move like this is pure Virus."

"How's the share price holding up?" I asked.

"Down ten percent."

"Damn."

"Exactly, Trace. How's the drilling coming? We need to put out some major good news, ASAP."

"Fish and I think we've figured out the problem. It's a fault. Red is drilling a steeper, deeper hole to see if our calculations are correct. We should know something later today."

"Okay, sounds good. Let me know if you re-locate the vein, and I'll get a press release out to the market."

"You do realize, Wally, that nobody but the directors and the drillers know we ever lost the vein. We haven't put out any drilling updates."

"Yeah, sure makes you wonder who the hell leaked this info."

"If the seller is Cyrus, the leak came from Malcolm. Keep digging Wally and check with Dominic. She has great contacts in the Caymans. If it is Cyrus, Malcolm is history."

"It's not easy to remove a director, Trace."

"Oh, I think he'll go of his own volition once we threaten to turn him over to the securities regulators. They're getting damned tough on insider trading. We'll Gordon Gekko his miserable ass."

"I'm all over it, Trace. Let me know as soon as you confirm we're back on the vein."

The Pantelli family worked out of a restored nineteenth-century mansion on Saint Louis Street, in the Quarter. Crispino Pantelli walked down the hall to his brother's office.

"*Buon giorno*, Al."

"Morning, Pino," Al replied, using his brother's nickname.

"Listen, my broker just called and confirmed a large short position was posted this morning against Montana Creek Mining shares."

"One thing about the Virus, he doesn't fuck around," Al replied, shaking his head.

"No, he doesn't, and neither do we. Whatever info Cyrus thinks he has is not yet public. It may just be a scam he dreamed up to knock down the share price. My guys are telling me to buy. The shares are down ten percent on word of the short sale. But they know of no negative developments with the company."

"So, whadda ya think?"

"I told them to start buying. Nothing too serious, just nibble a bit at these lower levels. See if we can make a few bucks when the stock recovers. By the way, I heard some sad news about Rosenburg. I understand he's no longer with us."

"Yeah, I heard he had some kind of seizure?"

Pino lowered his voice. "The Chemist?"

Al nodded.

"Well, we all gotta go sometime," Pino said, with a chuckle. "I'll keep you posted on Montana Creek. Maybe we'll get lucky and catch the Virus in a short squeeze."

Chapter 16

Between Red and Nick Wetzel they'd managed to drill down to 650 feet.

"Morning, Red," I said. "Looks like you and Nick made some serious hole?"

"Yep, she's drilling away, and we're catching a few drilling breaks now. The rock's drilling like it's fractured. You might want to check the cuttings. We could be getting close to the vein."

Fish and I checked the last twenty feet of drill cuttings. The last samples showed some alteration in the rock. The type of alteration that accompanies mineralization.

"You're right, Red," I yelled, over the rig noise. "Looks promising."

Red continued pushing the down-hole hammer bit through the rock.

"Trace," Red yelled, "feels like a transition. I'll stop drilling and circulate so you can check the samples from the bottom of the hole."

It takes a few minutes for the air compressor to lift the cuttings from the bottom of the hole to the surface. "Lag time" is what geologists call it. Right now, I'd have called it an eternity.

Finally the rock chips hit the splitter, and we were able to grab a sample. Through my ten-power hand lens I could see fragments of quartz and sulfides mixed in with the granodiorite.

"Bingo, boys!" I shouted. "Trip out of the hole, Red, and run the core barrel in. I think we're back in business."

"The core will tell the tale," Fish said, standing next to me, looking at the cuttings.

Red ran the core barrel and diamond bit into the hole, and started coring.

In about thirty minutes the core barrel liner was full, and Red used the wire-line to retrieve it.

"Grab your asses, boys!" Red yelled. "Here she comes."

Luke Johnson, Red's helper, decanted the core into the wooden core box.

"Holy moly," Fish said softly. "We are back in business."

I took a paint-brush from the supply table, dipped it in a coffee can full of water, and wetted down the entire five feet of core. "Damnation, it's pure pitchblende."

The next seven core runs were nearly identical. Nearly forty feet of the purest uranium ore neither Fish nor I had ever seen. On the eighth run we penetrated the footwall schist and were through the massive vein.

After a bit of celebration, Fish and I were on our cell phones, relating the good news to both James Lee and Wally.

"Send me the particulars, and I'll start drafting a news-release," Wally said, adding, "What about Malcolm?"

"Let's leave Malcolm out of the loop for now," I replied. "If we're wrong about him, I'll just have to fade the heat. And remember, Wally," I cautioned, "no press release until the core assays are back."

"But it looks good, right?" Wally asked.

"Yes, Wally, it's high grade, but hold the press release until assays are back."

"You got it. Boy oh' boy, I'd sure hate to be the short seller when this news gets posted."

"Yeah," I replied, "if it is Cyrus, he'll be in for a rude shock in a couple of days."

Chapter 17

A call came into FBI headquarters in Washington, DC.

"FBI, Agent Thompson speaking."

"Agent Thompson, this is Chief Constable Peter Rand with the Vancouver, BC, Police Department. Is Special Agent Beau Monroe available?"

"Hold one minute please."

Monroe punched the blinking light and picked up the receiver. "This is Special Agent Beau Monroe."

"Agent Monroe, this is Chief Constable Peter Rand. We spoke a week or so ago with regards to a homicide here in Vancouver."

"Yes, sir. The victim who was killed by exposure to VX."

"We're at pretty much of a dead end up here. I was hoping maybe your investigation might have turned something up?"

"Well, as I mentioned in our previous conversation, your case got moved to near the top of the totem pole. Anytime something as deadly as VX is involved, it get's the FBI's undivided attention."

"Any leads, Agent Monroe?"

"Well, whoever pulled this off is a very sophisticated customer. Most likely a chemist gone rogue, so to speak.

"Our thoughts as well," Rand replied.

"We've been running our databases, looking for a chemistry type who might fit the profile. Also, we've got three unsolved homicides, all of which involved sophisticated poisons. We're going back through those case files, looking for leads."

"Any of the open cases involve VX?" Rand asked.

"No, sir. But they're not run of the mill, either. One involved a synthetic replication of poison tree frog toxin, Allopumiliotoxin-267A."

"Bloody hell, the name's enough to kill you," Rand said, with a chuckle.

"Yes, sir, it's a mouthful. But like VX, it's a form of neurotoxin. It attacks the heart rather than causing complete muscle paralysis, as with VX."

"Both neurotoxins, huh? Well, Agent Monroe, it's a lead of sorts. The killer could be ex-military with chemical weapons experience? Or someone who worked at a university or research facility?"

"Our line of thinking too. We're reviewing records of people known to have worked on nerve agents, either in the military, or in the private sector. Possibly a disgruntled employee, someone with personal problems, history of depression, that sort of thing."

"The three open cases, any of the victims have a criminal history?" Rand asked.

"We believe the man killed by the synthetic tree frog poison had a mob connection. Of the other two, one we're pretty sure was a KGB hit. The third looked like a drug deal gone bad. The joint the victim was smoking at the time of death was laced with ricin," Monroe said, with a chuckle.

"Any of this ring any bells?" Agent Monroe asked.

"Possibly the mob connection," Rand replied. "Our victim was a well-known gambler both in the Vancouver penny stock market and at the crap tables in Vegas. I'll have my team dig deeper into his recent stock dealings and check into his gambling situation."

"What about William Thornton?" Constable Rand asked. "The man Rosenburg killed during an attempted robbery?"

"As Thornton was an American citizen killed in a foreign country, we checked him out thoroughly. Turns out he was the right-hand man for one Cyrus McSweeny. Cyrus operates out of Spokane and is well known to law enforcement. But this is way out of his league. He's basically a penny stock promoter, a pump and dump artist. He did five years for income tax evasion but no other convictions. Neither one of them fit the profile.

And to be frank, Constable Rand, we're a bit skeptical of the attempted robbery alibi Rosenburg put forth."

"How so?"

"Well, as I said, Thornton doesn't fit the profile. He wasn't above using a little muscle, but he wasn't a killer. We think it's more likely Rosenburg was into Cyrus for some serious cash, and he sent Thornton to collect. The one common denominator seems to be Montana Creek Mining Corp."

"Rosenburg's statement claimed Thornton tried to steal his shares of Montana Creek Mining before he shot him," Constable Rand replied.

"We did some checking, and it turns out at least one company controlled by McSweeny is also a shareholder in Montana Creek Mining."

"What's the name and domicile of the company?" Rand asked.

"Twisp River Resources, based in Vancouver. Malcolm Trueblood is the CEO, but the company is a wholly owned subsidiary of Carib International, a Cayman Island company we suspect is owned by Cyrus."

"So you think there is some kind of connection between McSweeny, Montana Creek Mining, and Rosenburg's death?" Rand asked.

"Not Montana Creek per se, but with some of the company's shareholders. We haven't put it all together yet, but we will." Monroe said, firmly.

"I see. Well, you've been a big help, Agent Monroe. We'll dig into Mr. Trueblood and Twisp River, as well as Montana Creek Mining. Please keep me updated on your end, and I'll do likewise."

A few days later, Thorny's PI buddy in Coeur d'Alene called Cyrus.

"Mr. McSweeny, this is Doug Masters over in Coeur d'Alene, Idaho. I worked for Bill Thornton on occasion. Have you got a minute?"

"Sure, Doug. What's up?"

"First off, I just wanted to thank you for taking care of Thorny and his family the way you did. He and I go way back, and, well, it was mighty good of you."

"Thanks, Doug. As you probably know, Thorny and I were pretty tight too, for nearly thirty years."

"Yes, sir, I did."

"So what else is on your mind, Doug?"

"I am sure Thorny told you of our arrangement with the gal at Mineral Valley Labs."

Cyrus took a deep breath. "Yes, is there a problem?"

"Oh, no, sir. It's just with Thorny gone, she's not sure where to send her reports."

"I see. Have her fax them to this number," Cyrus replied, giving Doug the fax number of a Spokane mail store. One he used for sensitive materials.

"Got it. She says she has some new results. I'll have her send them out today."

A shiver went up Cyrus's back. "New results?"

"Yes, sir."

"Okay, Doug, have her get them out today and invoice me for your time."

"Yes, sir. And you don't owe me anything. It's the least I can do for Thorny. I'll be sure all future reports are sent, ASAP."

Cyrus hung up and dialed Malcolm.

"Mal, Cyrus here. Do you know anything about new core results?"

"Hi, Cyrus. No, I don't. Last report I had, we were still trying to figure out where the vein had gone."

"Well, there's new assays coming my way. If they're not from previous cores, then they've relocated the vein."

"You want me to call Trace?"

"Yes, but you're going to have to be very careful how you question him on this. Otherwise he'll know I'm getting information from the lab, as well as from you."

"You're right. It might be better if I meet with Walter Wilkins here in Vancouver. Just two directors having lunch and discussing the drilling program."

"Perfect. Just do it fast and be very, very, careful."

Cyrus hung up the phone and opened his online trading account with Cayman Island Securities. He typed in Montana Creek's symbol. The shares were at a buck eighty with a little better-than-average volume. He dialed Nigel Cunningham.

"Nigel, Cyrus. What's the current status of Montana Creek Mining?"

"Hello, Cyrus. Well, your short sale knocked the price down ten percent, but there's been pretty steady volume at the lower levels. Looks like a few investors are averaging down."

"If I close out my short position, what am I looking at?"

"Stocks down ten percent from where you sold short. So, you're up twenty cents per share on a million shares."

"Two hundred grand profit?"

"Less our commissions."

"Okay, buy the shares back at one eighty. Close out my short position, now."

"Done. Tidy little profit, Cyrus. Congratulations."

"Yeah, well, it's not exactly what I had in mind. But, as my old man used to say, 'You never go broke taking profits.'"

Wally and Malcolm met at a restaurant on the top floor of Wally's office building, in downtown Vancouver. Both men ordered grilled salmon and salad.

Malcolm took a sip of his tea. "Damn, that's hot," he said, setting his cup back in its saucer.

"Yes, but feels pretty good on a cold day like today," Wally replied.

"That it does, Wally," Malcolm replied, dabbing his burned lip with his napkin. "I wanted to get together for a few minutes, Wally, and discuss operations down at the Sullivan Mine. I've not received any updates of late. And, as you no doubt do as well, I get the occasional shareholder query."

Wally's inner caution light started blinking. "Last report I got, they were doing some underground mapping on the first level. Looking for evidence of faulting. I believe the rig is on standby until they figure this out."

"I see," Malcolm said, pouring a bit of cream into his tea. "So no new drilling?"

"Trace may have moved the rig to a new location, just to save time later. As you know, anything is preferable to paying rig time for an idle drill."

"Agreed. What about the cores we've already cut? Have they all been assayed?"

"Yes. We're up to date, and all the assay data has been published and filed with the VSE."

"Just as I thought. Very good. Trace does run a tight ship."

The two men finished lunch and headed back to their respective offices. For Wally it was just a quick elevator ride down to his floor.

Wally arranged a conference call and had Trace, Will, and James Lee, who was in Los Angeles, on the line.

"Fellows, I just had lunch with Malcolm Trueblood. Actually, more of an interrogation than lunch."

"What's up, Wally?" I asked.

"He's very curious about new drilling. Wanted to know if we'd cut any new cores, or if any new assays from previous cores were forthcoming."

Jim Lee jumped in. "Fellows, he's got someone on the inside at the lab. Why else would he be asking about new assays?"

"I'm going to put you all on hold at my end," Wally said. "I need to check something. You all keep at it. I'll be back on in a sec."

Will, Jim, and I continued to discuss Malcolm and current operations at the mine while we waited on Wally.

"I'm back on fellows," Wally said, "and I've got some damned-interesting news. The million share short position has been closed. The seller, and I'm assuming it was Cyrus, bought his shares back this morning, at a dollar eighty."

"The son of a bitch made two hundred grand off our labors," Will said, disgustedly. "He found out we re-located the vein, before we announced it, and covered his short position."

"Well, boys, welcome to world of penny stocks," Wally said.

"Look, we can't begrudge a smart guy from playing the market," I replied. "What we can go after is an SOB getting insider information to formulate his play."

"So, how do we proceed?" Wally asked.

"Wally, I want you to call a board meeting as soon as possible. Can we use your conference room?"

"Absolutely. I'll send out the notice today. Can you all be here in two days?"

We all replied in the affirmative.

"What's the plan of attack, Trace?" Jim asked.

"We go to DEFCON three and front Malcolm. We tell him we have evidence he passed inside information to one of our shareholders. And we have reason to believe the same shareholder is getting copies of our assays before they're announced. We ask for his resignation. If he balks, we say we'll turn over our information to the securities regulators in Canada, and to the SEC and the FBI in the U.S."

"What about Cyrus?" Will asked.

"One bottom dweller at a time," I replied. "Once we take care of Malcolm, I'll have a sit-down with Cyrus."

Chapter 18

Pino Pantelli was enjoying a late afternoon aperitif with his brother when his cell rang. Al lit a Cuban cigar and sipped his drink while he waited for his brother to finish the call.

"Problems?" Al asked. after Pino hung up.

"Not a problem, but an interesting piece of news. Looks like Cyrus closed his short position against Montana Creek Mining. He bought back a million shares at a buck eighty."

"I'll be damned, a cool two-hundred-grand profit. Not too shabby. The Virus strikes again," Al said, with a laugh.

"Yeah. Good news for us too. The share price is heading back up."

"You know, I'm starting to like this penny stock bullshit. Anyway we can get a bigger piece of the pie?"

"You mean squeeze the Virus?"

"Damn right. I don't give two squirts about that *Il figlio di una femmina.*"

Pino laughed. "Yeah, he is a son of a bitch, but he's a smart son of a bitch."

"Smart or not, let's figure out a way to grab his shares in Montana Creek Mining. I got a good feeling about that company."

"Let me think about it, and you do likewise. We'll figure out a way."

Back in Vancouver, Peter Rand was pouring over Montana Creek Mining Corp.'s Vancouver Stock Exchange filings. He'd made a list of the major shareholders and insiders, and highlighted Rosenburg, Twisp River Resources, and shares purchased offshore through Cayman Island Securities.

His secretary buzzed him and said Special Agent Monroe was holding on line two.

"Special Agent Monroe, good to hear from you."

"Chief Constable Rand, if you've got a minute, I've got a bit of information for you."

"Shoot."

"As I mentioned, we've been reviewing open homicide cases where exotic poisons were used."

"Yes."

"Well, we may have found a link. In checking the medical examiner's notes, it appears one victim's steering wheel had been painted with a toxin."

"Which victim?"

"The one killed by synthetic tree frog neurotoxin. The toxin was absorbed through skin contact with the steering wheel. Sound familiar?"

"Bingo! Damn fine work, Agent Monroe."

"We were never able to confirm it, but there was some evidence the victim was involved in drug trafficking. Our information leads us to believe it may have been a mob hit."

"Any word on which crime family?"

"Nothing positive, but New Orleans kept coming up."

"The Pantelli family?"

"It's certainly possible. They're as rough as a Monday morning hangover, and they're certainly involved in the narcotics trade. There was one other notation on an old police report that caught my eye."

"What was it?"

"Just two words: the Chemist."

"The killer's *nom de guerre*?"

"Could be. We're running the name through our databases to see if anything pops out."

"Why would the Pantelli family have an interest in Rosenburg? Hell, he was just a penny stock promoter from Vancouver. Doesn't exactly make him unique."

"You mentioned he liked to gamble, especially in Vegas."

"Yes, word is he liked high-stakes craps."

"It could link him to the Pantelli family."

"How so?"

"Well, we've suspected the Pantellis are the money behind the Comstock Casino in Vegas. But, we've never been able to prove it."

"Interesting. The pieces are starting to fall together. I'll dig into Rosenburg's Vegas trips. See where he gambled and how far in the hole he might have been."

"Sounds good. If Rosenburg was into the Pantellis, for some serious money, they may have sanctioned the hit."

Chapter 19

Will and I flew up to Vancouver and met Jim Lee in the terminal. We grabbed a cab to downtown and went up to Wally's office. Wally and Malcolm were waiting for us in the conference room.

After a few cordialities, I called the meeting to order.

"Gentlemen, I called this meeting because we have a serious problem."

"Don't tell us you've lost the vein again." Malcolm said, with a chuckle.

"How'd you know we'd found it, Malcolm? We didn't notify you."

"What do you mean?" Malcolm replied, the color draining from his face.

"Malcolm, we know you contacted a large shareholder and told him we'd lost the vein. We also know this same shareholder shorted our stock a million shares. And he recently covered his short position when he found out we'd gotten back on the vein."

"That is preposterous!" Malcolm yelled.

"Malcolm, we know this shareholder has someone on the inside at Mineral Valley Labs. I've contacted the lab, and they're seizing all employee's' computers and reviewing all e-mails sent from the lab or from their personal computers. It's just a matter of time until we find the leak."

Malcolm looked stunned but remained silent.

"Here's the deal, Malcolm. I want your resignation now or we turn over all our findings over to the Canadian Securities Commission. And as we believe the shareholder you disclosed insider information to is an American, we'll do likewise with the SEC and the FBI. It's up to you, Malcolm. What's it going to be?"

Malcolm looked at each of the other directors in the conference room and then stared out across the harbor for a long moment.

"Done. You'll have my resignation within the hour. If you gentlemen will excuse me."

Malcolm rose and walked out of the conference room.

"I bet he's already on his cell to Cyrus," Will said, grimacing and shaking his head.

"Could be," I said. "I know he's on the top of my to-call list."

As I had the remaining board members in one room, I covered a few items with regard to the winter drilling program. I also informed them that from now on, all assays would come directly from the owner and manager of Mineral Valley Labs. Until the person selling our data was identified, only the owner would have access to our assay results. We'd also be getting a 20 percent discount on any future assays.

Will was right about the phone call.

"Cyrus, Malcolm here. We've got a problem."

"What now, Malcolm?"

"I just tendered my resignation to Montana Creek Mining's board."

"Why in the hell would you do that?"

"Because, Cyrus, they know everything. They know I called you when they lost the vein. They know it had to be you shorting the stock, and they know you've got someone on the inside at the lab. It was either resign or they would turn everything over to the CSC, SEC, and the FBI."

"Okay, don't panic. You did the right thing. They obviously don't want their shareholders, or the investment community, to get wind of the situation. Otherwise, they'd have gone straight to the authorities. Bad news is, you're off their board. Good news is, I made two hundred grand on the short sale, and Twisp River and Carib still own seventeen-plus percent of their company. And best news, they're back in ore. We took a shot and we fucked up. But we're still in the game, big time."

"What about my reputation?"

Cyrus laughed. "What reputation? You work for Cyrus the Virus, remember?"

Before Will, Jim, and I left Wally's office, I called Cyrus at his Spokane office.

"Cyrus, it's Trace Brandon. I'm in Vancouver but headed back to Ellensburg via Spokane. If you got some time tomorrow, I'd like to have a quick meeting with you."

"Sure, Trace. How about eleven at my office? I'm on the sixth floor of the Inland Empire Building."

"I know it well. See you at eleven."

Will wanted to come along, but I asked him to let me meet Cyrus one-on-one. I'd developed a bit of a relationship with Cyrus over the past months and while in the Caymans. He played hard-ball and mainly by his own rules. But I sensed I could deal with him.

At eleven sharp I entered the lobby of one of Spokane's architectural jewels, the Inland Empire Building. The office building was built in a V-shape with the sharp end of the V truncated to form corner offices. Naturally, Cyrus's office was on the sixth floor. Top of the V.

The sign on the door said Columbia Resources LLC. I opened the door and walked in. Cyrus was talking to his secretary and turned to greet me.

"Trace, good to see you again," Cyrus said, extending his hand. "This is Sally Friesen, my office manager."

I shook hands with Cyrus and then Sally.

"Let's go into my office," Cyrus said, patting me on the shoulder. "Can we get you anything?"

"Bottled water would be great," I replied.

"Sally, would you mind?" Cyrus asked.

Sally fetched me a chilled Cascadia, and I followed Cyrus into his office. His office was as I expected . . . plush.

"Cyrus, I asked for this meeting because I knew you and I could level with each other."

"Fair enough. What's on your mind?"

"I expect you already know this, but I kicked Malcolm off our board."

Cyrus's eye's didn't even flicker.

"Yes, Malcolm called me. It's an unfortunate affair."

"Cyrus, I don't have a problem with you or anybody else making money off our shares. Hell, if you're smart enough and have the balls to short a stock and make some cash, more power to you. But I do object when you use insider information from one of our directors to do it."

"That's a pretty strong charge, Trace."

"Look, all bullshit aside, we both know what went down. You made some money, Malcolm paid the price, and we all move forward. Currently, your companies own more than seventeen percent of Montana Creek Mining. Judging from all the mining deals you've been involved with," I said, gesturing to the photos of various mining projects on his office walls, "you're smart enough and experienced enough to know a good deal when you see it."

"And your point is?"

"My point is, get on the damn team. Work with us on building this company. Hell, you'll make millions on your shares, and you won't end up like Thorny."

"Are you threatening me, Trace?"

"Not at all. If I wanted a piece of your ass, I'd be at the SEC right now instead of here in your office. Hell, you came up through the mines and used your brains and guts to get to where you are now. Not unlike what I'm trying to do. I'm just saying, there's a better way to do this. We can all come out ahead, and you won't be looking over your shoulder the rest of your life."

"I appreciate your candor and the fact you have the balls to come to me like this. And I appreciate you're not running to the damn regulators. Not that you could prove any of this. But it's how I would have handled it, if our roles were reversed."

"Okay, so we're in agreement? You're on board?"

"I hate to admit it, but I've grown kind of fond of you, Trace. You remind me of me when I was starting out, and not so jaded. Okay, Trace. Let's declare a truce. No more dirty tricks on my end, and I'll vote my shares and proxies in the best interest of Montana Creek Mining."

"So, I could say I have your word on it?"

"Yes, you could say you have my word."

I extended my right hand, and we shook hands.

"By the way, Cyrus, you remind me a lot of my dad. He was a cantankerous, hard-headed SOB, but he always made money for his partners."

Cyrus laughed. "Very good, Trace. I think we'll leave it at that."

I smiled at Cyrus, and got up to leave.

"Oh, there is one more thing you should know, Cyrus. Your contact at Mineral Valley Labs is kaput. Save your money. You'll get the assay results same time as the other shareholders."

"I, of course, have no idea what you're referring to. But I do look forward to timely progress reports."

When I got back to my office in Ellensburg, I contacted the other directors and told them we wouldn't have any more problems with Cyrus. About ten minutes after the call ended, Wally called me back.

"Trace, I didn't want to spook Jim Lee, but I heard some interesting news."

"What's up?"

"Remember the papers up here saying Rosenburg died of a stroke or seizure?"

"Yep, I guess the guilt over popping Thornton got to him."

"Not quite. A contact of mine in the constable's office says it was a professional hit. And get this, Rosenburg was killed with some kind of nerve agent."

"What?

"You heard me right. Some kind of toxin supposedly only the militaries have."

"Jesus, we have shareholders shooting shareholders, and now we have a pro killing them too? What in *the* hell is going on?"

"Damn good question, Trace. I'd say Rosenburg pissed off some very bad individuals."

"You think the casino boys wanted more than just his shares?"

"Who else could pull off a hit like that, besides a government?"

"A guy like Rosenburg would have enemies from stock deals gone south. But I don't see any way a government would be involved. To me, it smells like he seriously pissed off someone in the Outfit."

"The Outfit?"

"It's what Al Capone used to call the mob."

"Jesus, I can't wait for our next shareholders meeting. Could be some interesting characters in attendance."

Chapter 20

Cyrus asked Malcolm to come down to the Spokane office. He wanted him to go through all of Thorny's business files. Cyrus told him to pull anything of interest, and shred anything that might be sensitive.

Malcolm was embarrassed and mad about being unceremoniously dumped from Montana Creek's board. He'd taken the hit while Cyrus had skated, and pocketed two hundred grand on the short sale. And to add insult to injury, he hadn't even offered to split the short-sale profit.

Digging through the files, an expense report for a trip Thorny had made to New Orleans caught Malcolm's eye. Checking through phone bills, he located several calls Thorny had made to New Orleans. All to the same number. He knew Cyrus had sent Thorny to New Orleans to meet with Al Pantelli. It was worth a shot.

"Mr. Pantelli please," Malcolm said to the secretary who answered his call.

"Which Mr. Pantelli, sir?"

"Al . . . Al Pantelli, please," Malcolm replied, a hint of nervousness in his voice.

"Yes, sir. One minute please."

"Al, here. Who's this?"

"Mr. Pantelli, this is Malcolm Trueblood. I run Twisp River Resources here in Vancouver, Canada, for Cyrus McSweeny."

Al's interest immediately peaked. "Sure, Malcolm, I know who you are. What can I do for you?"

"Well, sir, as you may know, both you and Twisp River are shareholders in Montana Creek Mining."

"Yes, we own about half a million shares. And as you may know, Cyrus has our proxy to vote those shares for the next three years."

"Yes, I do know that. He can vote your shares as long as he's alive. Upon his death the voting rights would revert to you. Correct?"

"Correct. Are you calling on a cell or from a land-line?"

"Land-line, sir."

"Okay, go ahead."

"Twisp River Resources took down a good chunk of the original private placement, which came with warrants attached. We exercised the warrants when the stock got to a dollar."

"Go on," Al said.

"As CEO of Twisp River Resources, I vote our shares. But as Twisp River is controlled by Carib International, that is to say, by Cyrus, I vote as instructed."

"I'm still listening, Malcolm."

"Well, I just thought, as both of us have a significant investment in Montana Creek Mining, and its future, it might make sense for us to meet and discuss our common interests."

Al's brother Pino opened Al's office door and stuck his head in. Al put his left index finger to his lips and motioned for him to come in and take a seat.

"Okay, Malcolm. I don't see what meeting and discussing our mutual interests could hurt," Al said, looking at Pino and raising his eyebrows. "Tell you what. My brother, Crispino, and I will be in Vegas the day after tomorrow. We keep an office in the Comstock Casino. Why don't you meet us there?"

"Thank you, Mr. Pantelli. I'll see you there. And, sir, I assume this conversation is in confidence?"

"All my conversations are in confidence. See you in two days."

"What the hell's going on?" Pino asked, after Al hung up.

"Sounded to me like the guy who runs one of Cyrus's companies wants a change in management. And there could be a lot of Montana Creek shares involved."

Chapter 21

Drilling was moving ahead at the Sullivan Mine. Each new drill hole extended the length of orebody and added additional reserves. I'd gotten the name of Twisp River's engineering firm from Malcolm before we'd lowered the boom on him. I put a call in to the firm's office in Vancouver. A young, very sexy-sounding gal answered the phone.

"Charter Engineering, may I help you?"

"Yes, ma'am, this is Trace Brandon with Montana Creek Mining. Could I speak to Gerald Smyth please?"

I heard the phone click, and then Smyth picked up.

"Jerry here."

"Mr. Smyth, this is Trace Brandon with Montana Creek Mining down in Ellensburg, Washington."

"Yes, Trace. Malcolm Trueblood said you might be calling. And please, call me Jerry."

"Okay, Jerry. Listen, we need a full-blown independent engineering report completed on our Sullivan Mine property. As you may know, we're up and trading and need to file a reserve report based on our drilling results to date."

"How soon would you like us to start?"

"Well, there's a hell of a lot of snow on the ground at the mine. But we're drilling away. We've got a lot of split core stored in a heated warehouse in Winthrop. And of course we've got all the core assays."

"Okay. Are there underground workings?"

"Yes, there's two levels, but only the upper adit is accessible. The lower workings are flooded. But you can map the rock types and the vein to the end of the upper adit."

"Perfect. As you know, Trace, we have to physically be on-site, inspect the geology, drilling, cores, and assay results. Plus, we'll also need to take a few confirmation core samples. Following which, we'll prepare a report for your review prior to submission to the VSE."

"Sounds like a plan. Can you put together a cost proposal and e-mail it down to me. I'll go over your proposal with the board and get back to you."

"You'll have something tomorrow morning. We look forward to working with you and with Malcolm again."

"Ah, Malcolm is no longer on our board. He's resigned for personal reasons. But his company, Twisp River Resources, remains a significant shareholder."

"I am sorry to hear that. I hope his problems aren't too serious."

"No, just some personal matters requiring more of his attention," I replied, envisioning Malcolm doing five years in the big house, without a shower.

Chapter 22

I received the engineering report proposal from Charter Engineering and reviewed it with Wally, Will, and Jim. The costs were as expected, and we all agreed to proceed. I contacted Gerald Smyth and arranged to meet him in Winthrop. From there we'd take him up to the Sullivan Mine. Jim Lee asked to be present as well.

I arranged to pick Jim up at the Spokane airport. We'd drive up together in my Bronco. Jerry was driving down from Vancouver in a four-wheel-drive Suburban crammed full of field and sampling gear. He'd meet us at the Winthrop House.

Jim was standing in front of the Spokane terminal when I drove up.

"Good flight, Jim?" I asked, while he stowed his gear in the back of the Bronco.

"Yep, no worries, mate. Smooth as a McGuire Sister's' harmony. So tell me about your meeting with Cyrus."

"Well, he's smart enough to know we could rock his boat pretty damn hard if he didn't shape up. He's also smart enough to know we don't want any kind of bad news, like lawsuits or SEC investigations. I'm convinced he'll play ball. It's in his best interest."

"You're right, of course. It's a slippery slope once problems like Cyrus and Malcolm's activities are made public. The investment community is a fickle beast and could just as easily turn against Montana Creek Mining as Cyrus."

"Agreed. From my point of view the most important thing we can do now is concentrate on drilling out reserves. Get the engineering report completed, and get listed on the Toronto Exchange."

"Couldn't agree more, mate."

Jim and I were having a beer in the W's bar around 7:00 p.m. when a character right out of *Alan Quartermain* walked in. This individual was decked out in bloused khakis tucked into leather boots that laced to just below the knees. He had on an olive-drab army winter field jacket with pencils, pens, and small notebooks stuffed in every pocket. A bright-red wool scarf was wrapped around his neck. His open jacket exposed what could pass for a Bowie knife hooked to his belt. He looked to be in his fifties, about five feet eight, heavy-set with a ruddy complexion and a bald head. To compensate for the lack of cranial hair, he sported a magnificent salt-and-pepper beard.

Jim took one look and laughed softly. "Bloody hell, that's got to be our engineer."

I waved the fellow to our table, and Jim and I stood up to meet him.

"Gerald Smyth, gents," he said, shaking each of our hands with an iron grip, "but you can call me Jerry."

"I'm Trace Brandon, Jerry, and this is Jim Lee, managing director of International Uranium Corp. Jim's one of our directors. You got a license for that pig sticker?" I asked with a chuckle, gesturing at his knife.

Jerry laughed. "Yeah, she's a whopper, all right. But she comes in pretty handy from time to time. Mainly for skinning young geologists," he said with a wink.

We all took a seat, ordered a round of beers, and got acquainted. Later, over steaks, I briefed Jerry on our drilling operation and the Sullivan Mine's history. We agreed to meet for breakfast at six and then head up to the mine.

The next morning, after a breakfast of eggs, bacon, hotcakes, and coffee, we loaded into our vehicles and headed up to the Sullivan Mine. When we pulled up, Fish came out of the core shack to meet us.

"Fish, this is Jerry Smyth one of the principal engineers with Charter Engineering out of Vancouver," I said.

"Glad to meet you, Jerry. I'm Tom Troutman. But everybody calls me Fish."

"Glad to meet you as well," Jerry replied. "How's the coring going?"

"We've just started coring a new location. You'll be able to get a look at the cores as they come out," Fish answered.

"Tom, good to see you again," Jim said, shaking hands with his young geologist. "Freezing your ass off, are you?"

"It's cold, but nothing compared to the Athabasca Basin," Fish replied. "Come on up to the rig, and I'll introduce Jerry to Red. And he can get a look at some fresh core."

After the intro's, Jerry took a serious look at the core from the hole Red was drilling.

"Jeezus—you boy's have hit the mother fuckin' lode. Excuse my language, but, sweet Jesus, this ore is incredible. You know the only bad part, though?" Jerry asked, frowning slightly.

My heart sank. "What bad part?" I asked.

"The bad part is, I can't buy any of your shares," Jerry said with a laugh. "I can't own an interest in any property I'm doing an engineering report on. And from the looks of this core, I wish I could."

Jerry spent the better part of two days either at the mine or in Winthrop poring over the cores and assays. To say he was thorough would be a gross understatement. He checked the underground workings and, watched and recorded our drilling and coring methods.

Finally on the third day, he'd seen enough. He loaded up his gear, along with some core samples for confirmation assays, and bid us adieu. He promised a draft report in two weeks.

Jim and I left Fish to carry on, and we headed to Spokane, where Jim would start his trek down under. After dropping him at the airport, I headed back to my office in Ellensburg to check on the corporate end of things. Hopefully, there were no more short sellers, or dead shareholders.

Chapter 23

Malcolm's flight touched down in Vegas at 10:00 a.m. He deplaned, cleared the terminal, and looked around to see if the Pantellis had sent a car. They hadn't. So, he took a cab to the Comstock Casino.

The concierge directed him to an office suite on the second floor of the casino. The name-plate on the door merely said *Private*. Malcolm knocked and walked in.

A secretary, who could have passed for a show-girl, showed him into Al Pantelli's office. Al was behind his desk, and his brother, Crispino, was seated on an adjacent sofa.

Al rose and came around his desk to shake Malcolm's hand.

"Malcolm, nice to meet ya. I'd like you to meet my brother, Crispino," Al said, gesturing toward his brother.

Malcolm took a step and shook hands with Crispino.

"Please, call me, Pino."

"Have a seat, Malcolm," Al said, pointing to the sofa. "Can I get you a drink?"

"No, nothing, thanks," Malcolm said, taking a seat on the sofa opposite Pino.

"So, Malcolm," Pino said, "my brother says we have similar interests in Montana Creek Mining. Especially an interest in the company's shares."

"Yes, and it's the purpose of my visit today. First, though, I'd like to thank you both for agreeing to see me. I know you're both busy men."

"So what's on your mind, Malcolm?" Al asked.

"To be frank, getting our hands on the Montana Creek Mining shares held by Cyrus McSweeny's offshore company, Carib International. And getting your voting rights restored."

Al glanced at Pino. "Why the hard-on for Cyrus?"

"The son of a bitch has ruined my reputation in Vancouver. I've been kicked off Montana Creek's board of directors, and to add insult to injury, he didn't even offer to split his short-sale profits with me. Profits, which without my help, he'd have never received."

"I see," Al replied, cutting a quick glance at Pino.

Pino got up and walked over to the bar and fixed himself a fresh Bloody Mary.

"And how do you propose to get control of Cyrus's shares?" Al asked.

"I found out Cyrus paid someone in the assay lab for copies of Montana Creek's core-assay results. Hell, he got the information before the CEO did, let alone the shareholders. A serious violation of insider trading laws," Malcolm replied.

Al and Pino both laughed.

"Well, what about information you passed on to Cyrus about drilling operations?" Al asked.

"My word against his. There's no document trail, no hard evidence I actually passed any information to Cyrus."

"I take it you're talking about blackmail?" Pino asked.

Malcolm took a breath and looked at both men; he knew he was about to cross the line, again. "Yes. We tell Cyrus we'll turn over our information to the SEC and the FBI if he doesn't cooperate."

"Hell, I know Cyrus," Al said, "I served time with him in a federal pen up in Oregon. He's not going to just turn his shares over to us."

"I agree," Malcolm replied. "We offer to buy all the shares held by Carib at a discount to market, and he agrees to return your voting proxy."

"And in return, we don't turn him over the feds?" Al asked, looking hard at Malcolm.

"Correct," Malcolm replied.

Al looked at Pino, who was shaking his head and frowning.

"I think I can give you our answer now, Malcolm," Al said. "And the answer is, no fuckin' way. I want you to get back on a plane and get the hell out of Vegas before dark, or we'll plant your sorry ass in the desert. *Capisce?*"

Pino took Malcolm by the arm and escorted him to the door.

"You see, Malcolm," Pino said, "the thing we hate more than anything, is a fuckin' rat. Get your sorry ass back to Canada and you keep your mouth shut. Or, we'll shut if for you—permanently."

Chapter 24

Special Agent Beau Monroe flew down to New Orleans, set up shop in the FBI offices on Leon C. Simon Boulevard, and started digging into the Pantelli crime family. He'd managed to get a couple of young agents seconded to him, and he put them to work looking at deaths of local underworld characters in the past ten years. Specifically, deaths reportedly caused by strokes or heart attacks.

It took ten days, but they found two deaths that fit the profile. Both of the deceased men were Pantelli family underlings and up to their ears in drugs and prostitution. Both had reportedly died of strokes, but no autopsies had been performed.

One of the dead men had been cremated and his ashes scattered all over Bourbon Street. However, the other man had been entered in a crypt in one of New Orleans's historic cemeteries. It took a bit of doing, but Monroe managed to get a local judge to sign a court order to open the crypt and allow a postmortem autopsy.

At 10:00 a.m. a call came into Monroe from the medical examiner's office.

"Agent Monroe, speaking."

"Agent Monroe, Art Cline, at the ME's office."

"Yes, sir. Any info for me?"

"Well, yes, but first let me say that without some idea of what we were looking for, we might have missed it."

"Neurotoxin?"

"Yes, and one we've never come across before. The victim was killed by an organophosphate. Similar in composition to an old pesticide from the 1950's. A product called OPP-D. Is this what you were looking for?"

"Dead-solid perfect. Thanks, Doc."

"So, we can repackage the deceased?"

Monroe laughed. "Yes, sir. Sew him up and stick him back in his crypt."

Beau called Chief Inspector Rand, in Vancouver, and filled him in.

"With the tree frog victim, this makes two cases where an exotic neurotoxin was used," Agent Monroe explained. "I think we're on the Chemist's home turf."

"Good work, Agent Monroe. Good hunting, and please keep me posted," Inspector Rand replied.

Monroe hung up, rounded up his trusty secondees, and commenced to shaking the trees.

Chapter 25

The core results at the Sullivan Mine continued to be good, and Montana Creek Mining's share price continued to climb. The asking price was now at three dollars.

Cyrus seemed relatively dormant, and I'd not heard a peep out of Malcolm Trueblood since the board sacked his sorry butt. Christmas was coming, and we'd be shutting the drill down next week, through New Year's. And, I had a date with Tina for Friday night. Everything seemed to be on very solid ground, which is usually when the bottom falls out.

I was deep in thoughts of Tina naked in my Airstream when my office phone rang. I jumped and nearly spilled my morning coffee.

"Montana Creek Mining, Trace speaking."

"Trace, it's Cyrus. Have you got a sec?"

"Sure, Cyrus. What's up?"

"A trader buddy of mine in Hong Kong sent me an encrypted e-mail early this morning."

My attention mode kicked into hyper-drive.

"Yes?"

"As you know, Trace, the Chinese are all over the damn place trying to tie up uranium reserves."

"Jim Lee and I were discussing that very thing when we were up at the mine last week. The Chinese just inked a deal to acquire a majority interest in an Aussie uranium company. They also bought a majority interest in a Namibian uranium mine, from a British company."

"Exactly. My trader tells me Montana Creek is on their radar. The Chinese are quietly acquiring a position in our company."

"Is it just an investment, or are they up to something more?"

"I think it's something more, Trace."

"Well, without my share block, there's no way for them to get control."

"True, but they could get what I call 'negative control.' Get enough shares to do what we did with Malcolm. Get a seat on the board. How many shares in the float?"

"Fully diluted, including warrants, about three million."

"They might do a tender offer, at a premium to the market, and pick up a good bit, it not all, of the three mil."

"What's your recommendation, Cyrus?" I said, not quite believing I was asking the Virus for his opinion.

"Well, I agree with you. Without your shares, they can't get control, and I won't tender my shares unless you, Wally, Will, and IUC decide to sell. Which I don't see happening at these levels."

"Thanks, Cyrus, and you're right. We're not sellers at these levels. Also, I know IUC is more interested in adding to their uranium reserves than in selling their shares. But, there could be a price at which their shareholders would force them to sell. At the end of the day, it's all about the bottom line."

"True enough. Okay, Trace, I just wanted to give you a heads-up. I'll keep you informed if I get more information."

"Thanks, Cyrus. I'll brief the other directors."

I hung up and sent an e-mail to Jim. He was in IUC's Melbourne office this week. I called Will and then Wally, who about had a heart attack. We decided to wait to hear back from Jim and then get everyone on a conference call, including the Virus.

Jim e-mailed back, and we arranged to have a conference call at 2:00 p.m. Thursday afternoon, our time, which would be 9:00 a.m. Friday morning in Melbourne.

It took a bit of doing and some help from an international operator, but we got all parties on the line.

"Fellows, I called this meeting to discuss the information Cyrus received from his trader contact in Hong Kong," I said. "Cyrus, can you bring the board up to speed?"

"Certainly, and I do have an update to what I passed on yesterday. The Chinese company buying our shares is URAN-China Nuclear Corp., or UCNC. They've recently acquired interests in uranium companies in Africa, Australia, and Kazakhstan. They're extremely aggressive and very well funded."

"I know the company," Jim said. "They are very active in the Australian uranium play. Their speciality is underfunded junior small caps with potential significant reserves."

"Except for the underfunded part, that's us," I said.

"Their MO," Jim continued, "is to get a minority position in the target company through open market share purchases. Then, they typically put together a tender offer for control of the company. They don't operate any mines they acquire. They prefer to contract with a major mining company to do the actual mining."

"Fits tight with your information, Cyrus," I added.

"What's the worst-case scenario?" Wally asked.

"Worst case," I replied, "is they acquire all of the shares in the float. Which would give them around thirty-seven percent of the company."

"Negative control," Cyrus said. "Not enough to take over, but certainly enough to get one or two of their people on our board."

"And then they'll tender for the rest," Jim added.

"But U.S. uranium can't, at least for now, be exported to China, can it?" I asked.

"Possibly as enriched uranium in fuel rods for nuclear power generation," Jim replied. "But they might be able to export yellow cake to a country with no export restriction to China. Or swap proven reserves here for reserves elsewhere. Or, they could merely be investing in our shares with an eye towards higher share prices down the road. The Chinese are buying up so much uranium. They know the price is going up, along with our share price. Another one of those self-fulfilling prophecies."

"So what's our defensive strategy?" Will asked.

Cyrus cleared his throat. "Well, fellows, we can't stop them from acquiring our shares. But as Trace pointed out, they'll fall short of control. My advice would be to wait a bit, see how this plays out. If it really gets nasty, we may have to seek out a white knight to better any tender they put forth."

"Jim, would IUC be interested in picking up additional shares to thwart the Chinese?" I asked.

"As I mentioned, when we agreed to acquire a twenty percent interest, we are interested in a larger ownership percentage," Jim replied. "That said, we couldn't wage a bidding war with the Chinese. They have very deep pockets."

We all agreed to run with Cyrus's wait-and-see approach. I, only half-jokingly, suggested we all re-read Sun Tzu's *Art of War*. Hostile takeover attempts were nothing short of corporate warfare.

Chapter 26

On Friday night I picked Tina up at her apartment near the university. I'd earlier hit the IGA for groceries, including two rib eyes, salad stuff, and two bottles of Cabernet Sauvignon. The cabernet was a local-boutique wine made by a Spokane entrepreneur turned winemaker. The wines were blended and bottled in an old converted warehouse in the historic district of Spokane. It was shaping up to be a hell of a night.

As Christmas was getting near, I'd decorated the exterior of my Airstream with colored Christmas lights. I even decorated a couple of small pine trees growing near the trailer and hung a wreath on the door. There was about six inches of snow on the ground, and the margins of the Yakima River were iced over. It looked and felt like Christmas.

When we pulled up to my Airstream, Tina was duly impressed.

"Boy howdy, cowboy, you went all out this year," Tina said with a laugh.

"Yep, even got a small Christmas tree inside. Might even be a present under it for you."

"Really?"

"Let's go in and take a look."

We got out of the Bronco and walked hand in hand to the door of the trailer. It was cold, and the snow crunched under our boots. The Christmas lights on my trailer reflected off the Yakima River. It was a pretty neat sight.

Inside we hung up our coats, and I grabbed a couple of wine glasses.

"Wine, babe?" I asked, holding up a bottle of cabernet.

"Wow, the good stuff," Tina said with a smile. "Trying to ply me with liquor?"

"Absolutely," I said, removing the cork and pouring us each a glass of the ruby-red wine.

I took a sip and walked over to the miniature Christmas tree I'd placed in the center of the dining table.

"Well, I'll be damned. There is a little something under the tree for you. You must have been a very good girl this year."

"Uh-huh. Let's have it cowboy. Can I open it now?"

"Absolutely."

I handed her the gift-wrapped package, and she tore off the paper but carefully set the bow aside. It must be a female thing; they all do it. Then she slowly opened the felt-covered jewelry box.

"Holy cow, Trace. Is this what I think it is?"

"Yep, Blackfoot Canyon sapphires from Montana. Do you like it?"

Tina held up the bracelet made of white gold and brilliant deep-blue sapphires.

"Of course I like it, Trace. But I don't have anything like this for you."

I smiled and raised my eyebrows in a suggestive manner.

Tina laughed. "Give me a couple of minutes and then meet me in the bedroom."

I spent a few minutes tidying up the kitchen and finishing my wine, and then headed to the front of the Airstream. Tina was lying on my queen-sized bed, wearing nothing but the sapphire bracelet.

"Damn, I knew I liked that bracelet," I said with a husky laugh. I shucked my clothes and slid in beside her.

She threw one leg over mine and pressed her full breasts into my chest. Her nipples were hard as thimbles, and so was I. I kissed her deeply and cupped her breasts. She ran her hand down my stomach and stroked my member.

"You'd better get on, if you're going to catch this ride," I said softly.

She rolled me on my back and mounted me like a comfortable saddle. Arching her back, she rolled her hips, taking me deeper into her. I felt the pressure building deep in my groin.

"Don't wait for me," she whispered. "Tonight is for you."

I didn't.

Chapter 27

Al Pantelli was having a quiet dinner with his brother, Pino, at Delmonico's in the Quarter.

"You know. Al, that Malcolm character bothers me."

"How so? Other than he's a freakin' rat?"

"I worry about him spilling his guts to the feds. We've got a chance to make some real dough with our Montana Creek Mining shares."

"I'm listening, brother."

"Well, if Malcolm starts spouting off about inside info going to Cyrus and payoffs to lab employees, it could cause a lot of problems, and knock hell out of the share price. Another thing, I don't think he owns any shares himself. The shares are all owned by Twisp River or Carib, which is to say, Cyrus."

Al took a sip of his wine and looked to see if anybody was listening.

"You think it's worth a hit?" he said, quietly.

"All I'm saying is, why take a chance?"

Al nodded. "I could send the Chemist to see him."

"Might not be a bad idea. Malcolm looked like he was under a lot of stress when he came to see us. Guys under stress have strokes all the damn time."

Chapter 28

I called Red and shut the drill down until after New Year's. Nothing much happens in the public markets during the holidays. Hedge fund guys and investment bankers flee New York in favor of some island paradise, and the dirty hula. It was a good time to shut down and catch up.

I asked Tina to join me on a little winter break to the Caymans. It took her all of a nano-second to say yes. We'd leave the day after Christmas and come back on January 2. Ellensburg is cold and windy in the winter. A bit of time in the sun with Tina in a bikini, or less, sounded pretty damn good.

I called Cyrus to see if he was going down to the islands for the holidays. He wasn't and kindly offered Tina and me the use of his George Town condo for a week. Which I thought was fair compensation for all the trouble he'd stirred up in the past.

Tina and I flew to Houston the day after Christmas. From Houston we caught an island commuter fight to George Town. We were safely ensconced in Cyrus's three-story, two-bedroom, two-bath condo in time to see the sun sink into the Caribbean. The view from Cyrus's balcony was breathtaking. Everything else aside, the Virus knew how to live.

We changed into bathing suits and hit the pool. Tina wanted to swim in the ocean, but I reminded her of what a Mexican fisherman had once told me. "No *señor*, there are no sharks at this fine beach, but do not swim after the sun goes down."

So, we swam some laps in the pool.

"Ready for some dinner?" I asked, Tina as we toweled off.

"Starved. Do you know a good place?"

"Jack's in the Colonial Hotel. It's just up the road. I made reservations while we laid over in Houston."

"Tough place to get in?"

"Without a reservation, or Cyrus, it's tough." I said with a laugh.

Something about swimming with a beautiful woman, wearing nothing but a skimpy bikini, makes me incredibly horny.

"We've got about an hour, and it's best to be fashionably late," I said, as I came up behind her and untied her bikini top. I ran my hands up her flat belly and cupped her firm breasts.

She turned and kissed me deeply on the mouth, while her right hand moved up the inside of my right leg.

"I think we've got time for a quickie, big fella," she whispered, in a sultry voice.

We were only twenty-five minutes late. Which, by island time, is right on time.

The week flew by. We jogged on the beach, swam, made love at least twice a day, and ate some of the best seafood in the world.

It was a shock getting off the plane back in Spokane to fifteen-degree temperatures and blowing snow.

Back in my Ellensburg office, tanned and fit, I set up a conference call with Wally, Will, and Cyrus. Jim Lee was en route to New York, and I'd catch up with him in the morning.

We would start drilling and coring again in a couple of days. It'd been pretty quiet, as expected, over the holidays. Cyrus reported that the Chinese were still steadily accumulating our stock. He figured they wouldn't tip their hand until they could attack in force. "Korean style," as Cyrus put it.

Chapter 29

Al Pantelli met with Peter Manetti, aka, the Chemist, in Al's office on Saint Louis Street, in the French Quarter.

"Peter, we've got another job for you. Almost a clone of the last one. Same city, similar type target," Al said, handing Peter a legal-sized manila envelope containing information on Malcolm Trueblood.

The Chemist took the envelope and looked through the contents.

"Read it over carefully," Al said, "then burn it all."

Peter nodded. "Any particular method in mind for this one?"

"It needs to look like a heart attack or stroke. This fellow is stressed out, business troubles, so it won't be any big surprise when he croaks. We'll wire the money to your offshore account. half now and half when it's done. Same as always. *Capisce*?"

The Chemist nodded, stood up, and shook hands with Al. "I'll let you know when it's done."

Not too far from where Al and the Chemist were meeting, Agent Monroe was meeting with his assistants in the New Orleans, FBI offices.

"Okay, boys and girls, what've you come up with?"

Agent Wilson Allen stood up.

"We interviewed every Pantelli family associate doing time in Louisiana. As bait, we used the possibility of a reduced sentence in return for any information on a hit-man with the nickname of the Chemist."

"Any luck?" Beau asked.

"The last guy, on our last day of interviews, gave us our only lead."

"Never fails. Go on," Beau said, his adrenaline starting to kick in.

"The guy's name is Vince Bugati. He's doing a nickel in Pollack for possession with intent to distribute. Says he heard about a hitter, called the Chemist. He said word on the street was this wacko had a PhD in chemistry. Bugati also said the fellow did wet work for the Pantelli family, and always used poisons."

"Anything else?"

"I told him if his information panned out, we'd look at trying to get his sentence reduced."

"How much time's he got left?"

"About three years."

"Okay, damned fine work people. Let's start checking local universities and colleges for PhD chemists with major malfunctions, personal problems, gambling or drug habits, ex-wives, dead wives. You know the drill. And start with Louisiana colleges and universities"

Chapter 30

It was already tomorrow in Hong Kong, and Lei Chang was deep into analyst's' reports on Montana Creek Mining. As managing director of URAN-China Nuclear Corp., he'd already initiated limited buying of the junior uranium company's shares.

The deeper Chang dug into Montana Creek Mining's core results, the more excited he got.

He punched ore grades and possible tonnages into his calculator, and whistled softly when he saw the numbers.

By the end of the day, Chang had made up his mind. UCNC would keep buying Montana Creek Mining shares until they were just below the 10 percent reporting threshold. Then he'd meet with his superiors in Peking and get the okay to make a tender offer for control of the company.

Once he got the okay, he'd show the imperialist Yankee dogs a trick of two.

Chapter 31

Red used one of Bob Malott's snow-plow trucks to clear the roads and drill pads at the Sullivan Mine. Old man winter had been in full force and effect over the break. Fish climbed up on Red's drill and set the mast angle using the clinometer on his Brunton compass. This hole would be drilled at a seventy-five-degree angle. He projected they'd intersect the vein at around seven hundred feet.

Fish lifted his Brunton compass from the mast, and looked over at Red.

"All set, Red," Fish said, closing his compass and putting it in the leather holster on his belt.

"Steady, ready, go," Red replied, grinning broadly as he fired up the compressor. "Let's see if we can make some hole before we all freeze to death."

"My thoughts exactly," Fish said, rubbing his gloved hands on his heavy flannel pants.

"When do you want me to start pulling core?" Red yelled, above the sound of the air compressor.

"Trip out at six hundred ninety feet and put the core barrel on," Fish replied. "If my calculations are right, we should be in the vein at seven hundred feet or so."

Red nodded and touched his index finger to his army-surplus, Korean-era winter hat. He released the clutch, and the down-hole hammer bit began pounding its way toward the vein.

Chapter 32

Peter Manetti entered Canada as Joseph Baglio, as before. He rented a car and checked into a downtown hotel, as before. Just a business-man on a repeat trip to Vancouver to check on his various investments. Everything routine, nothing to arouse anyone's interest.

Manetti staked out Twisp River Resources' offices in the part of downtown Vancouver known as Gastown. For five days he monitored Malcolm's comings and goings, including two evening visits to his girlfriend's house.

By week's end Manetti was ready. He placed a call to Al Pantelli, using a throw-away cell phone.

"Al, Peter. I'm all set. Any change in plans?"

"No. Close the account," Al replied.

"I'll call you when it's done," Peter said, and hung up. He dropped the phone on the pavement and stomped on it before tossing it into a nearby Dumpster. Malcolm's fate was now irrevocably sealed.

Manetti would use the same toxin as with Rosenburg but with a different method of exposure. The following Tuesday Malcolm left work at six in the evening. And as he had done the previous Tuesday, he did not go straight home.

Manetti smiled when he thought of the old maxim. *Bait the trap with chocolate or pussy, and you'll get 'em every time.*

The maxim was right. Malcolm headed straight to his girlfriend's house. Manetti watched him knock on the door and saw the same good-looking broad let him in.

"Enjoy it, Malcolm, because it's going to be the last piece of tail you'll ever get," Manetti whispered, as he watched from his parked car.

Manetti pulled on a pair of surgical gloves and took an official Vancouver police parking ticket from his shirt pocket. He'd lifted the ticket from a parked car in front of an expired parking meter. He planned to place the ticket under the windshield wiper on Malcolm's car. The top portion of the ticket would be impregnated with VX.

The street where Manetti was parked had little traffic, and he'd seen only one or two pedestrians since he arrived. It was perfect. He pulled on a hat, wrapped his wool scarf up over his mouth, and pulled up the collar of his overcoat. About all anyone would be able to see, should someone pass by, would be his eyes.

Manetti took the metal shoe polish tube containing the VX from the inside pocket of his overcoat. He held the tube low in his lap, well below the view of any passerby. Carefully, he removed the plastic cap and placed it on his left thigh. Holding the tube in his right hand, he turned the sponge applicator head with his left hand, a quarter turn counterclockwise.

He felt the metal give more than he heard the faint click. Oily liquid oozed between his gloved fingers and dripped onto the crotch of his slacks. Manetti held his breath. Inhalation of the toxin was even deadlier than contact with skin. The metal tube had failed. He could see a hairline crack, from which the VX issued. A manufacturing defect, or maybe the toxin had corroded the metal? It didn't really matter. He'd be toast as soon as the toxin reached his skin, if he didn't take a breath first.

He tossed the ruptured container on the passenger-side floor mat. With his left hand, he peeled the contaminated glove off his right hand and threw it in the same general direction. Needing to breath, he threw open the driver's side door and stepped out into the frigid January night. He exhaled, took a deep breath, and worked to unbuckle and unzip his slacks. He was just about to get his pants off when he felt a cold dampness on his lower belly. Manetti quickly pulled a pen and the parking ticket from his coat pocket. He scribbled two words on the back of the parking ticket and then sank to his knees.

"Forgive me, Julie," Manetti whispered softly. "I'm coming home."

The first seizure hit him like a freight train.

Chief Inspector Rand got the call in the middle of the night. A cab driver dropping off a fare had reported a man lying beside an open car with his pants part way off. Officer Malone, of the Vancouver Police Department, had responded to the call, and become the second casualty.

Rand drove to the location in North Vancouver. An emergency response team was already on-site when he arrived. Several of the ERT's were in hazmat suits with gas masks.

David Osgood from the Ministry of Public Safety pulled up near the chief inspector's car and walked over to where Rand was watching the operation.

"Inspector," David said, pulling off his right glove to shake hands, "don't tell me it's happened, again?"

"Looks that way, David. But this one's different. Looks like the assassin bought it, along with one of our own."

"What've we got so far?"

"Looks like the killer's vial of toxin, I'm assuming it's VX again, leaked and took him out. When Officer Malone arrived on scene, he managed to somehow get contaminated. Not sure if by inhalation or by contact with the skin, or both."

The hazmat team was putting Peter Manetti into a special body bag. Officer Malone was already bagged and tagged.

"They found a note, evidently written by the assassin just moments before his demise," Rand said. "They've bagged it in a chemical bag."

"What did it say?" David asked.

"Just two words: Pantelli slash Trueblood, and a partial word that could be chemical, chemist, or chemistry."

"Mean anything to you?" David asked.

"Pantelli, could be the Pantelli crime family in New Orleans. We're still checking on Trueblood. If the third word is chemist, it could be a nickname the assassin used."

A uniformed police sergeant approached Chief Inspector Rand and David Osgood.

"Excuse me, sir," the officer said, saluting the chief inspector.

"Yes, sergeant?" Rand replied.

"Sir, we've gone house to house in the immediate area. Looking for anyone who may have heard or seen something. There's a gentleman we're questioning who was visiting in the house just up the street."

"Did he see anything?" Rand asked.

"No, sir. But you may want to talk to him just the same. His name is Trueblood."

Chapter 33

My cell phone went off as I was unlocking my office. I looked at the caller ID; it was Fish.

"Damn, Fish, you're out of the gate early today." I said with a chuckle.

"I've got some news I thought you'd want to hear," Fish replied.

"Do I need to sit down?" I asked, blowing my breath out.

"No, no worries, Trace. It's damned good news."

"Okay, Fish, lay it on me."

"The core hole Red's drilling, at a seventy-five-degree angle, hit the vein around six hundred ninety-eight feet. We cored about thirty-five feet of high-grade pitchblende."

"I like it so far. Is there more?"

"Yeah, it gets better. As you know, I usually drill about ten feet into the footwall schist just to be sure we're completely through the vein."

"Yep. What'd you find?"

"Well, about three feet into the foot-wall, we hit a second vein."

"A splinter off the main vein?"

"No, it's a totally different system, Trace."

"Uranium?"

"No. This vein is about five feet of quartz with chalcopyrite and specs of visible gold."

"No kidding? Visible gold with copper sulfide?"

"I kid you not. I reckon the vein is about sixty-five percent chalcopyrite. Plus, there's visible free gold, and I'm sure the chalcopyrite will carry gold values as well."

"Great news, Fish, but not a total surprise. Remember, the Sullivan was originally a copper and gold mine. We've been drilling in a high-grade uranium zone but it figures we'd hit some copper and gold, sooner or later."

"It could be the two veins merge above where we're drilling," Fish replied. "Remember, this hole is at a seventy-five-degree angle. We're well below the second level of the original mine workings."

"This new vein didn't show up in the forty-five-degree hole we drilled from this location, did it?" I asked.

"No. All we saw in the core was the same uranium vein we've been chasing."

"Okay, drill another hole from the same location, this time at sixty degrees. Let's try and get an idea if the veins merge or if the copper-gold zone pinches out towards the surface. If we keep intersecting the gold zone along strike, we may want to go back and deepen some of our earlier holes."

"I'm all over it, Trace. I'll get the cores split and off to the lab in the morning. I think the gold values are going to knock our socks off. Plus we'll have the copper as a kicker."

"Good work, Fish. Keep after it and keep me posted. I'll get word to the rest of the board. I'm sure Jim will be on the next flight to Spokane," I said with a laugh.

I called Wally and Will, and filled them in. They both about busted at the seams. Jim was in a meeting in Chicago, so I left him a message. This time the Virus would have to wait for the press release, like all the other shareholders.

That evening I received an e-mail from Jim. He'd fly into Spokane in a couple of days and wanted to know if I could go up to the mine with him. I e-mailed him back to let me know his flight info so I could pick him up.

Three days later, I met Jim at the Spokane airport and we headed for Winthrop.

"Have you got any assays back yet from the cores in the gold-copper intersection?"

"Not yet, Jim. But they could show up anytime. I put an expedite order on the assays. It costs a bit more, but I figure it'll be worth it, especially if the assays are as good as Fish thinks they will be."

"It'll make a nice press release. Gold and copper on top of the extraordinary uranium grades. The bloody share price should make a healthy move upwards."

"My thoughts, exactly."

"Anything new from Cyrus on our Chinese friends?"

"Not too much. His trader buddy in Hong Kong says they're still buying. Nothing huge, just steady day-to-day buying. Especially on any dips."

"They could be a problem down the road, Trace. I've seen them in action in the Australian uranium market. They're sharp guys, with deep pockets, and they're ruthless. No quarter asked, none given."

I started to reply when my cell phone went off.

"Trace Brandon."

"Trace, Steve Bennet, Mineral Valley Labs. Got a sec?"

"You bet. What's up, Steve?"

"I have some assay info for you. The formal reports will go out to day, from my office."

"How'd the gold values look?"

"Are you driving?"

"Yes."

"Buckled up?"

"Yes," I said with a laugh, glancing at Jim.

"Okay. Looks like you're averaging about eight-tenths of an ounce gold and about two and a half percent copper."

"Wow! Not too damn shabby."

"You can say that again. I thought you'd be pleased."

"Yeah, it's really good news, Steve."

"Well, while you're in such a good mood, let me run one other item by you."

I raised my eyebrows and glanced at Jim. "Okay, shoot."

"I found the leak here at the lab."

"Good."

"Well, it's good and bad, Trace."

"How so?"

"The leak came from one of our senior people. A gal named Mary Johnson."

"Okay. And?"

"And, her daughter has terminal brain cancer. Mary's about exhausted her med insurance and is between a rock and a hard spot. She took the money for the assay data to keep her daughter alive."

"I see. So what's your plan?"

"She's a good gal, Trace. I'm not sure any one of us wouldn't have done the same thing in a similar situation. But, I leave it to you. If you say prosecute, we'll file a complaint."

"Are you going to keep her on?"

"Yes. On probation. If she screws up again, she's history."

"Okay, here's my thought. Keeping her on is your decision. I don't want to be telling you how to run your business. But I don't want her anywhere near our data. Understood?"

"Understood."

"Secondly, have her set up an account with a stock brokerage firm in Coeur d'Alene. When it's done, send me the account information, and I'll transfer one hundred thousand shares of Montana Creek Mining stock into her account. To use as she sees fit. Remember, she'll be a shareholder in Montana Creek. Another reason she can have nothing to do with our assays."

"Damn, Trace. That's a hell of a nice thing to do."

"Yeah, well, no kid should have to go through cancer."

"I'll tell Mary, and we'll get everything set up. Thanks, Trace. She really is a good gal. Just made a bad mistake."

"No worries, mate, as my Aussie friend always says. Hell, the only guy who never made a mistake lived two thousand years ago. And you couldn't have hired him anyway."

Chapter 34

Chief Inspector Rand followed the police sergeant to a squad car, where Malcolm Trueblood was waiting, and opened the squad car door.

"Mr. Trueblood, I'm Chief Inspector Rand. I need to speak with you," he said, sliding in beside Trueblood and closing the car door.

"What's this all about, Inspector?"

"We found a note the dead fellow, the guy with his pants around his knees lying in the street, evidently wrote just before he expired."

"What's that got to do with me?"

"Your name is on the note. Along with the name, Pantelli."

Chief Inspector Rand saw Trueblood flinch at the name Pantelli.

"I take it from your reaction, you're familiar with the Pantellis?"

"Am I being charged with anything?"

"Not at the moment. We're just trying to figure out why this fellow was watching you. Why he was carrying a vial of nerve toxin, and why he put your name on the last thing he ever wrote."

"I see. So you think I was the intended target?"

"Yes, I do. Do you remember a while back when a Mr. Richard Rosenburg died of a stroke in a department store parking garage?"

"Yes, I do recall reading of his death. He lived not too far from me in North Vancouver."

"Did you know the man? Have any business dealings with him?"

"I knew he was involved in penny stock companies and had done fairly well over the years. That's about it. Why do you mention it?"

"We think the fellow, lying in the street over there, killed Rosenburg. And you were his next target."

"Why would he want to kill me?"

"I think both you and Rosenburg are, were, involved in some way with the Pantelli crime family out of New Orleans. Look, we're going to run your passport, travel records, phone records, e-mails, the full-meal deal. If I were you, I'd be very cooperative. Just because they missed tonight, doesn't mean they won't try again."

"Jesus," Trueblood whispered, lowering his eyes and nodded. "Yes, I know the Pantellis. I had a meeting with them in Las Vegas a short time ago."

"What was the meeting about?"

"The company I run here in Vancouver, Twisp River Resources, and the Pantellis both own shares in a junior Vancouver-based mining company. I flew down to discuss our mutual holdings and to see how we might better benefit from our stock ownership."

"Uh-huh. What's the name of the mining company?"

"Montana Creek Mining, Corporation. It trades on the VSE. Symbol is MCM.V."

"Do you own the shares personally, or are they owned by Twisp River?"

"They're owned by the company."

"Do you control the company?"

Trueblood took a deep breath. "No the company is a wholly owned subsidiary of an offshore holding company."

"What's the name and domicile of the offshore company?"

"Carib International. It's based in the Cayman Islands."

"Who controls Carib International?"

"I'm not at liberty to disclose that information, sir."

"We'll find out."

"Good luck."

Inspector Rand smiled. "Okay, Mr. Trueblood. That's all for now. Do you need a ride home?"

"No, sir. My car is just down the street."

"Okay. Thank you for your help. We'll be in touch. And Mr. Trueblood, don't leave town without contacting me first," Chief Inspector Rand said, handing Malcolm one of his cards.

First thing the following morning Chief Inspector Rand was on the phone to FBI Special Agent, Beau Monroe.

"Agent Monroe, this is Chief Inspector Rand in Vancouver."

"Yes, sir. And what can I do for you this fine morning, Inspector?"

"Fine morning? You must not be in Washington. I saw on TV it was snowing like crazy in D.C."

Monroe laughed. "That's why you're the chief inspector, Inspector. I'm in our New Orleans office. What can I do for you?"

"I think we got Rosenburg's killer last night."

"No kidding? What happened?"

Chief Inspector Rand filled Agent Monroe in.

"The note had Pantelli and Trueblood written on it?" Monroe asked.

"Yes, those two names and the letters c-h-e-m-i. Which we're guessing was going to be the word *chemist*."

"Uh-huh. Any ID on the body?"

"Yes, a passport and a Las Vegas driver's license. Both in the name of Joseph Baglio. We think both documents are forgeries. We checked with immigration, and Baglio entered Vancouver about a week ago. He rented a car at the airport and a room at a downtown hotel. Then he more or less dropped off the radar screen."

"Can you send us his prints?"

"Will do, just as soon as we get him decon'd enough to take them."

"Jesus. He's a mess, huh?"

"Well, if he isn't, he'll do until a mess comes along."

Agent Monroe laughed. "Okay, Inspector, send us everything you can, as soon as you can, and we'll get on it. By the way, we may have a lead on our dead chemist friend. We located a small-time druggie doing a nickel in a federal pen here in Louisiana. He claims a hit-man, using the nickname of the Chemist, did wet work for the Pantelli Family."

"Good work, Agent Monroe. Please keep me posted, and I'll do likewise. Oh, one other thing. Share ownership in Montana Creek Mining keeps popping up. As you know, it's a Vancouver company, but according to Trueblood, their mining claims are in Washington State. And if you remember, Rosenburg supposedly shot William Thornton for trying to steal his Montana Creek Mining shares. Well, it turns out Trueblood's company, Twisp River Resources, is also a shareholder in Montana Creek Mining. And it gets better. According to Trueblood, members of the Pantelli crime family are also shareholders."

"The proverbial common denominator. Good work yourself, Inspector. I'll check on Montana Creek Mining's U.S. holdings from my end. Please keep me posted on anything else you turn up. With the Pantellis in the melee, it's likely to get even more interesting."

Chapter 35

Jim Lee and I pulled in near Red's drill and parked. Fish waved and walked over.

"Damn, Fish. It's so cold my dick's gone into turtle mode," I said with a chuckle. I didn't bother to take my glove off when we shook hands.

Jim nodded and punched Fish lightly on the shoulder. "Bloody good to see you, mate."

"Come on in the core shack, fellows. I've got something you'll want to see," Fish said, gesturing with his left hand toward the small Quonset hut-type building.

We walked into the warm exterior of the core shack. Fish had box after box of cores up on wooden saw-horses.

"This is from last night's core from hole Ten-C," Fish said, pointing to a wooden core box. "We drilled the hole at a sixty-degree angle. Sort of split the difference between the forty-five degree and seventy-five-degree holes."

Jim and I examined the mineral-laden core with our ten-power hand lenses'.

"Bloody, hell," Jim said, "this is some damned fine gold-copper ore. By the way, Fish, Trace hasn't had a chance to tell you yet, but the manager of Mineral Valley labs called while we were driving up here. The assays from the first gold-copper zone cores are back."

"What'd they run?" Fish asked, with a huge grin on his face.

"Eight-tenths gold and two and a half percent copper," Jim said with a chuckle.

"Hot damn, I knew they'd be good," Fish said, slapping his thigh.

"I think these will be just as good, fellas," I said, looking at a couple of specs of visible gold in the section of core I was holding.

"Yeah, I agree," Jim said, "really good-looking ore."

"I'll get a news release out to the shareholders and the VSE as soon as I get the official results from the lab," I said. "I think we'll see a hell of a lot of interest in our shares."

Jim laughed. "Yep, ought to drive the bloody chinks right up the wall."

Fish looked at us. "Chinks? You mean the Chinese are interested in Montana Creek?"

"Yep, looks that way," I said. "Cyrus has a contact in Hong Kong who tipped us off to buying by URAN-China Nuclear Corp. So far they're just nibbling away. But throwing some high-grade gold and copper into the mix, will likely kick things up a notch or two."

Chapter 36

My cell phone started vibrating. I flipped the phone open and answered.

"Trace Brandon."

"Mr. Brandon, this is Special Agent Beau Monroe with the FBI. Have you got a second?"

"Yes, sir. What can I do for you?"

"I wonder if we might meet in Spokane in the next day or two."

"Yes, sir, that shouldn't be a problem. I'm up on our mining claims, northwest of Winthrop, Washington, at the moment. But I've got to drop one of our partners off at the Spokane airport day after tomorrow. Would that work for you?"

"That would be perfect, Mr. Brandon."

"May I ask what this is all about?"

"We're working with the Vancouver police on the murder of Richard Rosenburg, one of your shareholders. And on the attempted murder of Malcolm Trueblood, also one of your shareholders, and until recently, one of your directors."

"Jesus, somebody tried to kill Malcolm? And I thought Rosenburg had a stroke or something."

"Rosenburg was killed with a nerve toxin. I'll explain when we meet. Spokane terminal, day after tomorrow?"

"Yes, sir. I'll be there."

"Good. Call me on this number, and we'll link up."

"Yes, sir."

I hung up. Both Fish and Jim were staring at me.

"That was the FBI. Somebody tried to kill Malcolm Trueblood. And they want to talk to me the day after tomorrow at the Spokane airport."

Jim and I spent the next day with Fish and watched additional cores come up. So far, we were still hitting the uranium vein followed by the gold-copper vein. The next morning we said goodbye to Red and his crew, told Fish to keep up the good work, and headed back to Spokane. Jim had a flight to catch to Los Angeles, and I had a meeting with the FBI.

I walked with Jim to security check-in, said good-bye, and called Special Agent Beau Monroe.

"Agent Monroe, it's Trace Brandon. I'm in the terminal."

"Okay, meet me at security between concourses A and B. I'm six one, salt-and-pepper crew-cut hair, and I'm wearing a blue suit."

"Got it. Be there in a couple of minutes."

Monroe was easy to spot. He looked like the prototype FBI agent.

"Agent Monroe? I'm Trace Brandon," I said, extending my hand.

"Mr. Brandon, thanks for coming. There's a wine bar slash restaurant just past security. Follow me."

Monroe showed his badge to security, said a few words to the supervisor, and gestured toward me. I went through the security screening. Monroe didn't.

We grabbed a table in a quiet area of the small airport restaurant and ordered soft drinks.

"Mr. Brandon, I wanted to chat with you a bit as we have one homicide, one attempted homicide, and a dead assassin on our hands. Not to mention an unlucky Vancouver police officer who tried to render aid and is also a fatality."

"Call me Trace, Agent Monroe. And you think ownership of our shares is somehow related to these killings?"

"We do. So far it's the only common denominator. Both Rosenburg and Trueblood owned, own, shares in your company, either directly or indirectly through their companies."

"That's true. Rosenburg was co-owner of the public shell we did a reverse merger with. As part of the transaction, he kept a significant number of founder's' shares. Trueblood is CEO of Twisp River Resources, which took down part of our initial private placement."

"We understand Twisp River Resources is a wholly-owned subsidiary of a Cayman Island holding company."

"Correct. We did some research on Twisp River to see who actually owns or controls our shares. Our findings indicated Carib International, out of Grand Cayman, controls Twisp River."

"Do you mind telling me how you were able to ascertain that information?"

"We employed a local, Cayman Island, securities analyst to do some digging."

"I see. All legal and above board, I presume."

I just smiled. "It *is* the Cayman Islands, Agent Monroe."

Monroe exhaled through his mouth and nodded.

"Yes, and thankfully out of my jurisdiction. Are you also aware the Pantelli crime family in New Orleans are shareholders in your company?"

"We're a publicly traded company, Agent Monroe. Anybody with a brokerage account and access to the Vancouver Stock Exchange can buy our shares."

"The Pantellis got their shares from Rosenburg."

"Look, I know Rosenburg used his shares to pay off a gambling debt he owed to a Vegas casino. I don't know which casino or who actually holds his shares," I said, omitting the fact that Cyrus had managed to get a proxy to vote those same shares, and would know exactly who owned Rosenburg's shares. I figured it was a two-way street. Monroe was trying to see what I knew, and I was doing likewise.

"You should get an updated shareholders' list from your transfer agent. You might be surprised who some of your shareholders are."

"I'll do that. Do you think the Pantelli family is behind Rosenburg's death, and the attempt on Trueblood?"

"Well, they do fall in the realm of usual suspects."

"But why would they want to kill Rosenburg after he squared his debt? Hell, the shares are worth more now than when he transferred them. And there's a damn good chance they'll be worth a lot more in the future."

"With the Pantellis, it doesn't take much to get whacked. Maybe Rosenburg said the wrong thing or threatened to go to the authorities. Or maybe they just flat-out didn't like him. These people are stone-cold killers. If there's a profit to be made by whacking someone, that someone usually gets whacked."

"What about Trueblood? How the hell does he fit in all this? He's about as straight as they come."

"Maybe, maybe not. We're just now digging into Mr. Trueblood. I've got to say, Trace," Monroe said with a smile, "you sure have one eclectic bunch of stockholders."

"Yeah," I replied, thinking to myself. Just wait till you find out Cyrus the Virus owns 17 per-cent of our company. And holds a proxy to vote the Pantelli's' shares. "Well, Agent Monroe, when you hatch a company on the Vancouver Stock Exchange, you're apt to end up with some rather colorful shareholders."

"No argument there, Trace. Listen, I appreciate your taking the time to see me. I'd also appreciate it if you'd get an updated shareholders' list and send a copy to my office," Monroe said, handing me one of his business cards.

"No problem, Agent Monroe. Do you think any of our other shareholders are possible targets?"

"I don't think so. Rosenburg and Trueblood had direct dealings with the Pantellis. I think something in those dealings got Rosenburg killed, and Trueblood nearly killed. I don't think they'd do anything to jeopardize the company's management, and thereby, their investment, in Montana Creek Mining. But if we turn up something that suggests otherwise, I'll let you know immediately."

179

Chapter 37

Since I was in Spokane, I called Cyrus as soon as I left the airport.

"Cyrus, it's Trace. Got a minute? It's important."

"Sure, Trace. Where are you?"

"I'm at the Spokane airport. I've been up at the mine with Jim Lee. I just put him on a plane. And then I had a coke with Special Agent Beau Monroe of the FBI."

"What? You met with the FBI at the Spokane airport?"

"Yep, they called while I was up at the mine and requested a meeting in Spokane. As I had to drop Jim off, we met at the airport."

"What did they want? Are we in some kind of trouble?"

"Not us, or the company. But Malcolm is."

"Malcolm? What the hell did he do?"

"First off, Cyrus, Rosenburg didn't have a stroke. He was killed by a pro."

"Look, I hated that prick for killing Thorny, but I didn't take him out."

"I know, Cyrus, because the guy that whacked Rosenburg evidently tried to kill Malcolm a couple of days ago, in Vancouver."

"Is Mal all right?"

"Yeah, he skated, but the assassin didn't make it."

"Police shoot him?"

"I don't think so. From what little Agent Monroe would tell me, there was some kind of accident."

"I'll call Mal and get the lowdown. Jesus, first Thorny, then Rosy, and now someone tries to hit Mal. What in the hell *is* going on?"

"Same question I've been asking. The FBI thinks the common denominator is Montana Creek Mining, and the Pantelli family."

Cyrus hung up, leaned back in his black-leather office chair, put his feet up on his desk, and dialed Malcolm Trueblood's cell phone number.

"Malcolm, it's Cyrus."

"I've been expecting your call."

"What in the hell is going on?"

"I got mad about being dumped from Montana Creek Mining's board. You know, Cyrus, it was quite humiliating. I've spent my whole life building my reputation. And then to get dumped like some two-bit shyster. Anyway, I compounded the problem by doing something stupid."

"You tried to cut some kind of deal with the Pantelli family?"

"How did you know?"

"The FBI met with Trace today, in Spokane. Seems Rosenburg didn't die of natural causes. They think the same guy who whacked Rosy tried to hit you the other night. The one common denominator that keeps popping onto their radar screen is all the parties of interest, dead or alive, are, or were, shareholders in Montana Creek Mining. What kind of deal did you try and cut with the Pantellis?"

"I wanted them to help me blackmail you. The plan was to get you to sell us your interests in Montana Creek Mining, at a discount."

"And why in the hell would I do that?" Cyrus asked, already knowing the answer.

"To keep us, me, from going to the regulators with information on insider trading."

"I see, and how did the Pantellis react to your proposal?"

"They threw me out of their office and told me to get out of Vegas by sundown, or they'd plant me in the desert."

"Jesus Christ, Malcolm. What in the hell were you thinking? You should have come to me. You're way out of your league with the Pantelli family."

"Look, Cyrus, I was pissed off, and I made a big mistake. Ever make one of those? A big mistake?"

Cyrus exhaled, blowing air from his cheeks. "Yeah, kid, once or twice. Okay, spilt milk, but we've got a big problem here. I suspect the Pantellis were worried you'd go public and the information would hurt Montana Creek Mining's share price. And therefore their investment."

"They'd kill me over that?"

"In a fucking heartbeat, Malcolm. Are you starting to get the picture here?"

"Yeah, I can see I'm in deep shit."

"Uh-huh. Okay, here's what we'll do. I'll call the Pantellis and tell them I've talked to you, and you're squared away. Not a threat of any kind. And that you're taking a transfer to the Caymans to manage some of my offshore interests."

"Caymans? Jesus, Cyrus, what is this, exile?"

"Look, Malcolm, it's offshore, out of FBI jurisdiction, and it should satisfy the Pantellis. You'll get to live, and you'll have plenty of company with other expats with similar problems. When the heat dies down, I'll bring you back to Vancouver."

"Why are you helping me like this? I tried to use the mob to blackmail you."

"Well, Malcolm, let's just say it's partly my fault you got into this predicament. I knew you weren't cut out for the down and dirty part of this game. I should have kept you above it. So, I'll help square it this time. But don't ever try and go around me again. Fair enough?"

"Yes, it's fair enough, and you're right. I thought I'd like the darker side, but I don't think I'm cut out for it."

CHAPTER 38

I'd submitted a news release to the Vancouver Stock Exchange and posted our latest assays, uranium, gold, and copper, on our website. It didn't take long for the investment community to take notice. Our shares hit four dollars Canadian the day after the information was released. Even better, the company now met all the qualifications for a Toronto Exchange listing.

I called Wally, and I got him working on the filings for a Toronto Stock Exchange listing. I also asked him to check in with Jerry Smyth and see how the engineering report was progressing. Wally said he'd get on both items. He also suggested we might want to amend the report to include the newly discovered gold and copper values.

I agreed. Then Cyrus called.

"Trace, it's Cyrus. Got a second?"

"Sure, Cyrus. What's up?"

"Couple of things, Trace. First off, damn good work on the news release and core results. The stock price has really reacted."

"Yeah, thanks. We've got a lot of happy shareholders today."

"Which brings me to the next item . . . Malcolm."

"Did you speak with him?"

"Yes, I did. Turns out he was really pissed about being dumped from your board and tried to take it out on me by cutting a little deal with our shareholders, in Las Vegas."

"Great."

"Yeah, he got in way over his head, and I'm going to have to try and bail him out."

"What's the plan?"

"Plan is, I call the Pantellis and convince them he's not a threat. And that he'll be transferring to my Cayman Island operations, for the foreseeable future."

"Think it'll work?"

"Yeah, I think it might. If the Pantellis did try and hit him, they probably won't try again if they don't have to. There's too much heat right now. Hell, the FBI's tossing their name around like confetti."

"Jesus, what a mess."

"Yeah, but I think it will all work out. The Pantellis are only interested in one thing, and that's making money."

"Well, they're making money today."

"Aren't they though?" Cyrus said with a chuckle. "Hot damn, four bucks a share."

Chapter 39

Al Pantelli walked down to his brother's office in their French Quarter office building.

"Pino," Al said, "we got us another damn problem."

"What now, brother?"

"I just got off the phone with one of the Outfit's capos in Vancouver."

"Yeah?" Pino replied, now paying full attention to his brother.

"Yeah. He's got a local detective on the pad. You know the reason we ain't heard nothing from the Chemist?"

"No, but I've been wondering what's taking him so damn long."

"He's dead. That's why we ain't heard nothing about the hit on Trueblood."

"Trueblood killed him?" Pino asked, in disbelief.

"Hell, no. There was some kind of foul-up with the poison he was going to use. He accidently killed himself."

"Jesus."

"Uh-huh, and it gets worse. The crazy bastard wrote out some kind of note as he was croaking. According to the detective, there were just two words on the note, two names. Trueblood's and ours."

"Holy crap. Why in the hell would Manetti do something that damned stupid?"

"Beats the shit out of me. But he sure as hell implicated us, and according to the detective, the FBI is involved."

"Damn, it just gets better and better."

"We need to give this situation some serious friggin' thought," Al said, pulling his vibrating cell phone from his shirt pocket. "Excuse me just a sec, Pino. It's Cyrus on the horn. Maybe he'll have some thoughts on this situation.""Cyrus, good-timing. We were just talking about our mutual friend, Mr. Trueblood."

"Exactly why I'm calling, Al. I've had a long talk with Malcolm, and he's seen the light. I'm going to pull him out of Vancouver and put him in the Caymans. He can do some work for me with Carib International. I'll keep him offshore until the heat fades."

"You know he's a freakin' rat? He tried to cut a deal with us to blackmail you and force you to sell us your Montana Creek Mining shares, on the cheap."

"Yeah, I know all that. He screwed up, thought he'd be a player in the big leagues. But I've straightened his ass out. If you agree, I'll take care of this."

"Give me a sec to run this by Pino. He's sitting right here."

"Sure, no problem."

In a couple of minutes Al was back on the line.

"Okay, Cyrus. Because you and me go way back, Trueblood gets a pass. This one time only. *Capisce?*"

"Thanks, Al. It's for the best all the way around."

"I want that SOB offshore, yesterday."

"Not a problem, Al. Malcolm's a pilot and flies his own plane. I'll have him packed up, airborne, and en route to the Caymans in twenty-four hours."

"What about his family?" Al asked, glancing over at his brother.

"His wife was killed years ago. A train hit her car and killed her instantly. They had no kids. I think he has a girlfriend, but that's about it."

"Okay, perfect. You tell the little prick we'd better not hear so much as a loud fart out of him, or he'll be off the board."

"Understood, and thanks, Al. I owe you one."

"No, you don't, Cyrus. But Trueblood does."

Al hung up and looked at his brother. "What'd ya think?"

Pino rubbed his chin with his right hand.

"Mixed feelings, Al. Getting Trueblood offshore is a good move. But, he'll always be a threat to both of us and to our investment in Montana Creek Mining. We had a face-to-face with him, and then we tried to whack him. Sooner or later, if they dig hard enough, the FBI is going to connect the dots. And sooner or later Trueblood is going to get antsy sitting on his ass on that damn island."

"Agreed. We hit him, but this time it has to look like an accident."

CHAPTER 40

Malcolm Trueblood had flown single-engine aircraft for more than fifteen years. He was instrument rated and had flown into remote mining camps all over Canada, Alaska, and Mexico. Now, on Cyrus's instructions, he was preparing to fly from Vancouver to George Town on Grand Cayman Island.

He planned to stop in Denver long enough to eat a bite, refuel his TurboAire, and then overnight in Houston. On the second day, he'd fly from Houston to George Town. It would be a 985-nautical-mile hop from Houston to George Town, well within the TurboAire's 1,300 nautical-mile maximum range.

So far, the hardest part of his trip had been convincing Chief Constable Peter Rand of Vancouver's finest to let him leave British Columbia. But since Malcolm was not an actual witness to the purported attempt on his life or the death of the assassin, or the police officer, there was little Inspector Rand could do.

In a way, Inspector Rand was glad to be rid of Malcolm Trueblood. He already had Thornton's death, Rosenburg's subsequent murder, a dead hit man, and a dead police officer to deal with. Good riddance, he'd let the Cayman authorities worry about Malcolm.

Malcolm shoved the last of his gear into the TurboAire. He'd be living in Cyrus's town house but would continue to keep his house in North Vancouver. His girlfriend, whom he'd been visiting the night of the attempt on his life, would keep an eye on his place till he returned.

Malcolm completed his pre-flight check-list and taxied the plane out to the main runway of the small municipal airport.

The TurboAire is a kit-built, high-performance aircraft. He'd purchased the single-engine aircraft from a former U.S. Navy pilot, who was now working for Boeing in Seattle. Malcolm had paid over four hundred grand, and felt it was worth every penny.

The plane was built of a carbon composite with retractable gear and was pressurized to a maximum ceiling of thirty thousand feet. The five-hundred cubic-inch, turbo-piston engine developed three hundred fifty horsepower. The plane could cruise at over three hundred miles per hour at twenty-five thousand feet. A very fast *mama jama,* and a cocaine smuggler's wet dream.

A low-level Vancouver mobster duly noted Malcolm's takeoff. Once Malcolm was airborne, the man placed a call to Al Pantelli in New Orleans.

Al took down the flight information and hung up.

"We'll make our move at Houston Hobby," Al said, looking over at his brother.

Chapter 41

Lei Chang sat in his lavish office on the fortieth floor of one of the most historic old bank buildings in Hong Kong. The building had been originally constructed in 1864, and torn down and rebuilt several times, with the last renovation completed in 1985. At the time, it had been the most expensive building on earth, having cost around $600 million U.S. dollars.

From his windows, Lei Chang had an unobstructed view of Victoria Harbor. A strict adherer to the principles of feng shui, he believed a view of water led to prosperity. So far he'd been right. Chang also believed his company's investment in shares of Montana Creek Mining would lead to even greater prosperity.

Under Chang's orders, URAN-China Nuclear Corp. continued acquiring shares of Montana Creek Mining. He knew the price for uranium ore would continue to rise, and along with it the price of Montana Creek shares. Chang knew this because his company was tying up enough uranium reserves to manipulate the price of uranium.

Chang looked at his computer screen and smiled at the closing price of MCM.V. Four dollars and ten cents. His investment in this little Canadian mining company had already generated healthy paper profits, with more to come.

On the other side of the globe, Trace was also monitoring the share price. Smiling, he flipped open his cell phone and called Wally.

"Wally, Trace here. Got a sec?"

"Sure, Trace. What's on your mind?"

"Toronto is on my mind. I think it's time for a road show, and the Toronto Annual Mining Convention is coming up. I think we should make a presentation and set up a booth."

"Hell of a good idea, Trace. There will be twenty or thirty thousand attendees over the four-day event. Every prospector, miner, promoter, and investor who can get there, will be there."

"I agree. It's a hell of a forum. We can present to a lot of private, as well as institutional, investors. It'll get a lot of interest cranked up just about the time we list on the Toronto Exchange."

"Perfect. I'll get us registered, get you signed up for a PowerPoint presentation, and reserve a booth."

"I'd like you to go with me, if you can get away."

"No worries. You couldn't keep me away with a sharp stick."

"Okay, Wally, I'll leave it to you. Would you mind e-mailing Jim Lee when you get confirmations? I'm sure he's planning on attending, but we should give him a heads-up on our plans. He may want to participate in the presentation. After all, IUC owns twenty percent of our company."

"I'm on it. I'll send you the confirmation information, and I'll book us some rooms in a nearby hotel."

"Perfect. Thanks, Wally. I'll put out a news release when I get your confirmations. Do you think the Chinese will make contact at the convention?"

"The commies usually blow a bugle before they attack," Wally said with a laugh. "Stay frosty. It could get real interesting."

Chapter 42

Malcolm was anxious to land in Houston and stretch his legs. He'd been flying most of the day, and it was getting near sundown.

"Damn," Malcolm said aloud as he massaged the tops of his thighs. "Time to land this puppy."

He contacted Houston Approach on 124.5. Air traffic control cleared him to land on runway 12L/32R. The wind was off the gulf from the southeast. He pushed the left-rudder pedal a tad. brought the plane to a heading of 120 degrees, and continued his descent. Cleared for final, Malcolm eased back on the throttle, lowered the gear, and dropped the flaps to full down. Three minutes later he touched down smoothly on the asphalt runway.

Malcolm taxied the plane down the south ramp to Houston Flight Support's hangar area. He parked the plane and killed the engine. A short, stocky man with a red goatee and a military-style haircut watched Malcolm's arrival from one of the nearby hangers.

Al Pantelli went outside his usual bull pen for the second attempt on Malcolm. He wanted a non-Italian, non-Outfit, killer with two very specific skill sets: locks and explosives. After a few phone calls, he found the perfect mechanic.

The assassin's name was Sean Flannigan. He was Irish and an expert with explosives and locks. Flannigan had made his reputation blowing up British installations in Northern Ireland.

He'd worked his way up the chain of command in the Irish Republican Army before abruptly walking away. Now, he sold his services to the highest bidder, irrespective of his or her political affiliations. He was perfect for the hit. And he was the man who watched Malcolm from the empty hangar.

Chapter 43

Malcolm went into Houston Flight Support's office, paid his ramp fee, and arranged to have his plane fueled at 8:00 a.m. the following morning. He called a cab and headed to a nearby hotel. He wanted a shower, a steak, and about eight hours of sack time.

While Malcolm slept, Flannigan went to work. He spotted Houston Flight Support's swing-shift fuel truck driver.

"Hey, bud, the office wanted me to double-check on fueling the TurboAire. Was it for seven or eight in the morning?"

"Eight sharp," the driver answered.

"Roger that," Flannigan replied, with a laugh. "Damned desk jockeys. It's amazing they can find their asses with both hands."

The driver nodded and laughed. "You got that right. See you in the morning."

Flannigan made his way back to an empty hangar and hid out until 4:00 a.m. The shank of the night, and the time to do evil deeds. He took one more look around. Satisfied the coast was clear, he made his way to Malcolm's plane.

An expert locksmith, Flannigan picked the plane's door lock in less than thirty seconds. There were a couple of duffel bags behind the co-pilot's seat. He opened the bottom duffel and carefully inserted the explosive device. The bomb was a simple timed device with a battery, electric cord, and primer. The primer was inserted into a block of C-4 plastic explosive. The whole mechanism fit neatly in an empty first-aid kit. Flannigan had used similar devices many times, with deadly results.

Flannigan set the timing device to go off at 10:00 a.m. Figuring twenty minutes to fuel and another twenty minutes for pre-flight and takeoff, the TurboAire would be about eighty minutes into its flight to Grand Cayman when the device would detonate, well past the continental shelf and the ubiquitous offshore oil rigs, and over the abyssal deep of the Gulf of Mexico.

Chapter 44

I got to my office and saw my e-mail inbox indicator flashing on my computer screen. I opened my e-mail to find Toronto Mining Conference confirmations from Wally. He'd also booked us rooms at a hotel adjoining the convention center.

I noted he'd copied the e-mail to Jim Lee. I rocked in my desk chair, thinking for a moment, then I picked up the phone and called Cyrus.

"Cyrus, Trace here."

"Hey, Trace. Any more gold assays?"

"A tad eager, are we?" I replied, with a laugh. "We just shipped a load of cores to the lab. We'll have some new assays in a few days."

"Good deal. I know uranium's the play, but I still get a hard-on when it comes to gold."

"I know the feeling, Cyrus. There is something mystical and powerful about that damned yellow metal."

"It's the history, Trace. Men have been fighting and dying over gold since time began. It doesn't corrode. It can be melted down and re-cast time and time again. Hell, the gold in some damn bankers Rolex may have been mined by some poor Egyptian slave a millennia ago. It is a mystical metal."

"Listen, Cyrus, gold aside for a minute, I'm going to the Toronto Mining Convention in a couple weeks. Wally's going too. Will's going to stick around in case there's any problems at the mine. And I was wondering if you were planning on attending."

"I am planning on attending. Probably not for the whole four days but at least for a couple. Why do you ask?"

"Well, I have a hunch our Chinese investors will be attending and will want to meet. If they pitch some kind of deal, I'd like you there to discuss it with me, Wally, and Jim. Counting me, there'll be three of our four directors there. Between our little group, including you, we represent the controlling interest in Montana Creek Mining."

"Sure, Trace, be glad to. Just give me a call on my cell anytime you want to meet. I'll be attending several presentations, but I'll make time."

"Okay, thanks, Cyrus. It'll be interesting to see if the Chinese seek you out. I'm sure they'd love to acquire your block of shares."

"Trace, at some point it's going to come down to a major company coming after Montana Creek. We don't have the financing or infrastructure to put the Sullivan Mine into production."

"I know that, Cyrus, but I want the best company possible tendering for our stockholders' shares."

"You also know, Jim Lee and IUC aside, it's going to come down to you, me, Wally, and Will tendering our shares to make any deal work."

"Yeah, I do, Cyrus. Sometimes you just have to take the good with the bad," I said with a chuckle.

Chapter 45

Malcolm walked out to his plane just as the fuel truck was finishing topping off his tanks.

"Good to go?" Malcolm asked.

"Yes, sir. Topped off with high test," the fuel truck attendant replied. "Hell of a nice plane, sir. I hear they'll cruise at over three hundred miles per hour."

"Yep, she's fast all right and very, very, responsive."

The attendant laughed. "I guess those damn DEA Cessna's won't have a chance of catching this bird."

"You're right about that, but I don't ferry contraband."

"Didn't mean anything by it, sir. Just nice to see a plane that can give them a run for their money. If you ever want to sell your plane, just let me know," the attendant said, handing Malcolm one of his business cards. "I know some people who'd be very interested."

Malcolm took the man's card and put it in his shirt pocket. "Thanks, I'll keep it in mind, if I ever decide to sell."

Malcolm did a walk around the aircraft while the attendant finished loading his hoses and drove off. He'd checked the oil, and tires, and drained gas from each fuel tank sump into a glass vial to check for water in the fuel.

Satisfied the fuel was good, Malcolm removed the wing tethers, pulled the wheel chocks, and climbed into the cockpit. He strapped into the pilot's seat and took a look around the cabin. Everything seemed in order. After his pre-flight check, he contacted Houston Hobby departure and was cleared to taxi to the same runway he'd landed on, 12L/30R.

He held while a Citation and a Cessna 210 landed.

"TurboAire, whisky mike two niner five, you are cleared for departure."

"Roger, Houston departure. TurboAire whisky mike two niner five is rolling."

Once airborne, Malcolm climbed to twenty-four thousand feet on a heading of 126 degrees. He set his GPS system's lat/long for Grand Cayman and engaged the auto-pilot. At three hundred miles per hour, assuming no significant head-winds, he should make George Town in about three hours and forty-five minutes.

About an hour into the flight, Malcolm stomach started growling. He checked the auto-pilot and did a visual check for traffic. Seeing none, he climbed out of the pilot seat and eased his way toward the back of the plane. He'd stashed a box of Little Debbie peanut butter cheese crackers in one of the duffel bags. Opening the bottom duffel, he immediately spotted the first-aid kit.

"What the hell?" he said, aloud. "Who the hell put that in there?"

Carefully he opened the plastic first-aid kit. When saw the contents, an icy chill ran down his spine.

"Holy shit," he whispered. "It's a bomb,"

Malcolm looked at the timing device. It appeared to be set to go off in twenty minutes. Very carefully he closed the first-aid kit and reached forward, placing it in the co-pilot's seat. He then carefully climbed back in-to the left seat and clicked his mike.

"Houston control, TurboAire, whiskey mike two niner five."

"TurboAire, whiskey mike two niner five, Houston control."

"Houston control, TurboAire, whiskey mike two niner five. I need to declare an emergency."

"TurboAire, whiskey mike two niner five, please change frequency to one twenty point two."

Malcolm switched to the emergency frequency.

"Houston control, TurboAire, whiskey mike two niner five on one twenty point zero."

"Roger, TurboAire, you may dispense with your call sign from here on. What is your emergency?"

"Houston control, I have a bomb on board. It has a timing device and is set to detonate in approximately twenty minutes. I'm sixty minutes from any landfall."

"Understood. Do you wish to ditch, or are you able to jettison the bomb?"

"Houston control, I would like to descend to ten thousand feet and eject the device over the Gulf."

"Understood. Wait one."

Malcolm waited. He knew Houston control was checking for any aircraft below his flight level. They'd also be contacting the Coast Guard for shipping in his vicinity. After what seemed like an eternity, but less than five minutes later, Houston control was back.

"TurboAire, you are cleared to descend and maintain ten thousand feet. Contact control once the explosive device has been jettisoned."

"Houston control, roger that, and thanks."

Malcolm reduced speed, lowered the plane's nose, and began rapidly descending. At ten thousand feet he would depressurize, level off, crack open the pilot's side window, and toss the bomb.

"Houston control, TurboAire, just passing fifteen thousand one hund . . ."

At fifteen thousand feet, a second bomb, taped to the bottom of the co-pilot's seat, and set to explode when the plane dropped below fifteen thousand feet, detonated.

"TurboAire, say again. Your transmission broke up."

But there was only static.

Air traffic control had lost radar contact with the TurboAire.

When Malcolm's plane failed to show up at the George Town airport, Lisa Miller called Cyrus.

"Cyrus, Lisa. Hey, was there a delay in Mr. Trueblood's flight?"

"No, not that I know of. He hasn't shown up yet?"

"No. No sign of him. His e-mail said he'd be wheels dry around noon. It's nearly three p.m. here."

"Okay, check with the local air traffic guys and see if he had a mechanical problem and returned to Houston. I'll call Houston Hobby and see what I can find out."

About an hour later, Cyrus called Lisa back.

"Lisa, hi, it's me."

"It's not good, is it, Cyrus?"

"No, I'm afraid not. His plane was about an hour out from Hobby when he declared an emergency, and then disappeared off radar. They won't tell me the nature of the emergency or what happened to Malcolm. All they would tell me is the Coast Guard is investigating. Anything on your end?"

"About the same. He'd declared an emergency and requested to descend to ten thousand feet."

"That means he wanted to get below where he'd need oxygen."

"You think the plane lost pressurization?"

"Could be, but knowing Malcolm, I think he'd have descended immediately and asked for permission later."

"What now?"

"Well, the Coast Guard is sending a cutter to search for the plane. He may have been able to ditch."

Pino Pantelli stuck his head into his brother Al's office.

"Got a second?"

"Sure, Pino. Come on in."

Pino walked into Al's office and sat in one of the side chairs.

"I just heard from our Irish friend. He's been monitoring FAA radio traffic. Seems they lost a small plane out over the Gulf this morning. And according to my contacts in George Town, Mr. Trueblood never arrived."

Al got up from behind his desk and walked over to the wet bar.

"I think that calls for a drink. Care to join me?"

"Sure. Make it Irish whiskey in honor of our Mr. Flannigan."

Chapter 46

I was in my office, working on the PowerPoint presentation I was going to give in Toronto, when my office phone rang.

"Montana Creek Mining, Trace speaking."

"Trace, Special Agent Beau Monroe."

"Good morning, Agent Monroe. Don't tell me another Montana Creek Mining shareholder bit the dust." I said, half-afraid I might be right.

"Your former director, Malcolm Trueblood, the one someone tried to whack in Vancouver."

"Yes," I interrupted, "what about him?"

"His plane never made Grand Cayman."

"His plane. You mean a commercial flight went down?"

"No. Trueblood was a pilot. He was flying to the Caymans in his personal aircraft."

"What happened?"

"This is what we know, and this is in strictest confidence, Trace. Agreed?"

"Agreed."

"Trueblood departed Houston Hobby Airport en route to George Town, Grand Cayman, at approximately eight a.m. About an hour out of Hobby he declared an emergency. He reported finding a bomb on board and requested permission to descend to ten thousand feet. He wanted to de-pressurize, open a window, and chuck the device into the Gulf."

"And?"

"And, as he descends through fifteen thousand feet, poof. He's gone. Off the radar."

"The bomb went off?"

"A bomb went off. He told ATC the device he found had a timer detonator. He thought he had twenty minutes before it was set to blow."

"So it went off early or he misread the timer."

"Or, there was a second, back-up, explosive device with a pressure trigger. And when he dropped through fifteen thousand feet—game over."

"Jesus, why kill him now? He was going into soft exile. Out of all but Cayman jurisdiction."

"Insurance. Dead men tell no tales."

"Don't tell me. Let me guess. The Pantelli family?"

"They're at the top of my list. Anyway, Trace, keep this information to yourself until it's published. And watch your six, just in case."

Confidential or not, I hung up and dialed Cyrus's number.

"Cyrus, Trace. Have you heard anything about Malcolm's flight?"

"Yeah, he had some kind of problem and called Houston air traffic control to declare an emergency. Shortly thereafter his plane disappeared from radar. Not a trace after that. He should've been on-island hours ago."

"He didn't make it, Cyrus. Special Agent Monroe just gave me a confidential heads-up. Malcolm did declare an emergency. He requested to descend to ten thousand feet and went off all the radar screens as he passed through fifteen thousand feet."

"Did Monroe know what kind of emergency?"

"Malcolm told air traffic control he'd found a bomb on board."

"Those goddamned bastards."

"Who?"

"The Pantellis. They knew he was flying his plane to the Caymans, because I told them.

"Why would they kill him now?"

"Because they don't like loose ends. Malcolm met with the Pantellis in Vegas. There would be records of his commercial flights, cab rides, credit card charges, et cetera. And it was just after their meeting, that someone tried to kill Malcolm. Too many connections back to the Pantellis. Like the old saying, Trace. 'Dead men tell no tales.' "

"Exactly what Agent Monroe said. Okay, how do we proceed?"

"Believe it or not, the Pantellis are keenly interested in the growth and success of Montana Creek Mining. Remember, they hold Rosenburg's shares, and they've bought more shares in the open market. The reason they killed Malcolm is because they perceived him to be a threat to Montana Creek Mining, as well as to themselves."

"Damn, so the mob's got my back."

Cyrus couldn't help but chuckle. "Yeah, I guess you could say that."

Two days later, it was in all the papers: "Canadian executive killed in plane explosion over the Gulf of Mexico." Two days after the story broke, it died. Seemed no one really gave a shit about some rich Canuck flying his high-performance rocket ship down to the Caymans. The article did mention Malcolm had served a short time on Montana Creek Mining's board. The net effect of his demise on Montana Creek Mining's shares— nil.

Chapter 47

It was cold, gray, and snowing lightly when Wally and I landed in Toronto for the Mining Convention. We caught a cab from the airport and checked into our hotel adjacent to the convention center.

Wally had arranged for us to have a booth with banners, brochures, and a repeating PowerPoint presentation. I was signed up to give a fifteen-minute presentation in one of the large conference rooms the next day. Nearly one hundred natural resource companies would be presenting over the four-day conference. Government representatives from nearly a dozen foreign countries were also slated to make a pitch. All were seeking investor dollars to help develop their prospects, mines, or national natural resources.

Wally and I ran into Cyrus in the main lobby of the hotel and filled him in on our game plan.

"Wally and I are going to man our booth, give out brochures, and visit with investors. I know you want to take in some presentations and get a feel for the tone of the convention. Why don't we meet at nine this evening and compare notes?"

"Good idea, Trace. And I don't mind filling-in for you fellows from time to time so you can catch a presentation of interest. I'm an old hand at these conventions."

"Thanks, Cyrus. We'll take you up on that."

Wally and I made our way to our booth. There were already a good number of interested parties in front of our table. We shook a lot of hands, fired up the continuous PowerPoint, and went to work promoting Montana Creek Mining.

About an hour into the melee, I spotted him. He was wearing an exquisitely tailored Hong Kong suit, a pair of Italian alligator slip-on's, and an expensive-looking silk tie. Not your dad's Chinese communist. I continued talking with several investors who'd bought shares in Montana Creek Mining. The investors couldn't keep their hands off the six-inch sections of core Wally and I had laid out. They kept picking up the core samples and were grinning like kids who'd just found a copy of one of their dad's girliey magazines in the trash.

I tapped Wally lightly on the shoulder.

"Wally, can you help these gentlemen for a minute?" I asked, nodding in the direction of the approaching suit.

I made my way along our booth to where the oriental gentleman was standing.

"Good afternoon, sir. I'm Trace Brandon, CEO of Montana Creek Mining," I said, offering my hand.

"Lei Chang, Mr. Brandon," Chang replied, shaking my hand with a dry and firm handshake.

"Do you have an interest in uranium, Mr. Chang?"

"Yes. My company, URAN-China Nuclear Corp., is quite active in that arena."

"I would agree, sir. And thank you for your investment in our company. It's quite a compliment for a small cap like us to have caught your interest."

Chang smiled. "My compliments, Mr. Brandon. I see you keep up with who's acquiring your shares."

"Yes, sir. We try."

Chang picked up a section of the high-grade core.

"Is this representative of the uranium mineralization, or is this a selected sample?"

"It's representative of the uranium vein. The lode runs eight to ten percent uranium, as does the sample you're holding."

"No offense meant, Mr. Brandon. But you must realize many of the junior companies present only their best grades. I believe you call it, 'high grading'?"

"Yes, that's what it's called. And no offense taken, sir. But this is run-of-mine ore. It's a hell of a vein, not something one sees every day."

"Maybe once in a lifetime," Chang replied.

"Maybe."

"Are you free for dinner, Mr. Brandon, after the conference closes for the day?"

"I was going to have a late dinner with Mr. Wilkins," I said, pointing to Wally, "and James Lee. They're both directors. Would you mind if they joined us?"

"No, not at all. Very well then. Shall we say nine at the front desk? I'll take you and your directors to one of my favorite Toronto restaurants. Excellent cuisine and a wonderful view of city."

"I look forward to it, and thank you."

Chang bowed slightly, turned, and melted into the crowd.

Wally walked up next to me.

"Well?"

"Slight change in dinner plans, compadre. Mr. Lei Chang, managing director of URAN-China Nuclear Corp. is taking you, me, and Jim to supper."

"What about Cyrus?"

"He's not an officer or director, so I'll ask him to sit this one out.

"Agreed. We've probably had enough insider trading from the Virus."

I laughed. "Come on, ease up, pardner. He's turned over a new leaf."

"Uh-huh. What time tonight?"

"Nine p.m. We're to meet near the front desk. Chang is taking us someplace special. I'll call Jim and have him meet us."

"Damn, I bet old Mao is spinning in his grave. Capitalistic communists. Who'd have believed it?" Wally said with a laugh.

I got hold of Cyrus on his cell phone and told him of the change in plans. He was fine with it, and quite excited that Lei Chang had sought us out.

"Trace, it will likely take Chang most of the evening to get to the point of the meeting. Just bear with him and go with the flow," Cyrus advised. "It's the oriental way."

"Got it. I'll be patient but interested."

"Perfect. I'll see you two for breakfast at seven, and you can fill me in. Good luck."

Wally and I met Chang by the front desk. Jim Lee showed up a couple of minutes later.

"Good evening, gentlemen," Chang said, bowing slightly.

"Good evening, Mr. Chang," I replied. "I'd like you to meet two of our directors, Mr. Walter Wilkins and Mr. James Lee."

Mr. Chang bowed again. "Very nice to make your acquaintance, gentlemen. Mr. Lee, aren't you the managing director of International Uranium Corp.?"

Jim Lee returned the bow, "Yes, I am. IUC owns a twenty percent interest in Montana Creek Mining. And as Trace mentioned, I sit on their board."

"Very good. It should be a most interesting evening. Shall we go? I have a car out front."

We walked out into the frigid Toronto night. Chang's black CLS 550 Mercedes was parked just outside the door. The valet handed him the keys, and we all climbed in. Chang pulled out and accelerated into traffic.

"Wow," I said, glancing back at Wally and Jim in the rear seat, "she's powerful."

Chang nodded. "Four hundred horsepower from a 4.6 liter twin turbo. She'll do zero to sixty in about five seconds."

Not your dad's Mercedes, either, I thought.

"I am taking you to the Beau Geste," Chang said. "Are you familiar with it?"

"Only by reputation," I replied, glancing back at Wally and Jim, who both nodded in agreement.

"I think you will be pleased," Chang continued. "The food is first class, and the view of the city is magnificent."

He was right on both counts. The view of the city from the fifty-fourth floor of the Dominion Building was dramatic. And the cuisine was indeed first-cabin.

I opted for roasted venison with spaghetti squash and huckleberries. Lei and Wally both tried the tea-smoked duck breast with northern-woods mushrooms, wheat berries, and foie gras. Jim had had an early dinner with some of IUC's shareholders and munched on cheese and fresh warm bread.

We washed it all down with a couple of bottles of Leaning Post Pinot Noir. Leaning Post was a very limited vintage wine made from the oldest Pinot Noir vines in Ontario.

Wally, Jim, and I finished with a house blend of dark, rich coffee, while Lei stayed traditional with tea. And as Cyrus predicted, talk finally turned to business.

"So, gentlemen," Lei said, sipping his hot tea, "as you know my company has been acquiring shares of Montana Creek Mining. We are up to nearly a ten percent ownership position and would like to announce a tender offer for the remaining shares at five dollars Canadian per share. Provided I can get a commitment from you, Mr. Brandon, to tender your personal shares."

I looked at Wally and Jim, neither of whom batted an eye at the offer.

"I appreciate the offer, Mr. Chang. At nearly a twenty-five percent premium to the current share price, it's a very generous offer. I will, however, need a few days to think it over, and to confer in private with our full board of directors."

"Perfectly reasonable, Mr. Brandon. Shall we reconvene this meeting at the end of the conference? Will that give you sufficient time to consult with your board?"

"Yes, I think so. Three of our four directors are here at this table. I will call the fourth director back in Washington State in the morning."

"Excellent. I trust the meal and wine were satisfactory?"

"Perfect," the three of us replied in unison.

"Then I look forward to hearing from you in the coming days. Shall we go, gentlemen?"

At seven the next morning, Jim, Wally, and I met in my suite. I'd called room service and had a variety of breakfast foods sent up. I thought it better to have Cyrus sit this meeting out as well. I'd brief him privately, later.

After everyone got a bite of breakfast and some coffee, I called Will and put him on the speaker-phone. I explained the potential tender offer, subject to me selling my share block to URAN-China Nuclear Corp.

Jim Lee tugged on his upper lip. "Well, boys, we all knew this was coming. It was just a matter of time. IUC can match the five dollar offer, but we couldn't go much more. And I feel certain Mr. Chang and the Chinese are prepared to go much higher."

I looked around the room. "Will, what's your take on this?"

"Well, five bucks a shares is a pile of cash. Especially for us founders. Even for IUC, with a two-dollar-twenty-cent cost basis, it's a hell of a profit. The fly in the buttermilk is, do we want to sell to the Chinese? Do we want them to control a major US uranium reserve? And that's assuming our government would approve the deal."

"Here's my take, fellows," I interjected. "I'm not going to sell my block of shares to the Chinese, period. If I sell to anybody, it will be to IUC, even if I leave a few bucks on the table. And without my shares, Chang's company can't get control."

"Thanks, Trace. I appreciate it," Jim said. "As you all know, IUC would love to increase our ownership and operate and develop the Sullivan Mine. We might not be able to be a white knight, but we could be a whiter shade of gray."

We all laughed.

"Could be a song there, Jim," I said, still chuckling. "Okay, then, I'll get back to Chang and tell him no deal. Just pray we don't hear any bugles."

Chapter 48

Special Agent Beau Monroe contacted the National Transportation Safety Board for an update on Malcolm Trueblood's crash. The NTSB agent in charge of the crash told Monroe they'd found traces of plastic explosives on some of the wreckage the Coast Guard had recovered from the Gulf. The composition of the explosive residue matched a common military explosive, C-4.

Monroe called his team together in the New Orleans office.

"Okay, people, listen up. We've got Mr. Rosenburg, with ties to the Pantelli family, killed with VX agent. Then we've got an assassin who dies in an attempt to kill Malcolm Trueblood, who also has ties to the Pantelli family. And, last but not least, Mr. Trueblood and his airplane explode over the Gulf of Mexico."

Special Agent Monroe looked around the room. "I'm all ears, people."

Agent Winston Allen spoke up.

"We're close to tying the Chemist to the Pantelli family. The information we obtained from Mr. Bugati led us to one Peter Manetti. I should say Dr. Manetti, as he holds a PhD in chemistry from LSU, and taught advanced chemistry for a number of years. About ten years ago, his wife died from colon cancer. After her death, Doc Manetti fell off the board. According to Mr. Bugati, Doctor Death began doing specialty hits for the Pantelli family."

"Did the information from Chief Inspector Rand confirm the Chemist's ID?" Agent Monroe asked.

"The photos, dental records, and finger-prints we got from the inspector matched records and photos we've obtained from LSU and Dr. Manetti's dentist. The assassin, aka, the Chemist, is Louisiana's own, Dr. Peter Manetti."

"Really good work, people," Agent Monroe said, nodding in approval. "Have we been able to confirm Manetti's ties to the Pantelli family?"

"We're working on it, sir," Agent Allen replied. "We're looking for the money trail. So far, we've found several wire transfers from Pantelli accounts here in New Orleans to an account in the Cayman Islands. The wires follow a pattern. They're always to the same account in the Caymans, always two equal payments, and the payments usually a week or two apart. When we looked at suspected mob hits in the same time intervals, we found several homicides matching the transfer of funds."

"Can you tie Dr. Manetti to the account in the Caymans?"

"Not yet, but we're working on it," Agent Wilson answered. "With the new money-laundering laws, the offshore banks are a bit more cooperative. But it's going to take a little time."

"Okay, keep pushing and keep me informed. Now, what about Mr. Trueblood and his flameout over the Gulf?"

Agent Wilson answered again.

"We know from the NTSB that there were traces of plastic explosives matching C-Four on some of the recovered debris. We've interviewed everybody working near Houston Flight Support's area at Houston Hobby. And we've reviewed all the air traffic control communications with Trueblood, before he went down."

"And?"

"A fuel-truck driver remembers a fellow he'd not seen before. The guy was wearing Houston Flight Support coveralls, and the driver figured he was a new hire. We checked with HFS. No new hires. And no one has seen this fellow since."

"Did the driver talk to our mystery man?" Agent Monroe asked.

"Yes, Sir. He said the fellow wanted confirmation on what time the next morning they were to refuel Trueblood's plane."

"Did he give you a description of the man?"

"He said the fellow was short, about five six, with a red goatee and short-cropped red hair. And he said he thought the guy spoke with an accent, maybe Irish."

Okay, damn good work," Agent Monroe said. "Check our files for an explosives expert fitting that description. Also, check with the Brits. See if they've lost an IRA bomber of late."

Chapter 49

I'd just finished giving my fifteen-minute PowerPoint presentation on the Sullivan Mine. The conference room was jam-packed with investors, and they gave me a nice hand. I knew many of them would gravitate to our booth for additional information and to get copies of the PowerPoint.

When I got to the booth, I saw my assumption was correct. Wally, Jim, and even Cyrus were answering questions and handing out copies of the presentation hand over fist.

"Bloody hell," Jim said with a huge grin. "What did you say in your presentation to stir up such a hornet's nest?"

"I told them you were personally going to buy all my shares at ten bucks a pop."

Jim laughed. "Done deal."

"Keep your knickers on, Jimbo. I'm just kidding. All I did was show them our updated PowerPoint. When I got to the new gold intercepts, on top of the high-grade uranium, they sort of went nuts."

"I guess so," Jim replied. "Have you seen the stock price today?"

I glanced over at Wally and Cyrus, who were both grinning like Cheshire cats.

"Okay, so tell me."

"Five-twenty Canadian," Jim said. "Kind of kicks ol' Chang in the nuts, doesn't it?"

I laughed. "Yeah, I guess it does. I wonder what he'll do now?"

Cyrus laughed. "I don't know, but it's fixin' to get real damn interesting."

Chang was in his executive suite, checking Montana Creek Mining's share price on-line. And he was not laughing. He called in the two junior executives traveling with him. In Chinese he told them to get a list prepared of all the holders of 5 percent or more of Montana Creek Mining Corp. shares. He'd find a weak link, someone who'd sell his or her shares.

Chapter 50

It took Scotland Yard less than twenty-four hours to get back to the FBI query and description of a bomber with possible IRA ties. Special Agent Beau Monroe read the reply and looked at his small, but eager group of agents.

"Okay, people, seems we may have hit a nerve because the Brits never respond this fast. I'm guessing they have a real hard-on for our bomber. Get a copy of this photograph to our Houston office and have them show it to the fuel truck driver. Let's get a positive ID," Agent Monroe said, holding up the photo of one Sean Flannigan, alias Sean McDougall, alias Thomas Finnagan.

Al and Pino Pantelli were having lunch at a small café, in the French Quarter.

"Al, I got a call from a guard we've got on the pad over at Pollack. He says the fed's have been in to see a small-time drug dealer named Vince Bugati. Does the name ring a bell?"

"Yeah, he's a two-bit hustler. Sells a little crack for us, from time to time. Got busted for holding with intent to distribute. He's doing a nickel at Pollack. What are the feds talking to him about?"

"The guard heard him say something about a chemist."

Al's face drained of color.

"They're talking to that little puke about the Chemist?"

"Yeah, that's what our man said. Does Bugati know anything?"

"Could be. He may know the Chemist did some work for us."

"Jesus, could he tie us to Manetti?"

"It's possible."

"Can we get to him?"

"Hell, yes. I could have him shanked tomorrow, but it might look suspicious. One day he's talking to the feds about the Chemist, and maybe us, and the next day he's dead. The hit would point right to us. No, we've got to find another way. See if Bugati's got any family, anybody we can use to keep his trap shut."

The fuel-truck driver confirmed the man in the Scotland Yard photo was the same man who had asked him about re-fueling Trueblood's plane.

Special Agent Monroe went into hyper-drive.

"Okay, people, I want a nation-wide APB out on this Flannigan character. Include his photo and all known aliases. I want this troll hauled in—now."

Chapter 51

The mining convention was winding down, and a lot of the players had already left town. I was still manning our booth, hoping for the odd straggler, when Lei Chang walked up.

"Mr. Chang, I was just thinking about calling you."

"With good news, I hope?"

"I'm afraid not, Mr. Chang. I've decided to hang on to my shares. And as you no doubt know, our current share price is above your proposed tender offer."

"Yes, I am aware of that fact. However, share prices go up and down. Sometimes quite rapidly, as yours have this week. But next week, when the frenzy of the mining convention is over, will your shares maintain this level?"

"I am sure we'll have peaks and valleys, but I have a feeling each valley will be a bit higher than the last. I think we could hit ten dollars once our engineering report is published."

"I see. Let me ask you this, Mr. Brandon. At what price would you tender your shares to us?"

"As I said, I think the stock will go to ten dollars a share. But if I were to sell, I would be more inclined to sell to Jim Lee's company. IUC believed in our project, invested early, and stuck with us through good days, and bad."

"I doubt IUC could pay you what we could for your shares."

"Agreed, but sometimes relationships are more important than money."

Mr. Chang smiled. "Are they?"

He held my gaze for a moment, then bowed his head slightly, turned, and disappeared into the crowd.

Cyrus came up a moment after Chang left.

"Hey, Trace. Any word from our communist friend?"

"Oh, yeah. Chang was just here, and he wasn't a happy camper when he left. I sense we haven't heard the last of him."

"Well, to hell with him and his red buddies. Have you seen our stock price this morning?"

"Yep, we're getting close to six bucks a share. I told Chang I thought we might go to ten dollars."

"I'll bet that fried his wontons."

I laughed. "Yeah, I think it probably did."

Chang returned to his suite and told one of his assistants to book a flight to New Orleans, and set up an appointment with a Mr. Al Pantelli.

Chapter 52

Flannigan left Houston as soon as he'd confirmed Trueblood's plane was splattered over the Gulf of Mexico. Everybody has a weakness, and Flannigan's was whores, and his favorite hunting ground was the French Quarter. He'd driven his old Ford F-150 pickup from Houston to New Orleans, where he kept a small apartment on the edge of the Quarter.

He parked his truck in the small garage adjoining the two-story pink stucco apartment building. His second-story apartment overlooked a small courtyard on the opposite side from the garage. The location was convenient to Bourbon Street and the skin joints he frequented, but far enough from the action so a person could get some sleep.

Flannigan took a nap, then showered, went on-line, and checked his bank account balance. One thing about the Pantellis, they paid well, and they paid on time. He smiled when his balance showed two recent wire-transfer deposits. He'd have a hell of a good time tonight.

Special Agent Beau Monroe played a hunch. Everything pointed to the Pantellis being behind the hit on Malcolm Trueblood. And he was betting they hadn't strayed too far from the reservation looking for a mechanic. It was human nature; people look for the easiest solution to a problem.

Monroe was betting the bomber was from the New Orleans area. He made sure every police and sheriff's department within fifty miles of New Orleans got the information on Mr. Flannigan.

Dressed in his best Tony Manero outfit, Sean Flannigan set out in search of a little action. He pulled up his right pant leg and slipped a .25 caliber automatic into an ankle holster. Sometimes a little action could turn in to a lot of action, and Sean Flannigan always came prepared. He walked out of his apartment and hailed a passing cab.

"Club Le Bon Temps, on Bourbon Street," he said, to the cabbie. Flannigan never drove into the Quarter. Too many cops looking to bust a drunk driver, and no damn place to park.

The cab dumped Flannigan off in front of Roddy Kincaid's Club Le Bon Temps. The doorman recognized him from past visits and smiled.

"Good evening, sir. Good to see you back."

"Top of the evening to you, Mike," Flannigan said, extending his right hand, in which he'd folded a twenty. "How's the action tonight?"

"It was slow earlier, but it's kicking into high gear now. You should have a good time tonight," Mike replied, expertly palming the twenty.

Flannigan smiled and nodded. "You never know."

Inside the club the lights were dimmed, and the air was heavy with the smell of booze and cigarette smoke. Kincaid had done a nice job fitting the joint out. The chairs and couches were red velvet sitting on expensive wall-to-wall carpet. Sconces on the wall provided soft light for the patrons, while a spotlight lit up the topless dancers' stage and pole.

Flannigan took a seat at the bar and ordered a drink.

"Glenlivet on the rocks, if you please, Jake."

A statuesque blonde had just begun her routine. Flannigan was watching her with keen interest.

"She's new, Mr. McDougall," the bartender said, setting Sean's drink on a glass coaster. "Her name's Misty Rowe. At least that's her stage name. I can introduce you to her when her set's over, if you like."

Flannigan always used the alias of Sean McDougall at the club.

"Hell yes, Jake. I'd love to meet her," Sean replied, pushing a twenty toward the bartender. "Keep the change, and thanks for the intro."

Jake smiled as he pocketed the change from the twenty, until he noticed a big fellow in a suit coming into the club. He leaned his head closer to Flannigan.

"See the guy in the suit just coming in?" Jake asked, in a low voice.

"Yeah, I see him. Gotta be a cop."

"You've got a good eye, Mr. McDougall. His name's Detective Frances Hebert. Don't let the Frances part fool you. He's tougher than boot leather, and he's not on the pad."

"Thanks for the heads-up, but I'm on the right side of the law."

"Ain't we all, brother."

Detective Hebert walked over to the bar and pulled up a stool. He was two places down from Flannigan. Flannigan could see the bulge under the left armpit of the detective's suit. Whatever he was carrying in his shoulder holster, it was big.

Detective Hebert motioned to the bartender.

"Jake . . . gin and tonic, but leave out the gin. And a fresh slice of lime, please."

"Coming right up, sir," Jake replied.

Hebert looked around the room, and then at Sean.

"Evening. How's it going?" Hebert asked.

"So far, so good," Sean replied, tipping his glass in the detective's direction.

"You sure look familiar to me," Hebert said. "Have we met before?"

"No, sir. I don't believe so. I'm Sean McDougall."

The detective pursed his lips and was obviously running the name through his on-board computer system.

"You're right. Doesn't ring a bell."

Flannigan knew immediately from the detective's body language there was some kind of problem.

"Watch my drink, will ya, Jake?" Sean asked, the bartender. "I've got to use the head."

Flannigan got up and walked over to the men's room. Pushing the door open, he took a quick look around. It was empty. Every swinging dick in the joint was glued to the performance Misty was putting on.

Flannigan pulled up his right pant leg and pulled the .25 auto from his ankle holster. As he walked to the farthest urinal, he worked the action and jacked a shell into the chamber. With his left hand he pretended to urinate. He let his right hand, holding the little automatic, hang limp beside his right leg. Just out of sight.

It didn't take long. The detective opened the door and looked at Flannigan. And then surveyed the rest of the unoccupied men's room.

"Sean McDougall, eh? You sure it's not Sean Flannigan?"

The detective moved his right hand toward the hog leg he had holstered under his suit coat. It was the last move he ever made. Flannigan spun and put two rounds in the detective's chest and a third through the bridge of his nose.

Flannigan holstered the automatic and walked out of the men's room. Misty Rowe was still on stage in full-tilt bump and grind, backed up by a pounding drum-beat. A few of the men were looking around like they'd heard something, but their attention quickly returned to Misty's bodacious *tatas*.

Flannigan went back to the bar and finished his Glenlivet. He was damned if he'd waste a drop of the single malt over a piece-of-shit New Orleans' detective.

"Any trouble with the cop?" Jake asked.

"The big fellow with the cannon under his coat?" Flannigan replied. "No. But I think he's got a hell of a case of the drizzles. I wouldn't go in there for a while if I was you. It really stinks."

Flannigan finished his drink and casually strolled out of the club. Once outside, he quickened his pace, then cut through an alley to a side street and hailed the first cab he saw.

When Misty's dance finished, several fellows headed for the men's room. A couple minutes later one of the men, a club regular, went over to the bar and signaled to Jake.

"Jake, you got a problem in the can," the customer said, in a low voice.

"What's up?" Jake said with a chuckle. "The cop shitting his pants, is he?"

"Could be. He's got three holes in him, and he's deader than last night's beer."

Flannigan stopped the cab a couple of blocks from his apartment and walked the rest of the way. Before going into his building, he took a good look around. Seeing nothing out of the ordinary, he went upstairs.

Once in his apartment, he headed straight to the bathroom. He pulled his Dopp kit from under the sink and went to work. Twenty minutes later the goatee was down the drain, and his red hair was now chestnut. He put the clothes he'd worn to the club in a trash bag and dressed in jeans, work shirt, and cowboy boots. The boot heels would make him a bit taller than the man they'd be looking for.

He pulled a small suitcase from under the bed and grabbed an old-style brief-case from the shelf in his closet. The briefcase contained about fifty thousand in cash and two sets of forged ID's.

Flannigan, now posing as William O'Connell, put his gear in his pickup and drove until he spotted a Dumpster in a quiet alley. He stopped and tossed the trash bag with his Tony Manero outfit into the Dumpster. Heading west, he started across the bridge over the Mississippi. Seeing no immediate traffic, he lowered the passenger-side window, slowed a bit, and tossed the .25 auto into the Big Muddy. In a few hours, he'd hit Houston and disappear.

Chapter 53

Pino Pantelli walked into his brother Al's office in the family-owned building in the French Quarter.

"Morning, Al. Hey, did you see someone smoked a police detective in Kincaid's place last night?" Pino said, handing the newspaper to his brother.

"No shit? Let me see that."

Pino watched his brother read the account of the homicide and saw Al's cheeks flush.

"Holy shit," Al whispered. "We got another problem, and this one could be real trouble."

"What problem? Hell, it's just one less fuckin' cop. And we sure as hell didn't whack him."

"No. But I know who did, and that's the fuckin' problem."

"Who hit him?"

"From the description the bartender gave, it's Sean Flannigan. The guy I hired to take care of our aviator buddy."

"Are you sure?"

"Pretty sure. The description fits, right down to the Irish accent."

"Do you know where this Irish idiot is?"

"He keeps an apartment near the Quarter, but he won't be there. Sean's tough and smart, and he's been on the lam for years. The New Orleans Police Department hasn't got a chance in hell of finding him."

"I hope you're right, because if our cops do get him, he'll likely try and cut a deal. And any deal could include him handing our asses to the feds."

"True enough, but I know Sean. He's got money and contacts all over the world. He'll disappear, blend in. He's probably out of the country already."

"But what if they grab his ass?"

"Then we'll have to take care of it. No sawed-off Irish prick is going to take this family down. *Capisce?*"

Chapter 54

Al's secretary knocked softly on the door and stuck her head in.

"Mr. Pantelli, you have a call on line one."

Both Pantellis looked at her.

"The call is for Al."

"Who is it?" Al asked.

"The caller said his name is Lei Chang. He said he's managing director of URAN-China Nuclear Corp."

Al looked at his bother and raised his eyebrows.

"Now what?"

"If he's in the uranium business, it must have something to do with Montana Creek Mining. You'd better take the call, Al."

"Okay," Al said, nodding to his secretary. He punched line one and picked up the phone. "Al Pantelli, speaking."

"Thank you for taking my call, Mr. Pantelli. My name is Lei Chang. I'm the managing director of URAN-China Nuclear Corp. We're a Hong Kong-based Chinese uranium company."

"I see," Al replied. "Do you mind if I put you on speakerphone, Mr. Chang? My brother, Crispino, is here in my office. We're partners, and I like him to be on this call."

"No problem, Mr. Pantelli."

Al hit the speaker button.

"Okay, Mr. Chang, you're on the speaker, and Pino and I are all ears."

"Very good, gentlemen. I am calling in regard to our mutual interest in Montana Creek Mining."

Pino nudged Al with his elbow and nodded.

"Yes, sir. We do own an interest in Montana Creek Mining. So what's on your mind?"

Direct and to the point. Crude, but in some cases effective, Chang thought.

"My company owns various interests in a number of major uranium deposits around the world. We've recently acquired nearly ten percent of Montana Creek Mining, and we'd like to acquire more."

"Call your broker and put in a buy order," Pino interrupted, slightly sarcastically.

"We are looking for an out-of-market acquisition, at a set price," Chang replied, showing no reaction to Pino's tone.

"Why don't you just make a tender offer, and pick up the majority of the shares?" Pino asked.

"We could do exactly what you suggest, but without certain key shareholders accepting the tender, we would never be able to obtain control."

"Have you discussed your proposal with Montana Creek Mining's management?" Al asked.

"Yes, I met with three of the four directors in Toronto a few days ago. Including the CEO, Mr. Trace Brandon."

"I see," Al replied. "And what was his, their, response?"

Chang paused for a moment. He didn't want to give away too much information.

"Mr. Brandon was not interested in selling his position. And without Mr. Brandon's shares, one cannot obtain control of the company."

"So why are you calling me?" Al asked.

"We would like to buy your shares, at a premium to the current price. And we'd like your help in convincing Mr. Brandon to sell us his shares."

Al looked over at Pino and grinned. "I see. And how much of a premium are we talking about?"

"Twenty percent over the last sixty-day average price," Chang replied.

"Uh-huh," Al replied, "and what kind of pressure could we put on Mr. Brandon to induce him to sell you his shares?"

"I would leave that to your discretion. But my understanding is, you can be most persuasive."

Al looked again at Pino. "If the situation warrants. Why don't you give me a number where I can get back to you? We'll need a couple of days to kick your proposal around."

Chang gave them his unlisted cell phone number.

"I look forward to hearing back from you. One more thing, gentlemen. As time is of the essence, this proposal will be withdrawn in ten days. Good day, gentlemen."

Al hung up his phone. "Jesus, talk about out of the blue. Whadda you think, little brother?"

"I think it could be a hell of an opportunity. Remember, we got a half a million shares from Rosy for his gambling note. Hell, the casino has already washed his debt off the books. Anything we get for old Rosenburg's shares is gravy for you and me. Plus, there's the shares we've acquired in the open market."

"What about leaning on the CEO? Sounded to me like we have to get Brandon to sell to the Chinks, or no deal?" Al asked.

"Yeah, that's what the man said," Pino replied. "Leaning on Brandon could cause problems . . . of which we already have a couple on our plate."

Al laughed. "Yeah, we do. But this sounds too good to pass up. Let's you and me kick this around a bit. We got ten days to get back to the Chinaman."

Chapter 55

Wally and I left frozen Toronto at the close of the mining conference. We'd met with hundreds of potential and current investors. The presentations had gone well, and our share price was steady in the upper five-dollar range, well above Lei Chang's proposed tender price.

All in all, a hell of a good trip, but we'd both be glad to get home. I'd asked Tina to check on my Airstream to be sure it didn't freeze solid in my absence. I was looking forward to thawing out my bed with a little help from her.

We landed in Spokane, and Wally caught a flight to Vancouver. I located my trusty Bronco in the long-term parking lot, and, thankfully, she fired right up. In a couple hours I was back in my office.

I called Tina and arranged to have dinner with her. Then I checked my snail mail delivered while I was in Toronto. I was just about to shut down and head to my trailer for a shower and a change of clothes, when my cell started vibrating.

"Montana Creek Mining. Trace Brandon, speaking."

"Mr. Brandon, this is Al Pantelli calling from New Orleans. My family owns a considerable number of shares in your company. I'd like to speak with you for a moment, if you have the time. And may I call you, Trace, Mr. Brandon?"

"By all means, Al," I replied, using his first name. Fair's fair.

"Okay, Trace, here's the situation. We've been approached by a group that would like to buy our shares, and at a significant premium to the current share price."

"Good for you."

"Yeah, well, it could be good for the both of us. See, this group would like to buy your shares as well. Matter of fact, they won't buy our shares unless you sell them your shares. It's a very good price, Trace. You'll make a hell of a pile of money."

"Trouble is, Al, I don't have any interest in selling my shares to Lei Chang's company."

"Touché, Trace. I'm impressed."

"Yeah, well, Chang pitched me a similar deal in Toronto, but our share price blew through his tender offer. I turned down his offer, and I think I offended him. Fried his wontons, I believe is the term one of my directors used."

Al laughed. "Is there any room to negotiate on this? Can we work something out where both you and me, and of course the other shareholders, make a shit pot full of dough?"

"Look, Al, my advice is hang on to your shares. Our share price is headed north, right along with the price of uranium. The company has a lot of very positive developments pending. Hell, Al, there's no guarantee the US government would let a Chinese company take control of domestic uranium reserves. And, I think it would be fair to say there could be other, more suitable, suitors."

Al paused and absorbed what Trace was telling him. "You make a number of very good points, Trace. Listen, do you like Vegas? My brother, Pino, and I go to the Comstock Casino in Vegas from time to time. How about we meet in Vegas and get to know each other better. After all, we're a large shareholder in Montana Creek Mining. We'll get the casino to comp your trip, RFB. You can bring your wife, girlfriend, whoever. Whadda you say?"

"What's RFB?"

Al laughed. "Room, food, and beverages, and I'll even introduce you to some very nice show-girls."

"Tell you what, Al. I need a few days to get caught up and to check on the drilling. Once I'm caught up, I'd be glad to meet with you. I'll bring a whoever with me by the name of Cyrus McSweeny. He's also a big shareholder and an advisor to the company. I believe you may already know Mr. McSweeny?"

Al paused for a second. "Sure, Trace . . . Hell, Cyrus and I go way back," Al said with a snort. "Bring him along. I'll have the concierge at the Comstock get in contact with you, and you can give him your arrival info."

"I look forward to meeting you, Mr. Pantelli."

I hung up and immediately called Cyrus.

"Cyrus, you're not going to believe who just called me."

"The CIA?"

I laughed. "The CIA?"

"Yeah, well, last time you asked me that question, it was the FBI. I just moved up a notch."

"Uh-huh," I said with a chuckle. "No, this time it's the other end of the spectrum. Try Al Pantelli."

"What in the hell did he want?"

"He wants to meet with me in Vegas in a couple of days. Seems Lei Chang contacted him about acquiring their Montana Creek Mining shares. And from what Al told me, Chang's offer was contingent on me selling Chang my shares, at the same price."

"What price?"

"All he'd say was Chang told him it would be at a significant premium to the current share price."

"Hells bells. Maybe you should go down and hear what they have to say."

"My thoughts, exactly, Cyrus. We'll leave as soon as I get caught up on the drilling."

"We?"

"You got it, compadre. Al said I could bring whoever, so I told him I would bring you."

"How did he react?"

"It took him by surprise, but it didn't take him long to recover."

"I'll bet. Don't forget, I hold Al's voting proxy for three years. I wonder if Chang would be so hot for their shares, if he knew that."

"Good question. Let's just keep that between us and the Pantellis for now. We may want to play that card later."

"Okay, but just keep one thing in mind, Trace," Cyrus said, his tone now very serious. "We're moving into the big leagues with these fellows. Both Rosenburg and Trueblood had face-to-face sit-downs with the Pantellis, and they're both dead."

"Should be an interesting meeting," I replied, and hung up.

The next day, I threw some clothes and gear in the Bronco and headed up to the Sullivan Mine to get an update from Fish.

I checked into the W hotel in Winthrop and drove up to the mine. When I pulled up to the rig, Red waved and pointed in the direction of the core shack. I nodded and waved back.

I walked over to the core shack, my knees just about recovered from last night's après-dinner romp in the sack with Tina, and opened the door.

"Hey, Fish. How's it going?"

"Hi, Trace. Good to see you. How was Toronto?"

"Almost as cold as here," I said, noting I could see my breath, even in the core shack, "but a damn good conference. We visited with lots of shareholders and tons of potential investors. Even the Chinese came by."

Fish wrinkled his brow. "The Chinese, huh? The same Chinese Jim said were buying Montana Creek Mining shares?"

"One and the same."

I explained Chang's tender-offer proposal and my subsequent rejection.

"How'd he take it?"

"Not too damn good. He's contacted a couple of our more nefarious shareholders about buying their shares."

"Sounds like you could be lining up to be between the proverbial rock and a hard spot."

"Could be. I wanted to check in with you and get up to speed, then Cyrus and I are heading to Vegas to meet up with a couple of our more nefarious shareholders."

Fish laughed. "Okay. Well, on this end, the drilling is going good, and we're coring great-looking ore. One thing, though. By spring were going to be drilling on our northwest-most claims. If we're still in ore, we should think about staking some additional claims."

"I thought about doing just that, Fish. I had our mineral surveyor run the claim files at the Bureau of Land Management and at the Okanogan courthouse."

"What'd he find out?"

"Seems every Tom, Dick, and Harry with enough money to stake and file a claim has tied up all of the open ground on trend with our vein. If we're still in ore when we get to the boundary of our claims, we'll have to make a deal with some of those claim owners."

"Agreed, but, honestly, I'd be surprised if these grades continue beyond our claim block. It's already a world-class deposit; it won't go on forever. Plus, we've still got a fair number of claims to the southeast of Montana Creek to drill."

"My thoughts exactly. If a little ore does run over on to mom and pop's claims, good for them."

I spent the next day with Fish and Red going over the upcoming drill locations and looking at cores. As usual, the fellows had everything under control. I told Fish I'd be heading back to Ellensburg early the next morning.

"Good luck in Vegas, and watch yourself. A lot of folks involved with this company seem to get knocked off."

"Amen, brother, but not to worry. I've got Cyrus the Virus to cover my ass."

The following Friday morning I met Cyrus at the Spokane airport and we caught a flight to Vegas. When we exited the McCarran Airport terminal, a Comstock limo was waiting.

I looked at Cyrus as the driver stowed our gear in the trunk.

"First class all the way."

"Uh-huh. Just be sure we don't end up in the trunk on the return trip."

In twenty minutes we were checking in. Al Pantelli arranged for the Casino to comp us a two-bedroom executive suite. When we entered the suite, I saw the red message light blinking on the bedside phone.

"Looks like we've already got a message," I said, to Cyrus

"More likely a summons," Cyrus replied.

I dialed the message center and was connected with Al's office.

A man, whose voice I immediately recognized, answered.

"Mr. Pantelli, it's Trace Brandon. Cyrus is here with me, and we're at your service, sir."

"Trace, damn glad you're both here. Listen, my brother Pino and I have a pretty busy afternoon. How about we meet for supper in the Ruby Silver dining room? And check the desk drawer in your suite. There should be two velvet bags in the drawer. Each bag has a grand's worth of chips. Try your luck on us, and we'll see you at seven."

"Okay, Al. Thanks for the comp's and for the chips. We'll do our best to give them back to the house."

Al laughed. "You do that. See you this evening. Business casual is fine. Pino and I keep it pretty low key."

Cyrus and I freshened up and went down to the casino. We were both hungry and ate a burger in a small fast-food restaurant in the casino. After the burgers, we split up to do some gambling, on the house. I hit the blackjack table, while Cyrus wandered over to the craps table.

By five in the afternoon, I was down five hundred, and I started feeling a little guilty about losing Al's money. So, I went to find Cyrus.

He was at the craps table with a crowd of people around him. The gamblers betting with him were laughing and urging Cyrus on. Those betting he'd crap out didn't look too happy.

"Damn, Cyrus. I guess you're winning?"

Cyrus just smiled and shifted his eyes left and right to the two buxom beauties hanging all over him.

"You're guess would be correct."

I laughed. "It's getting late. I'm down five hundred and heading up to the room."

"I'm right behind you, kid," Cyrus said, tipping the croupier and slipping a hundred-dollar chip into the cleavages of his two ardent admirers.

"How much are you up?" I asked, while we walked to the elevator.

"About eight hundred, less the titty tips," he replied, with a laugh.

We each grabbed a shower and changed. I put on a pair of cream-colored slacks with a black silk-and-cotton-blend sport shirt. Cyrus wore gray slacks and a white-linen shirt. Decked out in our business causal finery, we headed downstairs to the Ruby Silver dining room.

The restaurant was reminiscent of a mining boomtown eatery, circa 1890's, with soft lighting, heavy-wood tables, and chairs. Period paintings of mine headframes, grizzled miners holding chunks of high-grade silver ore, and dance-hall girls doing high kicks, adorned the walls.

My kind of place, I thought, following the maitre'd to the Pantelli's' table.

Al and Pino both stood up to greet us. They were both big men with dark hair and olive complexions, not quite handsome but pretty close, especially in their Armani slacks and sport shirts.

"Hello, Cyrus, my old friend," Al said, shaking Cyrus's hand. "I don't think you've met my brother, Crispino?"

"No, but you talked a lot about him while we were guests of the state of Oregon."

"Yeah, that's one way of saying it," Al said, as Pino and Cyrus shook hands.

"Al, Crispino," Cyrus said, "this is Trace Brandon, founder, CEO, and chairman of Montana Creek Mining."

"Nice to finally meet you, Trace," Al said, firmly shaking my hand.

"Same goes for me, Trace," Crispino said, extending his hand. "And please call me Pino."

"Have a seat, gentlemen," Al said, sitting back down. "What'll you have to drink, gents?"

"Crown and water on the rocks for me," I replied.

"Ditto," Cyrus said.

Al motioned a waiter over and gave him our drink orders. He and Pino were both drinking red wine.

Al started the dialogue.

"First off, just let me say, Pino and I are very pleased you'd both take time from your busy schedules to come to Vegas to meet with us. And just to clarify, Pino and I are partners in all our family business ventures, including our investment in Montana Creek Mining."

"Our pleasure gentlemen," I replied. "I'm pleased to meet you both. I'd like to thank you for your investment in Montana Creek Mining, and for inviting us to this meeting. Same goes for the comp's, and for the chips." I paused and smiled. "I've managed to donate half of mine back to the casino, but Cyrus is a winner."

Al laughed. "Cyrus always was a good gambler. It's one reason I'm glad he's also a shareholder, and an advisor to you." Al looked across the table at Cyrus. "You've been involved in mining for, what, forty years?"

"Just about," Cyrus replied. "Long enough to know a good deal when I see one."

"Well put, Cyrus," Al said, opening his menu. "Let's order, and then we can visit a bit. I think you'll find everything on the menu is first class."

I'd eaten so much seafood in Toronto, I was craving a steak. I ordered a porterhouse with all the fixin's. Cyrus did likewise while the Pantelli brothers both had the veal.

Al was right; the meal *was* first class.

"My compliments to the chef, Al. I come from Black Angus, country up in Ellensburg, Washington. But this is as fine a steak as I've ever sunk a tooth into."

"Thanks, Trace," Al replied. "We brought in a hell of a chef from New Orleans, and we have access to some of the best beef in Nevada."

We all ordered coffee and then got down to business.

"Trace, as I mentioned on the phone, the offer we received from this Lei Chang character is quite impressive. He's talking a twenty percent premium to the market price of the shares, and I sense he'll go higher. But, there's no deal unless you commit to sell your shares too."

I nodded. "Yes, I am aware of Lei Chang and the company he heads, URAN-China Nuclear Corp. And, as I mentioned on the phone, there could be some roadblocks to a Chinese company taking ownership of US uranium reserves. Uranium is a strategic mineral and closely regulated by the feds. I'm not sure the government would allow UCNC to take control of Montana Creek Mining."

Pino put his coffee down and looked at me.

"Trace, Chang said if he acquired our shares, yours and ours, he'd tender for the balance of the outstanding shares at the same price. Don't you have a fiduciary responsibility to allow your shareholders to decide if selling to Chang's company is in their best interests?"

"Look, Pino," I said, "I appreciate your situation, but Chang's proposition is predicated on me selling my shares. Neither you all, nor the shareholders, are going to dictate when or to whom I sell my shares."

I turned to Cyrus. "What's your take, partner?"

"Well, if we sell to the Chinese, we could make a lot of money, provided the U.S. government lets the deal go through. On the other hand, we could approach International Uranium Corporation to match Chang's offer. IUC's managing director, Jim Lee, sits on our board, and they already own twenty percent of Montana Creek Mining."

I nodded in agreement. "Keep in mind, Jim Lee will not get into a bidding war with the Chinese. However, neither will they have any regulatory problems taking control of Montana Creek Mining. We might get a bit less than the Chinese could offer, but we'd know the deal will close."

"One other point, gentlemen," Cyrus added. "There may be other suitors who show up once the word's on the street that Montana Creek Mining is in play."

I looked around the table. "Okay fellows, I'll cut to the chase and save us all a lot of time. I'm not inclined to sell my shares to the Chinese. If Chang wants to put out a tender offer for all of our outstanding shares, more power to him. If all the other shareholders agree to tender their shares, I'll do likewise. I won't stand in the way. Majority rules with me, but the ball is in Chang's court. I won't agree to a separate sale of my shares, not to anybody."

Al exhaled loudly and clasped his large hands together.

"You know, Trace, if Chang doesn't make an offer for all the outstanding shares, we could lose this opportunity. It could cost my family a lot of dough."

"Maybe in the short run, Al. But in the long run, I think you'll make more by holding your shares."

Al looked over his clasped hands at Pino for a long moment and then returned his gaze to me.

"Fair enough, Trace. My brother and I appreciate you and Cyrus taking the time to come down here to discuss this situation. For now, I believe we'll, as you said, leave the ball in Chang's court, but we'll be monitoring the situation . . . very carefully."

As we all stood to leave, Cyrus looked over at Al. "Too bad about Malcolm, wasn't it?"

"What, that the fuckin' rat has to spend a few years in the Caymans drinking piña coladas and banging native girls?"

"He didn't make it to the Caymans, Al. His plane exploded en route. He's scattered over a couple hundred square miles of the Gulf."

Al didn't flinch. "No shit. His plane blew up?"

"Yeah, first Thorny, then Rosenburg, and now Malcolm," Cyrus replied. "It's getting to be dangerous being involved with Montana Creek Mining, isn't it?"

Al extended his hand to shake with Cyrus and looked him directly in the eye.

"Sometimes bad things happen to good people, my friend."

"Yeah, they sure seem to, especially lately." I said, looking at Al and Pino. "Beats any actuarial table I've ever seen. Three dead shareholders in less than six months. Hell, I decided I should take some precautions. So, I set it up where if my plane goes down or I eat a poison tree frog, all my shares go to the general fund at Central Washington University, my alma mater."

Al and Pino looked at me.

"Very generous of you, Trace," Al said, glancing from me to his brother. "You're not insinuating we had anything to do with those deaths, are you?"

"Nope, but like Cyrus said, owning shares in Montana Creek Mining seems to come with a bit of risk. I'm just making sure my shares are well-placed should something happen to me."

Back in our room Cyrus looked at me as he mixed a Crown and water.

"Your shares really go to Central if something happens to you?"

"Yep. I had Will Coffee update my will. Kind of surprised Albert a tad, didn't it?"

"Yeah, I believe it did. It's a smart move, Trace. Take away the Pantelli's fancy clothes, cars, and money, and you've got a couple of bottom-dwelling scum suckers. I told you, killing is just a tool with them. We need to be very, very careful from here on out."

"I've got to believe the FBI is going to tie the Pantellis to Rosenburg and Malcolm's deaths."

"Maybe. Problem is, the guy who hit Rosenburg and tried to snuff Malcolm got snuffed himself. So he's not around to testify against the Pantellis."

"What about whoever planted the bomb on Malcolm's plane?"

"My guess is he, or she, is already out of the country."

I nodded in agreement. "By the way, that little jab about Malcolm hit a nerve. I could see Al's jaw tighten, just a bit."

"They're both very cool customers, but they killed Malcolm and Rosenburg just as sure as we're standing here."

Chapter 56

Sean Flannigan checked into a cheap hotel near Houston's Intercontinental Airport. He opened a throw-away cell phone and dialed Al Pantelli's number.

"Al, it's Sean."

"Jesus, Sean, are you out of your fuckin' mind? You hit a cop, a senior detective, in my town, without asking me first. Do you know how much heat this is going to bring down?"

"It was me or him, Al. There must be a warrant and a description out on me. The cop recognized me, called me by name, and went for his piece. I was damned lucky to tag him first."

"Okay, okay, shit happens. Where are you now?"

Sean hesitated. He knew he was on thin ice with the Pantellis.

"I'm getting ready to take a little vacation. I'll let you know where I end up."

"Good plan. Lay low till the heat blows over. And goddamn it, Sean, don't do anything else stupid."

"It wasn't stupid, Al. It was necessary. You'd have done the same damn thing."

"Maybe. It's just we've got a relationship with you, and naturally we want to protect it."

Sean knew Al meant *protect the family*. Which meant he'd be a dead man if he got captured.

"Don't worry, Al. They won't find me. I'll be in touch."

"You do that, Sean."

*****

Since Sean Flannigan was considered a terrorist, FBI Special Agent Monroe and Agent Allen were working closely with the New Orleans Police Department on the shooting of Detective Hebert. They re-interviewed both the bartender and the doorman at the Club Le Bon Temps. Both of the club's employees knew the suspect as Mr. McDougall, and both were able to ID him from photos of Flannigan.

Agents Monroe and Allen were seated at the bar in the Club Le bon Temps, having a coke after completing their questioning of the bartender.

"It was Flannigan, all right," Monroe said. "It looks like Detective Hebert made him at the bar and followed him into the head."

"Yep, and Flannigan was ready. Two in the chest and one in the head. Very tidy."

Monroe's cell phone buzzed.

"Special Agent Monroe, speaking."

Monroe listened for a minute, then pulled a pen from his shirt pocket and grabbed a napkin from a stack on the bar.

"Give me that again."

Monroe hung up and looked at Agent Allen. "The NOPD located Sean's apartment. They're waiting for us before they go in."

Monroe threw five bucks on the bar, and the two agents hauled ass.

The New Orleans Police had Sean's apartment building sealed off. Monroe and Allen pulled up, parked near a police cruiser, and walked over to a uniformed lieutenant, who appeared to be running the operation.

"Lieutenant, I'm Special Agent Monroe, FBI, and this is Agent Allen," Monroe said, opening his badge holder.

"I'm Lieutenant Decker. We're ready when you are."

"Let's go have a look-see," Monroe said.

Four uniformed cops, along with Lieutenant Decker, Monroe, and Allen, entered the apartment building and cautiously ascended the stairs to the second floor.

"It's number twenty-two," Lieutenant Decker whispered, pointing two doors down.

"Are we going in hard or soft?" Monroe asked, softly.

"Hard. Standby," Decker replied, in a low voice, motioning his men to get in position.

"Guns out and up," Decker whispered, pulling his .357 service revolver and positioning himself just to the left of the apartment's door.

Lieutenant Decker did a last check of his men, then shouted, "Police!" And kicked the apartment-door open. The uniformed officers followed, guns at the ready. Monroe and Allen were close on their heels.

"Spread out. Check every room, closet, everything," Decker ordered.

In a few moments, shouts of "Clear!" came from all quarters.

"He's not here, Agent Monroe," Lieutenant Decker said, the disappointment obvious in his voice.

Monroe figured if he and Allen weren't present for the raid, and if Flannigan had been in his apartment, he'd have been shot about twenty times . . . trying to escape. Cops hated a cop killer, above all else.

"No, not now, but he's been here since the shooting. Look at this," Monroe said, pointing to a few red whiskers stuck around the drain in the bathroom sink. "He's shaved his goatee and dyed his hair from the looks of it," Monroe said, picking an empty hair-dye bottle from the trash. "Our red-headed Irishman is now a brunette. Agent Allen, update the APB with this new information. Make sure security at all the major airports within a six-hundred-mile radius get the revised info."

Special Agent Monroe had the right idea, but he was about four hours too late. Earlier that morning, William O'Connell, aka, Sean Flannigan, boarded an Island Air 737 bound for George Town, Grand Cayman. As the updated description was being delivered to security personnel at Houston Intercontinental Airport, Flannigan was checking into the Colonial Hotel on Grand Cayman Island.

While he was waiting to get a hit on Flannigan's revised APB, Special Agent Monroe decided to go see Mr. Bugati. He called the warden at Pollack Federal Prison near Alexandria,

Louisiana, and got permission to interview Bugati. Monroe knew it was his last best chance. The Chemist was dead and buried, but Bugati might be able to give him enough to implicate the Pantellis.

Monroe met with Bugati in a special interview room. The convict was thin and wiry with short-cropped hair and jailhouse tats on his forearms. His close-set dark eyes and narrow, pinched face reminded Monroe of a weasel, which he hoped would be the case.

"Mr. Bugati, I'm Special Agent Monroe. I believe you've already spoken to Agent Allen?"

"Yes, sir, I have."

"Uh-huh. I'll get right to it, Mr. Bugati. I think you're a slime-ball, and I'd love to see you sit around here for a few more years, and maybe get shanked out in the yard or anally explored in the showers. But, if you can help us build a case against the Pantellis, I'll arrange an early release, and you'll be back on the street. You've got this one chance. I won't be back. Are we clear on that?"

"Yes, sir, I understand. I already told the other agent what I'd heard about the Chemist doing wet work for the Pantellis."

"Yeah, well, the Chemist is dead. I'll need you to agree to testify as to your knowledge of his association with the Pantelli family."

"Jesus, they'll kill me."

"No, they won't. We'll put you in the witness protection program, after you testify. You'll get out of this place and get a fresh start. It's up to you, and I need your answer right now."

Bugati clasped his hands between his thighs and looked down at his prison-issue shoes for nearly a minute.

"Okay, I'll do it. But, you've got to get me out of here, and I mean fast. Word will get out I've been talking to the feds. Hell, I won't last long enough to testify."

"I'll get the paper-work drawn up for you to sign. You'll be out of here in a couple of days. Just sit tight and don't do or say anything out of the ordinary. Got it?"

"I got it. Just don't take too fuckin' long. The Pantellis have big ears and long arms."

Bugati was right to be worried. Pino Pantelli closed his cell phone and walked down the hall to his brother's office. He knocked twice and opened the door.

"Got a sec, Al?"

"You bet," Al replied, looking up at Pino. "Jesus, you look like death warmed over. What's up?"

"Yeah, well, you remember when I told you a guard we have on the pad up at Pollack said the feds had visited with Vince Bugati?"

Al thought for a moment. "Yeah, I do. They were asking him questions about the Chemist?"

"Yep, well they came back. Only this time they sent a big-gun agent by the name of Monroe."

"Our guy on the inside is a senior officer. He says Bugati is going to be transferred to FBI protective custody."

"Holy shit," Al said, shaking his head. "The little prick's going to rat us out, isn't he?"

"Looks that way. The fuckin' Chemist is pushing daisies, but Bugati may know enough to implicate us in a couple of hits."

"How long have we got?"

"The guard says a couple of days, at most."

"Jesus, it's piss-poor timing, but we've got no choice.

"Agreed. I'll take care of it," Pino replied. "I know just the man for the job."

Pino arranged for a woman to be at the prison visitors area the next day. She was to meet with an inmate named Anthony Delucia, and pass on Pino's instructions.

Delucia was doing twenty years for manslaughter after a drug deal went south, a Pantelli drug deal. He took the bust and refused any deal to testify against the Pantellis. In return for his loyalty, the Pantellis made sure his wife and two kids wanted for nothing.

Delucia would do the hit on Bugati.

Chapter 57

When I got back from the Sullivan Mine, I'd received an e-mail, with an attached photo, from Special Agent Monroe. His e-mail said the fellow in the photo was a person of interest in Malcolm's plane crash. He also listed a number of aliases. I opened the attachment but didn't recognize the man, or any of the names listed. I forwarded the e-mail on to Cyrus and Wally.

Wally e-mailed me back within fifteen minutes. He'd never seen or heard of the individual in the photo. Cyrus called a few minutes later.

"Trace, it's Cyrus. I looked at the photo and names, but neither rings any bells with me."

"Yeah, same here."

"Listen, I'll forward the photo on to some of my pals who run more in the shadows and see if I get any hits."

I chuckled. "Okay, Cyrus. Let me know if you turn up anything."

Sean Flannigan needed to find more permanent quarters. The Colonial was great but too expensive, and too high profile, for a long stay. He decided to look for a condo he could rent on a monthly basis. After a few days of looking, he found a nice building on the beach with a great pool. The property manager said there was only one vacant condo in the building. The owner was from Spokane, Washington, and occasionally let friends and business associates use the condo. She said she'd check about the possibility of a month-to-month rental.

*****

Cyrus got the call a day later.

"Mr. McSweeny, this is Doris Wright in George Town. Have you got a minute?"

"Sure, Doris. Everything okay with the condo?"

"Yes, sir, it's just fine. I'm calling because I've had an inquiry from a gentleman who'd like to rent it on a monthly basis, for a few months. Would you have an interest in doing that?"

Cyrus thought about it for a few moments. "As a matter of fact, I'm not planning on using it for some months. So, yes, I would be interested. What's the going rate for a monthly rental?"

"I think three thousand a month with a seven-hundred-fifty-dollar deposit would be in line."

"Okay, go ahead and rent it, but make it a maximum of three months. I may be coming down for a bit, after that."

"Okay, I'll contact the renter. He's staying at the Colonial, and I'll e-mail you a copy of the lease. Do you want me to hold the funds in our account until you come down, or set up something else?"

"No, that'll be fine. It'll give me some spending money when I come down," Cyrus said with a laugh. "By the way, is it just one person or a couple?"

"Just one man. He seems very nice, and has a wonderful Irish accent. I believe he said his name is William O'Connell."

"William O'Connell? Boy, that name seems familiar to me."

"Well, I'll get everything taken care of and send you the documents."

Cyrus hung up, still trying to remember where he'd seen or heard that name before. Then it came to him. He quickly re-opened Trace's e-mail and scrolled down. William O'Connell was the third name on the list of aliases.

Cyrus hit Trace's number on speed dial.

"Trace, it's Cyrus. You're not going to believe this."

"Hell, Cyrus, I've got the commies trying to take over my company. I just got back from having supper with the Pantelli crime family, and I'm on a first-name basis with the fucking big Indians. I'll believe damn near anything."

Cyrus laughed. "Fucking big Indians?"

"When I was working on my masters, I was mapping along the Yakima River, and I wanted to cross a suspension bridge over the river. I sent one of the undergrad students over to see if it was okay to cross. The kid came back and said the FBI was on the other side, and told him we couldn't use the bridge. I said, 'The FBI?' And he replied, 'Yep, a fucking big Indian.' "

Cyrus laughed. "Well this is even better. My property manager in the Caymans just called to see if I'd consider renting my condo out for a couple of months. I don't have any plans to use it, so I told her sure. Guess who the renter is?"

"Jimmy Hoffa?"

"Very funny, but not too far off. Try, William O'Connell."

"William O'Connell? Where do I know that name from?"

"Check the e-mail from the fucking big Indians."

"Holy shit, you're right. It was one of the names in the e-mail from Agent Monroe."

"Exactly right, and it gets better. The guy's got an Irish accent. I am going to send his picture to my property manager and see if it's our man."

"Ah, I'd hold off on doing that, Cyrus. You could be putting her in harm's way. And, two, if your manager starts acting differently around him, he may get suspicious and disappear."

"Yeah, you're right, Trace. It's just I want to get this son of a bitch for killing Malcolm."

"So do I. But I think our best course of action is to get Agent Monroe on the phone. Can you hold while I try and conference him in?"

"Sure."

I pulled Special Agent Monroe's card from my desk and called his cell number.

"Hello, Trace," Monroe answered, seeing my name on his caller ID. "Did you get the e-mail I sent?"

"Morning, Agent Monroe. Yes I did, and I forwarded it to Cyrus McSweeny to see if he recognized the photo. I've got Cyrus on the line with us."

"Mr. McSweeny, Special Agent Beau Monroe here. What have you fellows got for me?"

"We think we've located Sean Flannigan, aka, William O'Connell," I replied.

"Did you recognize him from the photo?" Agent Monroe asked.

"You tell him, Cyrus," I replied.

"Okay. No, not from the photo," Cyrus said, "but from one of the aliases on the list."

"Which name?" Monroe asked.

"William O'Connell," Cyrus replied.

"I see," Monroe said. "And how do you know where he is?"

Cyrus snickered. "He just rented my condo in George Town, Grand Cayman."

"Are you sure?" Monroe asked, his voice deadly serious.

"Pretty sure, Agent Monroe," Cyrus replied. "My property manager confirmed the name and mentioned the fellow had an Irish accent. I was going to send her his picture to confirm, but Trace thought we should contact you first."

"You thought right. This guy is an IRA killer. He'd likely kill your property manager and skip the island, if he thought his cover was blown."

"So, if it is him," I asked, "can you arrest him and extradite him back to the US?"

"The Cayman police will have to make the arrest. Possibly with FBI or Interpol assistance, if requested," Monroe answered. "As to extradition, it's a commonly held misconception that we don't have a treaty with the Caymans. However, in 1976, Gerald Ford signed an extradition treaty with the Caymans, as did the UK and Northern Ireland. So, you bet, we can grab his sorry ass."

"What can we do to help?" Cyrus asked. "I'd really like to see this fellow pay for what he did to Malcolm Trueblood."

"Best thing for you to do now, is nothing," Monroe replied. "Don't say anything to your property manager. Don't send her Flannigan's photo. Just keep it business as normal. We'll get an agent on the island to make a positive ID, and notify the local authorities. Then mother justice will bring the hammer down on

Mr. Flannigan's Irish ass. And hopefully, the scumbags who hired him."

"The Pantellis?" I asked.

Agent Monroe paused. "As we say in the trade, 'They're definitely persons of interest.'"

Chapter 58

Flo Fabrini pulled her car into the visitor's parking lot of Pollack Federal Prison and followed the signs to the visitor's area. Once inside, she filled out a form and was given a visitor's badge. Senior Corrections Officer, Sam Savoie, a huge Cajun, who'd been on the Pantelli pad for years, spotted Flo and directed her to a table.

"You'll have ten minutes, ma'am. Don't pass anything to the prisoner and keep your voice low."

A prison guard brought Anthony Delucia in and sat him across the table from Flo. The guard glanced at Savoie and then backed off, out of earshot.

"I'm Tony Delucia, Miss . . . ?"

"It's Flo, and I've got a request from Pino."

Tony leaned forward a bit. "What can I do for him?"

Flo filled Delucia in on the situation with Bugati.

"I see," Delucia said, leaning back in his chair.

Flo started to say something more, but Delucia put his index finger to his lips and shook his head slightly.

Leaning forward again, he spoke in a barely audible voice. "I understand the situation. You may tell Pino it will be resolved in the required timeline. Please leave now."

In his cell that night, Delucia planned the hit. He would do it during the mid-day exercise period in the yard. Concealed behind a thin slit in his mattress was a shiv made of quarter-inch-thick plastic. Delucia had worked the plastic into a needle-pointed blade. In close quarters it would be lethal.

At two the next afternoon, Delucia was in the exercise yard with the shiv tucked up his right sleeve. He spotted Bugati talking with a small group of cons. Walking toward his target, Delucia let the shiv slide, butt first, into the palm of his hand. As he closed on Bugati, he looked across the yard and pretended to wave at another con. The movement caught Bugati's attention, causing him to shift his eyes in the direction Delucia waved. A slight diversion, but enough. To a casual observer, it looked as though Delucia accidently bumped into Bugati.

Looking directly into Bugati's eyes, Delucia drove the shiv deep into Bugati's solar plexus. The air rushed out of Bugati's lungs at the force of the blow, allowing the weapon to penetrate even deeper into his body.

"This is from Pino," Delucia whispered, in Bugati's ear as he pushed the shiv deeper into his body, stopping only when the handle was flush with Bugati's skin.

Bugati gasped at the pain and clawed at the wound, trying in vain to grasp the bloody hilt of the shiv. Blood began to stain the front of Bugati's faded prison-issue denim shirt. Delucia took a half-step to his left and blended into the morass of convicts milling about the yard.

Several of the men standing around Bugati could see the blood oozing from between his fingers, as he tried to stanch the bleeding. They immediately backed away from him. No one called out. No one moved to help him.

Bugati slumped to his knees, his hands and clothing now soaked in blood. He died before the guards could get to him.

Special Agent Monroe got a call from the warden a couple hours after Bugati died. He hung up the phone and cursed under his breath.

"What is it, Beau?" Agent Wilson Allen asked, looking up from his desk.

"They hit Bugati. He's dead."

"Jesus. He was going into protective custody in the morning."

"Somebody found out we were talking to him and must have gotten word to the Pantellis."

"Had to be somebody who works at the prison. No one else knew about the meetings."

"Yeah, probably some damn guard on the take."

"Great—now what?"

"We go, and we go fast, after the only lead we've got left, Mr. Sean Flannigan."

Agent Allen nodded. "Yeah, before the Pantellis find out he's in the Caymans."

"See if we have an agency plane available for tomorrow morning. I'll alert the local authorities and set up a joint operation to arrest Flannigan on suspicion of murder. Once we get a positive ID from the Brits, we'll move to extradite his ass."

"You know the Brits are going to want him pretty bad, and they're part of the bilateral extradition treaty, along with Northern Ireland."

"Yeah, well, they can have him. But only after he gives us the Pantellis."

Sean Flannigan signed the lease on Cyrus's condo as William O'Connell. He'd paid one month's rent plus a security deposit in cash. So far everything was copacetic, but he was in no hurry to fill the Pantellis in on his whereabouts. He knew from Al's tone on the phone that, he was in deep shit.

As Sean lounged by the pool the next day, a white Cessna Citation touched down at Owen Roberts International Airport, in George Town. Other than tail numbers, the bird carried no identifying features. The co-pilot opened the main door and Agents Monroe and Allen stepped out into the warm humid island air.

"Let's clear Customs and grab a cab," Monroe said. "We've got a meeting with Chief Inspector John Thomas in thirty minutes."

Both agents grabbed their carry-on luggage and headed for customs. They showed the immigration officers their FBI identification, and were out front at the cab-stand in less than five minutes.

"Police headquarters on Elgin, please," Monroe said, to the cabdriver.

In a few minutes the cab dropped them off in front of the Royal Cayman Island police headquarters.

"Agents Monroe and Allen to see Chief Inspector Thomas, please," Monroe said, to the attractive female officer at the reception desk.

"Right this way, gentlemen," the officer replied. "The chief inspector is expecting you."

The female office led the two agents down a hallway and opened the door to the chief inspector's office.

"Go right in, gentlemen," she said, gesturing with her left hand.

Chief Inspector Thomas got up from his chair and came around in front of his massive and paper-covered desk. The inspector stood about six feet tall; he was, trim with fair hair and freckles. And, Agent Monroe guessed, a more or less ongoing case of sunburn.

"Chief Inspector Thomas at your service, gentlemen," Thomas said, extending his right hand.

"Agents Monroe and Allen, sir," Monroe said, both showing their badges after they shook hands with the chief inspector.

"Have a seat, fellows," Thomas said, gesturing to two side chairs. "So we've got a bad actor on the island?"

Thomas hiked up his left trouser leg and sat on the edge of his desk.

"Yes, sir. You do. I assume you've received the information from our New Orleans office?" Monroe asked.

"Yes, Agent Monroe, we have," Thomas replied. "And I must add, your Mr. Flannigan, aka, Mr. O'Connell, is at the very top of the UK fugitive list."

"Understood, sir," Monroe replied. "He's also a prime suspect in the recent bombing of a private aircraft over the Gulf of Mexico, and the killing of a New Orleans police officer."

"Ah, yes. The small plane bound for George Town out of Houston?" Thomas replied. "I hadn't heard about the officer. Sorry."

"Yes, sir. We have an eyewitness putting Flannigan at the aircraft, just prior to take-off," Allen replied. "And, as you eluded, he's wanted in the UK for his activities with the IRA."

"We've had Mr. O'Connell under surveillance since we received your alert," Thomas said. "We can pick him up at your convenience."

"Would it be possible for us to be on-site for the arrest?" Monroe asked.

"I shouldn't think that would be a problem, Agent Monroe. Give us a few hours to coordinate the operation. I assume you're both armed?"

"Yes, sir," Monroe replied. "But if you've got a couple extra vests, it would probably be a good idea."

"Expecting some resistance, are we?" Thomas asked.

"Sir," Monroe replied, "Flannigan put three rounds in a very experienced New Orleans detective before he skipped town. So, yes, I would expect the unexpected. He's got nothing to lose."

Monroe and Allen checked into the Colonial, changed into tactical clothes, and waited for the chief inspector's call. They didn't have to wait long.

"Special Agent Monroe, it's Chief Inspector Thomas. We're ready to move. We'll pick you up in five minutes. Are you ready?"

"Yes, sir, we are. We'll be out in front of the entrance," Monroe replied, looking over at Agent Allen. "Let's go, Wilson."

A police SUV pulled up near the hotel entrance, and Monroe and Allen climbed into the back-seat.

Chief Inspector Thomas turned to the two FBI agents. "We've sealed off the compound. There's no way out unless he wants to swim to Cuba. We'll be there in six or seven minutes."

Sean Flannigan, aka, William O'Connell, was warming himself on a pool-side chaise lounge after doing thirty minutes of laps. He was just about to nod off when the RCIP stormed the compound.

"That's him by the pool!" Agent Monroe shouted, pointing to the reclining figure.

Flannigan heard the shout and jumped up, looking around frantically.

"Don't move or we will shoot to kill!" Chief Inspector Thomas yelled. "Get on your knees and lock your hands behind your head."

Sean could see there was no escape. He dropped to his knees and clasped his hands behind his head. One of the uniformed officers came up behind him and quickly cuffed his wrists.

"Mr. O'Connell, or is it Flannigan?" Chief Inspector Thomas said. "You're under arrest for the murders of Malcolm Trueblood and Detective Decker. Please stand up."

"You don't have jurisdiction for crimes committed outside of the Cayman Islands," Flannigan protested.

"Maybe not," Chief Inspector Thomas said, gesturing toward agents Monroe and Allen. "But these two gentlemen are with the FBI, and they do."

Flannigan looked at the two FBI agents and nodded in acquiescence.

"Look, for the record, I just want you to know the plane bombing was strictly business. And the cop in New Orleans was just plain bad *ádh* . . . bad luck. He recognized me and went for his piece. It was me or him. However, the fuckin' Brits, now they . . . they were a pleasure. I wish I'd killed a passel more."

Flannigan looked directly at Special Agent Monroe and grinned sardonically. Then he opened his mouth as if he was going to say more, but instead used his tongue to pry the cap off a hollow molar at the back of his mouth. Flannigan bit down hard on the rubber-cased glass vial of potassium cyanide. A small amount of white foam containing tiny flecks of glass oozed from his mouth as he crumpled to the ground and died.

"Jesus," Agent Monroe said, dropping to Flannigan's side. "A cyanide ampoule."

Chapter 59

My cell phone went off at about ten in the morning.

"Mr. Brandon, Special Agent Beau Monroe. Have you got a minute?"

"Yes, sir, I've always got time for the FBI."

"Uh-huh. I promised I'd keep you updated on our efforts to arrest Mr. Flannigan."

"Yes, sir. Did you get him?"

"Yes and no. With the aid of the Cayman Island authorities, we grabbed him at Mr. McSweeny's condo."

"Man, that's good news."

"Well, the good news is, we arrested him. The bad news is, he had a cyanide capsule hidden in a hollow molar. He was able to bite down on it before we could stop him. He died instantaneously."

"Damn, just like Herman Goering. Did he say anything about Malcolm?"

"Just that it was only business."

"Did he implicate the Pantellis in any way?"

"Nope. He took any information he may have had with him. Which leaves us with no living witnesses. We'd also been working on turning a low-level drug dealer doing time in Louisiana. He claimed he could tie the Pantellis to Rosenburg's murder, but he's dead too. Killed the day after our last meeting with him."

"Damn, the Pantellis don't leave any loose ends, do they?"

"No, and neither do we. Do you mind telling me why you and McSweeny met with the Pantellis, in Vegas?"

"No, I guess I don't," I said, exhaling softly. "The Pantellis asked to meet with me because they'd been approached by a Chinese uranium company who wanted to buy their Montana Creek Mining shares. The fly in the buttermilk being, the deal hinged on me agreeing to sell my control block to the Chinese. The Pantellis asked me to come to Vegas to discuss the Chinese proposal. I took McSweeny with me as back-up."

"And?"

"I told them I currently had no interest in selling my shares to the Chinese, or anybody else."

"How'd they take it?"

"I don't think they were too happy about. Especially after I mentioned that if anything happened to me, like an explosion or eating a poison tree frog, all my shares would go to my alma mater's general fund."

Agent Monroe laughed. "Poison tree frog?"

"Yeah, well, I wanted them to know I knew they killed Rosenburg, and probably Malcolm."

"You like to live dangerously, Mr. Brandon?"

"No, not really, but they pissed me off."

"Well, with all the suspects dead, we're going to have a tough time making any kind of a murder case against the Pantellis. All we can do for now, is keep an eye on their moves and see if we can nail them on some kind of lesser charge. When all else fails, there's always the IRS and the SEC. Maybe we can nail them on some kind of tax evasion charge, or a securities violation."

"Hey, that's how you finally nailed Al Capone."

"Exactly so, Mr. Brandon. Watch your back, and stay in touch."

"Roger that."

I hung up and called Cyrus.

"Cyrus, it's Trace. Got a sec?"

"Sure, Trace. Anything new from the fucking big Indians?" Cyrus asked, with a chuckle.

"As a matter of fact, that's why I'm calling. They caught Flannigan slash O'Connell at your condo."

"Damn good news. Are the sending the bastard back to the States?"

"Yep, in a body bag."

"Jesus, they had to shoot him?"

"Nope. The son of a bitch pulled a Herman Goering and bit down on a cyanide capsule. Agent Monroe said he was dead before he hit the deck. And get this, the FBI had a snitch in a Louisiana pen who was evidently going to cooperate, and testify against the Pantellis."

"Let me guess. He's dead too?"

"Good guess. Killed after Agent Monroe's last meeting with him."

"I told you, Trace. The Pantellis have a long reach, and murder is just a tool to them. What else did Monroe have to say?"

"He said to watch my ass and call him if the Pantellis made any kind of move against me or Montana Creek Mining. He also mentioned possibly being able to nail them on some kind of tax evasion or securities violation."

"Hmmm, interesting idea. I don't have a clue about their tax situation. And so far, I don't see where they've violated any SEC reg.'s. However, the situation could change in the future. Al or Pino don't have a lot of experience with securities. Maybe they'll do something stupid."

"One can only hope," I said with a laugh. "But we do have an ace in the hole."

"And what would that be?"

"You hold the Pantelli's voting proxy for nearly three more years."

"True enough. If properly played, the proxy could well be a trump card. One other thing, I doubt we've heard the last of Lei Chang and his band of immortals."

"Agreed. Chang gave the Pantellis ten days to respond to his offer, and their time is about up. I suspect when they turn him down, he'll be contacting me again."

"Well, our stock price is holding pretty steady in the high fives to low sixes, and we should get our listing on the Toronto Exchange shortly. The listing will allow some of the larger funds to buy our shares."

"Yeah, it will be interesting to see what Chang, and the Pantellis, do next."

I didn't have to wait too long to find out. About forty-eight hours later I received an e-mail from Chang, requesting a meeting in Spokane followed by a site visit to the Sullivan Mine. He said he was bringing along his chief mining engineer, Mr. Zhoa. I guess he wanted a firsthand look at his investment.

I contacted Cyrus and got his okay to use his offices for the initial meeting. Will Coffee and I would drive over to Spokane for the meeting. Following the meeting, we'd haul Chang and Zhoa, up to the Sullivan Mine. For this trip, I decided to leave my Bronco at home and rented a Suburban from an Ellensburg car-rental agency. With the Suburban, I could get everybody and their gear in one vehicle.

A few days later, Will and I left Ellensburg at 8:00 a.m. and headed east on Interstate 90, to Spokane. We got to the airport before Chang's plane landed and met him and Zhoa at baggage claim.

From the airport, I drove the entourage to Cyrus's office in the Inland Empire Building in downtown Spokane. I parked the Suburban, and we walked to the lobby and took the elevator to the sixth floor.

"Right this way, gentlemen," I said, motioning down the hall. "It's the third door on the left. The one marked Columbia Resources."

I walked ahead and opened the door to Cyrus's office.

Sally Friesen rose from her desk to greet us.

"Good morning, Sally," I said. "We've got a meeting scheduled with Cyrus."

"Yes, I'll let him know you're here," Sally replied, walking over to the door of Cyrus's private office.

She knocked softly on the door and then opened it just enough to stick her head in. "Cyrus, Trace and the gentlemen from Hong Kong are here."

"Okay, thank you, Sally. Would you see if they would like a cup of coffee or tea?"

"Certainly, sir."

Cyrus got up from his desk chair, straightened his tie a tad, and walked into the outer office.

"Good morning, gentlemen," Cyrus said, looking very dignified in his charcoal suit, white dress shirt, and blue silk tie.

I shook hands with Cyrus and gestured to my guests.

"Cyrus, you remember Mr. Chang from the conference in Toronto?"

"Of course. Good to see you again, sir. And welcome to the Pacific Northwest."

Chang and Cyrus shook hands.

"Thank you, Mr. McSweeny. I would like you to meet our chief mining engineer, Mr. Zhoa," Chang said, gesturing to the bespectacled, short but very stout, engineer.

"Nice to meet you, sir," Cyrus said, shaking hands with the engineer. "Please come into my office, gentlemen, and have a seat at the conference table."

Sally got Chang and Zhoa cups of hot tea while the rest of us drank coffee.

Chang took a sip of his tea, set his cup down on the glass-covered mahogany conference table, and started the meeting.

"Gentlemen," he began, "I asked for this meeting to reaffirm to you my company's continued interest in acquiring a majority interest in Montana Creek Mining. And secondly, to get an on-site look at the Sullivan Mine, especially the coring operations."

I glanced quickly at Cyrus and then back to Chang. "We are keenly aware of your interest in acquiring a control position in Montana Creek Mining, Mr. Chang. This interest was reinforced after our recent visit with Al Pantelli. Both Al and his brother, Pino, strongly suggested I should sell my shares to URAN-China Nuclear Corp. in order to facilitate your proposed purchase of their shares. An offer, I respectfully declined."

"I wonder," Cyrus added, looking directly at Chang, "if you are fully aware of the type of people you're dealing with. And I am speaking of the Pantelli family."

"We are not suggesting we wish to join the Pantelli family in any type of business venture," Chang replied, calmly. "Rather, we merely wish to acquire the shares they own in Montana Creek Mining. Simply put, we would prefer to have a controlling interest in your company prior to making such an acquisition."

"My advice to you would be to go ahead and acquire the Pantelli's' shares, regardless of whether or not you're able to get control," I replied. "The Pantellis have no interest in uranium or any commodity, except cash. I can assure you, we are not too happy about a crime family holding a large block of our shares. And I suspect, at some point, the SEC will share our concern."

"Everybody in this room believes both uranium and the value of our shares are going higher," I continued. "It could be a very astute investment to acquire the Pantelli's' shares at this time."

Chang rubbed his chin with his right hand and looked at Zhoa.

"Well said, Mr. Brandon, and worthy of serious consideration."

"I would appreciate it," I replied, looking directly into Chang's jet-black eyes.

Okay, fellows," Will interjected, seeking to take the rhetoric down a notch or two. "If we're to get to the mine in time to see much this afternoon, we'd better adjourn and continue this conversation on the way to Winthrop."

"Bathroom is down the hall, fellows," Cyrus said. "It's several hours' ride to the mine."

Chang and Zhoa left Cyrus's office and headed for the restroom. Cyrus motioned Will and me closer to his desk.

"I think you got his attention," Cyrus said, softly. "And I think they're beginning to realize they don't want a Mafia family as significant shareholders in Montana Creek Mining, either."

"I agree," Will added. "Maybe they'll go ahead and buy out the Pantelli's' shares unconditionally?"

"Could be," I replied. "Let's get them to the mine and dazzle them with some high grade. When they get all touchy-feely with ten percent uranium ore, it just might solve our Mafia shareholder problem."

Both Cyrus and Will chuckled.

"Stranger things have certainly happened with this company," Cyrus said, shaking his head.

"Ya, think?" Will replied, with a snort. "Only if you call a mad chemist, an IRA bomber, and you two characters having supper with a Mafia don, strange."

We were all chuckling when Chang and Zhao came back into the office.

On the drive up to Winthrop, I gave Chang and Zhao a brief history of the Sullivan Mine and updated them on drilling operations to date. By the time we pulled into the Winthrop House, both men were up to speed.

"Let's check in, and then we'll run over to our core storage warehouse," I said. "It's a little late in the afternoon to head up to the mine."

"Excellent," Chang replied, "Both myself and Mr. Zhao are very anxious to view the cores."

"Okay, let's get checked in and re-group here in the lobby in, say, fifteen minutes?" I replied.

Twenty minutes later we pulled into Bob Malott's construction yard and parked in front of the warehouse holding our core.

Bob saw us pull in and walked over from his office.

"Bob, I'd like you to meet Mr. Chang and Mr. Zhao," I said. "They're with URAN-China Uranium Corp., one of our larger shareholders."

Bob stuck out his right hand. "Nice to meet you fellows. You're in for a hell of a treat. Just wait 'til you see the cores."

I unlocked the warehouse door and flipped on the interior lights. Fish had several core boxes open and sitting on a long table.

"Fish is still logging these," Bob said, gesturing at core in the open boxes.

"Take a look, gentlemen," I said, walking over to the tables. "Just be sure to put any core you remove back in the same slot and orientation. We don't want to foul up our geologist's logging."

Chang and Zhoa took out their hand lenses and pulled small sections of the high-grade uranium ore from the core boxes.

For a moment both men were silent. I glanced over at Cyrus and Will, and raised my eyebrows.

"Trace, if I was not holding this ore, I would not believe it," Chang said, glancing at his engineer, who appeared to be in a nearly orgasmic state. "The uranium grade is unbelievable, and there are gold values as well?"

"Yep, in an adjacent vein system," I replied, trying not to gloat too much.

"Very impressive," Chang kept repeating.

I looked over at Cyrus and Will, and smiled.

After about an hour of salivating over the cores, I finally got Chang and Zhao back into the Suburban.

"Well, I gather you liked what you saw?" I asked, heading back to the W.

"Very impressive," Chang said, for the umpteenth time.

I laughed. "Yes, sir, It's what we call the 'mother lode.'"

Chang said something in Chinese to Zhao, which I guessed to be a translation of *mother lode.*

"Okay, fellows," I said. "Let's get back to the hotel, have some supper, and get some sleep. We'll head up to the mine first thing in the morning."

At supper, I introduced our two Chinese friends to Washington State Black Angus steaks.

"Trace, this steak is like Kobe beef. It's very delicious," Chang said, between mouthfuls of medium-rare rib-eye.

"Yep, it's hard to beat," I replied, glancing over at Cyrus. "I've only found one other place with steaks this good."

"And where was that?" Chang asked.

"One of the casinos, in Las Vegas."

"The Comstock?"

I nodded and smiled. "You do your homework, Mr. Chang."

"I like to know my adversaries, Mr. Brandon."

"As do I," I replied, making eye contact with Chang.

After the steaks and coffee, I suggested we retire and meet for breakfast at six sharp. I wanted to be done with the mine tour by late afternoon, and be back in Spokane by evening. Chang and Zhao had an early flight out the following day.

The next morning we all had a light breakfast and loaded into the Suburban. In about thirty minutes we were at the Sullivan Mine.

Fish walked over as we were climbing out of the truck.

"Morning, fellows," he said with a wave.

"Mr. Chang, Mr. Zhao," I said, gesturing toward Fish, "I'd like you to meet our project geologist, Tom Troutman. Tom's been seconded to us from International Uranium. Who, as you know, owns twenty percent of Montana Creek Mining."

"Good morning, Mr. Troutman," Chang said, shaking Tom's hand. "Please meet my chief mining engineer, Mr. Zhao."

Fish shook each man's hand. "Good to meet you, and please call me Fish. Come on over to the drill. We're just pulling some core from the ore zone. It should be pretty good."

We all ambled over to Red's drill as his helper decanted five feet of fresh core into a wooden tray.

Fish took a paint-brush, dipped it into a coffee can full of water, and wetted the cores.

"Wow," Chang said.

Fish laughed. "Wow is right. Have you fellows ever seen uranium ore like this?"

"Only in the Athabasca mines, in eastern Canada," Zhao replied, kneeling to get a better look at the shiny, wet core.

I gently nudged Cyrus, who I knew was thinking the same thing I was. Chang would make an unconditional tender for the Pantelli's' shares. I couldn't blame them. It was the mother lode.

Chapter 60

Will and I were having lunch at the First Inn a couple of days after we'd deposited Chang and Zhao at the Spokane airport.

"Well, I think the guys from Hong Kong were well pleased with what they saw at the mine," Will said, wiping some ketchup from his upper lip.

"Yep, I thought old Zhao was going to pee his pants when he saw the cores," I replied.

"You think they were dazzled enough to try and buy out our shareholders down in New Orleans?"

"I think they'll try. They know none of us insiders are selling, and that includes Cyrus. If they want to acquire a chunk of shares, outside of the market, they'll have to deal with the Pantellis."

I'd just finished my observation when my cell phone started vibrating.

"Speak of the devil," I said, finishing a french-fry. "Our good buddies from the Big Easy. Hello, Mr. Pantelli. What can I do for you this fine day?"

"You can tell me what kind of smoke you blew up the Chink's' asses on their visit to the mine?" Al Pantelli said with a laugh.

"Oh, just the usual dog-and-pony stuff. Why? What's up, Al?"

"What's up is, our commie friend, Chang, called me and offered to buy my shares outright, no strings attached. And at a twenty percent premium to today's price."

"Well, Al, all I can tell you is they got quite excited when they got their hands on the cores. There was some serious Chinese being tossed around," I said with a chuckle.

"I'll bet. So what do you think?"

"What'd you mean, Al?"

"Should I sell to the fuckin' commies, or not?"

"Hell, Al, it's up to you. I've already told you what I think about the mine and the company's future, but there's always the unexpected."

"What unexpected?"

"If I knew that, it wouldn't be unexpected."

"Goddamn it, Trace. We're talking about a hell of a lot of money here."

"I know it, Al, but it's your call."

"What about you? What're your plans?"

"You're talking apples and oranges. I have different goals and responsibilities than you all."

"How so?"

"My first priority is to the shareholders of the company. Your first priority ought to be, and rightly so, making a profit. The Chinese have just presented you and Pino with that opportunity."

"I see, and what about you, Trace? Would you ever consider selling your shares to the Chinese?"

"As I said before, Al, at this point in time, I'm not interested in selling my shares to anyone."

"Well, you're consistent, I'll give you that. Okay, Trace, thanks for your time. I'll let you know what Pino and I decide."

I hung up and looked across the table at Will.

"Just like we figured, huh?" Will said, between bites of his hamburger.

"Sort of. Reading between Al's lines is not easy, but I get the feeling he's going to have a hard time letting go of his shares. He's afraid to pull the trigger, afraid he might leave something on the table."

"Damn. I was hoping we'd get those fellows out of our company."

"We'll just have to wait and see how this all plays out."

Chapter 61

Special Agent Beau Monroe was not one to wait and see. He'd piled up a ton of bureau hours trying to nail the Pantellis, and so far all he had to show for his efforts were two dead hit men. Not exactly a home run, but maybe a solid double.

Monroe leaned back in his chair and put his feet up on his desk. He looked over at Agent Wilson Allen, who was finishing up the report on Sean Flannigan.

"Wilson," Monroe said, "I think we need to change course on the Pantelli investigation. I think we need to get those bastards the old-fashioned way."

"We can't just shoot 'em, Beau," Wilson said with a smile.

"No," Monroe said, chuckling. "Although not a half-bad idea. No, I mean the way the government took down Capone and some of the other capos. We need to get the IRS involved. I know someone in the criminal investigation division. I'll give him a call. Maybe we can get the Pantellis on tax evasion."

"Good idea, Beau. Listen, one other thing has been bothering me. How the hell did the Pantellis end up with their Montana Creek Mining shares? Rosenburg's debt was to the Comstock Casino. So how'd the shares end up with the Pantellis?"

"Good question. Do the Pantellis have a reported ownership in the Comstock?"

"Another good question."

"Get the team on it. Also, see if Al or Crispino have any felony convictions that would preclude them from ownership in a Nevada casino."

"Will do. What did old J. Edgar say? 'Always follow the money.'"

Al and Pino were sitting in Al's office, trying to figure out whether to take the money.

"Damn, Al, it's a hell of a profit. Maybe we should sell to the fuckin' Chinks."

"Mixed feelings, little brother, like seeing my ex-wife drive off a cliff in my new Caddie," Al replied, with a chuckle. "If the Chinese want our shares bad enough to pay a premium, they must figure the shares are going to go a hell of a lot higher."

"True, but remember what Pop always said. 'You never go broke taking profits.' Plus, as Trace told you, there's always the unexpected."

"What could happen that'd fuck up the deal?"

"Another Three Mile Island, or a terrorist attack with a dirty bomb or a nuke."

"Yeah, that would fuck everything up, wouldn't it?"

"It would."

"You know the other thing that chaps my ass about this?"

Pino laughed. "No, Al, what?"

"Selling anything to the fuckin' Chinese commies."

"Hey, we've sold shit to a hell of a lot worse."

Al nodded. "Yeah, I know. But my gut says we should let the commies sit a bit. Hell, maybe they'll raise the bid."

Agent Allen dropped a pile of documents on Special Agent Monroe's desk.

"You're not going to believe this, Beau," Allen said. "The Pantellis don't have any felony convictions. They've been indicted for murder, extortion, drug dealing, the whole shiteree. But no convictions."

"Unbelievable. What about the Comstock? Are they listed as owners?"

"Not directly. The Comstock is a privately held company. The majority shareholder is an LLC named Black Chip Investments. You'll never guess where the LLC is domiciled."

"Cayman Islands?"

"Confirming once again why you get the big bucks, sir."

Monroe laughed. "Can we find out who's behind Black Chip?"

"Maybe, but it won't be easy."

"Okay, good work, Wilson. Keep on it."

"Will do, sir. Oh, and one more thing. The IRS is going over the Pantelli's' individual tax returns for the past seven years, as well as the casino's. Maybe they'll turn up something of interest."

"I'll settle for anything that keeps them picking prison cotton for the next twenty years."

Chapter 62

I hadn't seen Tina Hart in weeks, and decided to give her a call to see how she was doing, and hopefully arrange a date.

"Tina, it's Trace. Sorry it's been so long, but I've been tied up with investors and operations up at the mine."

"I understand, Trace. You've got a lot on your plate."

I knew from her tone this conversation was headed south.

"Listen, I was wondering if we could get together later this week. Have supper, take in a movie?"

"Trace, I can't. I've met someone, and we're getting pretty serious. He's in education like me, and he wants to get married and have a family. I know you. After the Sullivan project, you'll likely be off on another project to God knows where. I care about you, Trace, but our lives are just too far apart."

"I understand, kiddo. It's not easy trying to hang with an exploration geologist, and you're right. I'm nowhere near ready to settle down and start a family."

"Thanks for understanding, Trace. Good luck in the future and please be careful."

She hung up before I could say anything else. Not exactly out of the blue, but still not a hell of a lot of fun, either.

The next day I called Will and told him about Tina.

"Well, hell, amigo. What'd you expect? You're on the road most of the time, and if she knew about all the shit going on with killers, the FBI, and the mob, you'd have been out on your ass a long time ago," Will said with a chuckle. "Besides which, you've still got me, Wally, and the Virus to pal around with."

I laughed. "Yeah, you're right. What in the hell was I worried about?"

"Exactly. Be at the First Inn at noon. Lunch and beers are on me."

I did paper-work in my office until around eleven thirty. I was just getting ready to head over to meet Will when Wally called.

"Hey, Wally, how's it hangin'?"

"Down, slightly to the left, and quite large."

I laughed. "Uh-huh. What's up?"

"Well, I just got off the phone with Jerry Smyth over at Charter Engineering."

"Yeah, how's he coming with the engineering report?"

"Good. He's sending you a zip file with the final draft for your review."

"How'd the numbers look?"

"Awesome. Try five hundred twenty million pounds of drill-indicated uranium."

"Jesus, we just hit the big leagues. What about gold and copper?"

"It'll be in the report, but he said the values are damn good too."

"Wow! Great news, Wally. Let's push to get this puppy on the Toronto Exchange and start trading with the big boys."

"I've got everything lined up. All I need is the final, signed, sealed report."

"Good work, compadre. I'll get on the draft like a duck on a June bug."

I called Cyrus on my way to the First Inn and filled him in.

"God-damn, Trace. We're peeing in the tall grass with the big dogs now."

I laughed. "Yes, sir, we sure are. Listen, I'm about to go have lunch with Will. I'll call you later."

"Okay, Trace. Say howdy to Will and keep up the good work."

I walked into the First Inn and spotted Will at a table. I looked around to see if Tina was working but didn't see her. Probably a good thing.

"She's not working today, Trace," Will said, noticing me glancing around. "Lucky for you."

"My thoughts exactly. By the way, I just got off the horn with Wally. The final draft of the engineering report is on the way."

"Did he say what kind of reserves they're giving us?"

I looked around and rubbed my hands together, stalling.

"Come on, Trace. It's good . . . isn't it?"

"Only if you call half a billion pounds of uranium good."

"Holy shit! Are you kidding me?"

"Not a pound, partner. Five hundred twenty million drill-indicated pounds. Plus the gold and copper values."

"Jesus, when this gets out, the shares will go to twenty bucks."

I nodded. "How's it feel to be rich?"

Will took a big pull of his Tumbleweed Ale and wiped his mouth with the back of his hand. "Not too goddamned bad."

After lunch I went back to my office and called Jim Lee's cell phone. With the time difference I figured he'd be in bed. The phone went to voice mail, and I left him a detailed message. I was pretty sure who my first caller would be in the morning.

As I closed up shop for the day, I couldn't help wondering what the Pantellis would do if they knew about the results of the reserve report. The Chinese would have about as much chance of buying their shares as a fart in a whirlwind.

Al and Crispino wouldn't know about the reserve report until I put out a news release to the Vancouver Stock Exchange and our shareholders. But they'd already made their decision.

"Are you sure, big brother?" Pino asked.

"Yep, I am. The Chinks smell money, and so do I. We'll hold our shares and take the ride."

"Okay, Al. Works for me. Besides, the casino's already written off Rosenburg's debt. Hell, we've basically got no cost basis in his shares. How can we miss?"

"My thoughts exactly. As Rosy used to say at the crap table, 'Let it ride.'"

"Beau, we may have turned up something," Agent Allen said, looking at a fax from the FBI's Las Vegas field office. "Seems our boys in the Vegas office have had an eye on the Comstock for some time."

"Damn, wouldn't it be nice if one hand knew what the other was doing?" Monroe replied.

"Be that as it may, we may have a lead. It's the old disgruntled employee shtick. Seems the Comstock canned a croupier for palming chips at the craps table. In return, the gentleman filed a wrongful-termination suit. Somewhere in all the BS was a passing reference to the Pantellis possibly pulling the old 'skimeroo.'"

"Really?" Monroe said, now giving his full attention to Agent Allen.

"Yep. One of our Vegas field agents picked up on the reference during a review of the grievance. If the Comstock hadn't already been on their radar, it's likely nobody would've noticed the accusation."

"Get out there, Wilson. See what you can come up with. This could be the opening we've been looking for."

"Color me gone, sir."

If there was a quality Lei Chang did not possess, it was patience. He hadn't heard a peep out of the Pantellis. Lei cursed in Chinese and flipped open his cell phone.

"Hey, Mr. Chang," Al said. "What can I do for you today?"

"Mr. Pantelli, we'd like an answer on selling us your Montana Creek Mining shares."

"Uh-huh, well, I'm afraid I've got bad news for you, Mr. Chang. My brother and I have decided to hang on to our shares. We think there's a lot more upside in the share valuation."

Chang's face flushed, and he bit down on his bottom lip to keep from exploding.

"Perhaps a higher offer would change your mind?"

"No, sir. We're going to run with Trace on this one, but thank you for your interest. If anything changes, I'll get back to you."

"I see," Chang replied, the bitterness oozing from his voice.

Pino walked into Al's office just as Al was hanging up on Chang.

"What's up, brother?"

"That was Chang. I told him, in polite terms, to go fuck himself. We aren't going to sell him our Montana Creek Mining shares."

"How'd he take it?"

Al laughed. "Not too damn good. But then I really don't give a shit how the commie bastard took it."

"Made you mad, huh?" Pino said with a chuckle.

Al smiled at his brother. "Yeah, I guess he did. He's a condescending little prick, isn't he?"

"Uh-huh, he most certainly is. Would be kind of fun to kick his slant-eyed ass."

Al laughed. "Hell, he's probably a kung fu motherfucker. He might kick both of our asses."

"Maybe, but I doubt he'd kick Mr. Colt's ass."

"Righty-roo, but I don't think we want to go nuclear with the Chinese," Al said, laughing harder.

I finally got the zip file to open and was working my way through the draft-engineering report. Smyth had done a 4.0 job. A full-blown engineering report on a mining property, is something akin to a PhD dissertation. I couldn't wait to see the bill for this monster.

Wally's numbers were right on. We were looking at around a half billion pounds of drill-indicated uranium reserves, plus the gold and copper values. But few would look past the uranium reserves; they were *that* good.

I made a few minor edits and e-mailed the whole mess back to Smyth. In a week or so, we'd be able to file the report with the Vancouver Stock Exchange and apply for our listing on the TSX, a major milestone for Montana Creek Mining.

I sat back in my desk chair and realized I was caught up, for now. Fish had the drilling program under control, and Wally was on top of the TSX listing. Of all the times for Tina to give me the deep six. Here I was with a bit of free time and no girlfriend to share it with. The situation required drastic action. So, I called Cyrus.

"Cyrus, it's Trace. Got half a minute?"

"Sure, Trace. What's up?"

"Nothing serious. I've got a little downtime and was thinking about disappearing for about a week."

"Uh-huh. Need the condo?"

I laughed. "Only if you're not using it."

"Hell no, I'm not using it. Grab Tina and head on down. I'll call my property gal and tell her you're coming."

"Tina won't be coming, Cyrus," I said, explaining the situation.

"Well, I can't blame her. Hell, you're always on the god-damned road. What'd you expect?"

"Yeah, I got the message. But still, she was one hell of a gal."

"Uh-huh, well, *que sera sera*, pardner. Listen, the Caymans are full of hot women. Hey, wait a sec. You liked Dominic Rinquet, didn't you?"

"What's not to like?"

"Exactly so, my boy. Look, I know her at least as well as Wally does. I'll call her and set you up. First date is on me. After that, you're on your own."

I laughed. "Okay, Uncle Cyrus. "I appreciate your help, and the use of your condo."

I hadn't thought about Dominic since we'd met on Grand Cayman. I'd sensed some good karma between us, but we'd both backed off and stuck to business. This time, I reckoned, might be different.

I flew from Spokane to Houston and then grabbed an Island Air 737 to George Town. Upon arrival, I took a cab to the Colonial, checked in, and called Dominic.

"Hey, it's Trace. Are you busy?"

"Do you mean at the moment, or tonight?"

"Both," I said with a chuckle.

"I'm free tonight. By the way, your uncle called and filled me in on your situation."

I laughed. "By my uncle, I take it you mean, Cyrus?"

"Uh-huh. He said you were heartbroken, worn out from work, and needed some R & R."

"The latter two are true. My heart's okay. Tina and I were good buddies, but I guess I always knew she wouldn't put up with my job and travel."

"Okay, enough of that. Where are you taking me tonight? And I warn you, I'm starved."

"What's the old quote? 'Forewarned is forearmed.'"

"Good looking and well-read too. I am impressed. Are you at the Colonial?"

"Yep, me and a bunch of movie actors. There goes Bart Yancey now."

"Uh-huh. I'll be in the lobby at seven sharp. Jack's is fine. I'll make the reservation."

I chuckled. "What? I don't have enough clout to get us in?"

"You got it, babe. See ya."

At seven sharp I was in the lobby. Dominic strode in, wearing white-linen slacks with a navy blouse. Every guy in the lobby turned to look. Eat your hearts out, fellows, I thought, as she shook my hand and kissed both my cheeks. I'd been right on the previous trip' she was an eleven.

"Hi, Trace. I'm very glad you decided to come back to the island."

"Ditto, Dominic. All the cards just fell into place, and of course Cyrus offering his condo, didn't hurt."

Dominic nodded and laughed. "You know he's got a terrible reputation. They call him Cyrus the Virus."

"Yeah, so I've heard. But I can tell you, he's changed."

"Uh-huh," Dominic said, pulling me in the direction of Jack's. "Come on, Trace, let's eat."

We ate a wonderful meal of sea bass accompanied by an excellent sauvignon blanc. To cap off the feast, we ordered steaming mugs of Caribbean coffee, a blend of dark rum, whipped cream, sugar, and coffee.

"Wow," Dominic said, using her napkin to dab a bit of whipped cream from her upper lip. "Excellent meal, good coffee, and pretty-fair company."

I chuckled and took a sip of the coffee concoction. "Thanks, Dominic. I can't think of a meal I've enjoyed more, or better company, either."

"How's the ocean-view from Cyrus's condo?"

"You have to see it to believe it," I said, grinning mischievously.

"Let's take a look."

We watched the moon come up over the Caribbean from Cyrus's balcony. Followed, against my better judgment, by skinny-dipping in the surf. I don't know if it was the cool water, the fear of a sea turtle looking for a dangling tender morsel, or the thought of a tiger shark taking off a leg, but my equipment was definitely shriveled when we got back on the beach.

Dominic noticed my plight and laughed softly. "I think I can remedy that."

Damned if she wasn't right.

The next four days were paradise in paradise. We made love, swam, dined, and lounged around in tee shirts and shorts, watching old movies we'd rented from a local vendor. We'd both fallen hard for each other and were already planning my return trip.

It was tough to say good-bye at the airport, but business was business. Wally had our listing on the Toronto Exchange confirmed, and I needed to be in Toronto next week for the opening bell. And our first day of trading on the big board.

Chapter 63

Agent Wilson Allen had been working out of the La Vegas FBI field office for nearly two weeks. The local FBI office along with the Criminal Investigation Division of the IRS were hard into investigating the Comstock Casino.

Agent Allen called his boss to report his findings.

"Special Agent Monroe, it's Wilson Allen here."

"Morning, Wilson. Anything new?"

"Well, I've reviewed both of our investigation here in Vegas and the IRS-CID findings. I think it's pretty clear someone is skimming some of the casino profits."

"Black Chip, LLC?"

"That's the consensus around here."

"Any luck on tracing ownership of Black Chip?"

"Negative, sir. So far the Cayman authorities haven't been much help. I think it'll take an indictment of the Comstock to get them to act."

"Do we have enough to go in front of a grand jury?"

"With the croupier's testimony, I think so."

"Put him in protective custody. I don't want another potential witness against the Pantellis to get knocked off. Coordinate with the local authorities and raid the Comstock. Seize their computers and grab all the employees in sight."

I invited, Wally, Will, James Lee, and Cyrus to join me for our first day of trading on the Toronto Stock Exchange, usually just called the TSX. The exchange would have an opening bell ringing ceremony announcing the addition of Montana Creek Mining Corp. to the nearly fifteen hundred other companies listed on the exchange. It was a big deal for the company, and our shareholders.

Our cash-burn rate with just a single drill operating left us in good shape financially. I felt the founders and our biggest investors should enjoy this milestone, so I pulled out all the stops.

Will, Cyrus, and I flew in together and would meet up with Wally and Jim Lee at the Frederick Arms Hotel, one of the finest hotels in Toronto. I excluded the Pantellis from our little soiree.

As Will, Cyrus, and I collected our luggage and cleared customs, we ran into Jim Lee.

"Hey, Jim," I yelled, waving to get his attention.

Jim waved back and pointed to an area beyond the crowed customs area.

In a few minutes we all met and shook hands with Jim.

"Where's Wally?" Jim asked.

"He's flying in directly from Vancouver," I replied. "No customs hassles for Wally. He's a native."

We all laughed and then headed out to the curb to hail a cab.

"Frederick Arms, eh?" Jim said.

"Yep, I decided we should go first-class on this one," I replied. "Not too many times in a career do you get a listing on a major exchange. I thought it deserved a little ceremony."

"Speaking of ceremony," Jim replied, "you fellows will get to ring the opening bell in the morning, and watch Montana Creek Mining start trading with the big boys."

"You'll be there too," I added.

"True, but I've been there before when IUC got listed here in Canada," Jim replied. "I'll be in the background. I want you all front and center. As you said, Trace, it's a very special milestone in the company's history."

At around seven we all met for dinner.

"I hope none of you mind," Jim said, "but I went ahead and made us reservations at the Rancher's Restaurant, here in the hotel. "Best Kobe beef in Canada."

Jim was right; the Kobe beef was primo. As were the several bottles of cabernet we washed it down with. After the meal we adjourned to a nearby lounge for brandy and to discuss a little business.

"Anything new on the Chinese front, Trace?" Jim asked.

I laughed. "Damn, sounds like we're discussing the Korean war. Nope, all quiet on the eastern front. Not a peep since their visit to the Sullivan Mine. I made it crystal clear to Chang I have no intention of selling my shares, at this point in time. And since neither of my legs have been broken, I suspect the Pantelli family may have told Chang the same thing."

Jim snickered. "Who was it who told you we had an eclectic bunch of shareholders?

"Uh . . . that would be FBI Special Agent Beau Monroe," I replied, with a chuckle.

"Yeah, well, eclectic is a damn sight better than dead," Will chimed in. "Anything new from Monroe on the investigation into Rosy or Malcolm's deaths?"

"Well, Agent Monroe said they now know for sure that the guy who killed Rosenburg died in the botched, first attempt, on Malcolm," I replied. "The bombing of Malcolm's plane is still under investigation. Monroe won't tell me too much, but he did say everything they've uncovered so far seems to point to our shareholders, in New Orleans."

Jim Lee took a sip of his brandy, "Trace, I wish you'd sell IUC your block of shares. We'd tell Lei Chang to bugger off, and we'd make the Pantellis an offer they couldn't refuse."

I smiled and looked around the table.

"First things first, gents. Let's get this puppy trading on the TSX, and then we'll deal with the Chinese and the Pantellis. Hell, you never can tell. The FBI may bust the Pantellis for the deaths of Rosy and Malcolm. And I believe they still have the death penalty, in Louisiana."

"And, Jim," Cyrus added, "if you do end up with the Pantelli's' shares, don't forget yours truly owns their voting proxy for nearly three more years. Of course, I'd be glad to transfer the proxy to IUC for what I paid for it, plus a small profit."

We all laughed.

"Thank you, Cyrus," Jim said with a grin. "You'll be the first one I call should we buy out the Pantellis."

The next morning at nine sharp found us all decked out in our Sunday-go-to-meeting best. I rang the opening bell, and Montana Creek Mining, under its new symbol of MCM.TO, was off to the races.

I made a short promotional speech to the assembled brokers, who, I could tell from their expressions had heard it all before. But they were gracious listeners and gave all of us a rousing hand as our symbol posted and the first trade was completed.

The IRS and the FBI hit the Comstock Casino like it was Normandy on D-day. Full-meal deal, guns out and up, and enough yellow crime tape to wrap up an elephant. The agents sealed off the cashier's cages and counting room, and grabbed every computer in sight. They also arrested as many casino employees as they could catch.

When the dust settled, Agent Allen called Special Agent Monroe.

"It went off without a hitch, Beau. We seized all the computers plus hand-written ledgers in the counting room and about seventy-five employees. We also got a court order ordering the casino to cease operations, until further notice."

"Damn good work, Wilson," Monroe said with a chuckle. "Hell, we may not have to arrest Al Pantelli. He'll probably have a heart attack when he hears about the raid."

Special Agent Monroe wasn't too far off. One of the dealers who'd evaded arrest called Mr. Pantelli.

Al hit Pino's call button on his phone.

"Pino, come down to my office. The Comstock just got hit."

"Robbed?"

"No. A federal raid. IRS, FBI, local cops, a whole fuckin' army of badges. Get down here."

Pino sprinted down to his brother's office and burst through the door.

"What the hell is going on?"

"I don't know, but my guess is the feds couldn't find enough evidence to pin Rosy and Trueblood on us. So they went after the casino."

"The skim?"

"That, and our ownership interest."

"Hell, our ownership is through Black Chip, LLC. They'll never penetrate the Cayman corporate veil."

"Don't be too damn sure, Pino. If the feds can prove illegal funds were funneled to the Caymans, all bets are off."

"So what's the plan, brother?"

"Two things," Al said. "We need to find out what the feds have. Something or somebody must have tipped them to the skim. And secondly, we need to raise a shit pot full of dough. This is going to cost us a hell of a lot of money."

Pino nodded. "Hey, let's call our buddy, Lei Chang. Tell him we've changed our minds and sell him our Montana Creek Mining shares, before he finds out we're in deep shit."

"Damn good idea, brother. I'll call that condescending son of a bitch myself. I'll squeeze every dime I can out of him."

Chapter 64

I was just back from the Toronto listing ceremony when Special Agent Monroe rang me up.

"Trace, Agent Beau Monroe. Got a sec?"

"Yeah, sure, Agent Monroe. What's up?"

"I just wanted to give you a heads-up. The FBI and the IRS raided the Comstock Casino in Vegas. I'm telling you this because it may cause you some problems with the Pantellis. Off the record, Trace, we think they've been skimming profits from the casino and sending the money offshore."

"How could it affect Montana Creek Mining?" I asked.

"Well, if we indict the Pantellis, they may seek to get liquid to pay their defense lawyers, or fund a little vacation."

"You're thinking they might dump their Montana Creek Mining shares?"

"Could be, Trace, but I don't think they'd sell it in the market. A block that big might drive the share price down. No, I think they'll be looking to make a private sale. Sell the whole block in one fell swoop. Anyway, just a heads-up, Trace. As you know those fellows are unpredictable, to say the least."

I was way ahead of him.

"Listen, Agent Monroe. I really appreciate the information."

"No problem, Trace. One other thing. If you do see some selling on their part, I'd like to know about it."

"The least I can do, Agent Monroe. Good luck in nailing those bastards."

*****

It took Al Pantelli a couple of hours to track Lei Chang down. He finally caught up to him in London.

"Mr. Chang, it's Al Pantelli, in New Orleans. Sorry about the late hour on your end."

"Not a problem, Mr. Pantelli. What can I do for you?"

"Well, in our last conversation I told you I'd get back to you, if we changed our mind on selling our shares in Montana Creek Mining."

"And have you changed your mind?"

"Yes, sir, we have. Pino and I don't know a damn thing about uranium mining, or any other kind of mining, for that matter. We operate in totally unrelated fields."

"Yes, I know that."

"So, after reconsidering your generous offer, we are prepared to sell you one hundred percent of our holdings."

"How many shares in total?"

"Five hundred thousand we acquired in a private transaction, and another two hundred fifty thousand we've purchased in the market."

"I see. Well, Mr. Pantelli, I'll make you a onetime offer, good until this conversation is over. I'll pay you twenty percent over the last thirty days' bid price. Stand by please," Chang said, as he checked his stock charts. "The average price of the shares over the last thirty days is five-eighty. A twenty percent premium would bring it up to six-ninety-six, Canadian dollars. I need your answer now."

"I calculate a total purchase price of five million two hundred twenty thousand dollars. Do you concur, Mr. Chang?"

"Canadian dollars, and yes that is correct. Do we have a deal?"

Al smiled. It was a hell of a profit. Especially on Rosy's shares.

"Yes, sir. You've got a deal, but it has to be in cash. Delivered to our office here in New Orleans. Is that going to be a problem?"

Chang had expected it would be a cash deal. The Pantellis, after all, were criminals.

"No, not a problem. I'll have a courier in New Orleans three days hence. Have the stock certificates and signed, signature-guaranteed, stock powers ready to hand over. And no funny business, Mr. Pantelli. I am well connected with a Hong Kong triad. It will go badly for you should you try anything stupid."

Al hung up and looked over at Pino, who'd listened in on the call.

"Triad, my ass," Pino growled. "Who the hell does that slant-eyed bastard think he is . . . Bruce fuckin' Lee?"

Al smiled. "I think we may need to teach Mr. Chang a little lesson in messing with the Outfit."

Jim Lee called me the day after I'd spoken to Agent Monroe.

"Trace, remember when I joked about calling Cyrus if we, IUC, bought the Pantellis' Montana Creek Mining shares?"

"Yes," I said, wondering if Jim was going to say what I thought he was going to say.

"Guess who called me this morning?"

"Vito Corleone?"

Jim cracked up. "No, but you're pretty close. None other than Albert Pantelli and his sidekick, Crispino."

"No shit. They pitched you a deal to buy their shares?"

"Lock, stock, and barrel. Seven hundred fifty thousand shares."

"At what price?"

"Seven dollars and fifty cents per share."

"Damn, Jim, that's about a thirty percent premium to where we've been trading. What'd you tell them?"

"I told them I'd have to run it by my board. But the SOB's only gave me twenty-four hours to make a decision. I've already sent the details to all our board members and asked them all to get back to me, before the deadline."

"What do you think?"

"In the short term, it's a stout premium. But in the longer term, I think the shares will blow through seven-fifty without much of a problem."

"I do too, Jim, and I'd sure like to get the Pantellis out of our company. But it's up to you. Just keep me posted, will you?"

"Will do, Trace. Of course there is also the matter of Cyrus holding the Pantelli's' proxy to vote a half a million of those shares. Do you think he'll transfer or cancel his proxy?"

"Yes, I do, but you'll have to pay him what he paid the Pantellis, plus a little profit. Look, if you decide to buy the shares, let me talk to Cyrus. I've developed a pretty good relationship with him, and I think I can get him to work with you."

"Thanks, Trace, I was hoping you'd say that. It'll be a big help in convincing our board to move on this. Without the proxy, it won't happen."

Eighteen hours later, Jim Lee had board approval to buy out the Pantellis. He called Al Pantelli, to confirm the deal.

"Mr. Pantelli, Jim Lee with International Uranium Corp. How are you this morning?"

"Depends on what your answer is, Mr. Lee. Do we have a deal, or not?"

"Our board approved the acquisition late last night. We have a deal."

"Excellent. How soon can you come to New Orleans and pick up the shares, and pay us?"

"I can be in New Orleans in forty-eight hours. Please have the certs ready along with an executed, signature-guaranteed, stock power. Just one other item. How do you want the cashier's check made out?"

"Don't suppose you'd consider paying us in cash?"

"No, we wouldn't."

"Okay, no harm in asking. Make the check out to Albert A. Pantelli. I'll see you day after tomorrow. Do you have our address?"

"Trace has it in our shareholder files."

"Trace knows about the deal?"

"Absolutely. He was the first person I called. Is that a problem?"

"No, it's not a problem. Hell, my brother and I have grown quite fond of Trace, and we'll like him even better after we cash your check."

"I'm sure the feeling's mutual. See you in a couple of days." Al hung up and called his brother's office.

"IUC will be here in forty-eight hours with a cashier's check for five point six mil, and change."

"Jesus, Al. We're cutting this a little close, aren't we? Chang's courier is due to arrive at about the same time."

Al laughed. "I'm afraid the courier's going to have a very bad accident, and Chang's dough is going to get stolen. If we're careful and do this exactly right, we're going to have over ten mil, and about half of the dough in cash."

"Damn, that ought to cover any legal bills from the casino bust."

"My thoughts exactly, and Chang's cash won't be reported to the IRS, so add another thirty-five percent to the pot."

Jim Lee called me back and wanted to know if Cyrus and I could meet him in New Orleans the day after tomorrow.

"I'd like both of you there to witness the transaction, and we'll need Cyrus there to transfer his proxy."

"Okay, Jim. I'll call Cyrus and fill him in. I haven't mentioned anything to him yet. I wanted to be sure the deal was going to happen."

"Okay, call me if there's any problems. This will be an in-and-out trip, Trace. I want the shares out of the Pantelli's' hands and into our brokerage account the same day."

I hung up and called Cyrus.

"Cyrus, Trace here. Got a sec?"

"Yep, what's on your mind?"

"Are you sitting down?"

"Jesus, there wasn't another Three Mile Island, was there?"

I laughed. "No, no, the uranium market is strong. But there is a deal pending that could reach critical mass. I'm going to need a couple of things from you, Cyrus."

"You got it, kid. What'd you need?"

"I need you to transfer or cancel your proxy on the Pantelli's' shares. Second, you and I need to be in New Orleans, in about forty-eight hours."

"Uh-huh, so who's taking the Pantellis out of the equation?"

"IUC, provided you'll transfer or cancel your voting proxy."

"I can and I will. Of course, it'll cost them what I paid for it, plus a bit for my trouble."

"Not a problem, Cyrus. Jim will pay you when we meet in New Orleans."

"Can I ask what IUC is paying for the shares?"

"I'd rather Jim told you, but it's more than what Chang offered. Which, if I recall correctly, was a twenty percent premium to our recent share price."

"Correctamundo, Trace. Which means IUC is paying north of a twenty percent premium. Kind of makes you feel all warm and fuzzy, don't it?"

I chuckled. "Yeah, I guess it does. But what really makes me happy is to see an outfit like IUC think our share price is headed north of seven-fifty a share."

"Their bean counters would've never let them do the deal, if they didn't think so. Hot damn, son. We're going to make some serious loot."

"Yeah, if we can get Jim out of New Orleans with the shares, and in one piece."

"No worries, Trace. We won't have a problem with Al or Pino. That's not the way they operate. They'll be cool. But what I am curious about is our commie buddy, Chang. URAN-China can certainly outbid IUC, so why is Al selling to Jim's company? If Al is playing both ends against the middle, there could be trouble with Chang."

"Some kind of scam, double-cross?"

"Always a possibility. They don't call the Pantellis a crime family because they're straight shooters, no pun intended."

Chang's courier, Ri Wu, boarded the chartered Citation at JFK Airport. Handcuffed to his left wrist was an aluminum briefcase holding more than five million Canadian dollars. Wu was unarmed, but he *was* one of the kung fu mother fuckers Al had joked about.

In about four hours, Wu's jet touched down at Louis Armstrong International Airport and taxied to the general aviation ramp. A black limo waited with a uniformed chauffeur standing to the side and holding a placard with Wu's name neatly printed on it.

The very attractive flight attendant opened the cabin door, and Wu descended the ramp.

"Mr. Wu?" the chauffeur asked, holding the rear door of the limo open.

Wu nodded and climbed in. The limo was empty except for Wu and the driver.

"I'm to take you directly to Mr. Pantelli's office. It'll take about twenty minutes."

"Very good."

Traffic was light, and less than twenty minutes later, the limo pulled into the underground parking garage beneath the Pantelli's' office building. The driver pulled into a parking space marked reserved for A. Pantelli. The parking space was immediately adjacent to the elevator.

"Right this way, Mr. Wu," the chauffeur said, opening Wu's door. "I'll accompany you to the main office."

Wu nodded and said nothing, but his radar was on full alert. If there was to be trouble, he knew it would likely happen here.

The chauffeur hit the up button, and the elevator door opened. Wu immediately took a half-step back. A workman in coveralls was in the elevator. His tools were lying on the floor, which had been covered in plastic to keep the surface clean.

"Sorry, gents," the workman said. "I'm just doing a little maintenance. Come on in. You can use the elevator. I'll stop work for a couple of minutes. It's not a problem."

The chauffeur stepped in. Wu hesitated for a minute and then followed.

"Which floor, gents?" the workman asked.

"Three, please," the chauffeur replied.

The workman pushed the button for floor three and then stepped back and slightly behind Wu. As the elevator passed the first floor, a chime sounded. It was the last sound Wu would ever hear. The two pops from the silenced .22 were barely audible above the chime. Both hollow points hit Wu in the back of the head. He was dead before he crumpled on the plastic liner.

The chauffeur hit the emergency stop button and locked the elevator between the first and second floors.

The chauffeur looked at the shooter. "Wrap a towel around his head. He's bleeding like a stuck pig. And find the key to the cuffs."

The shooter tied a dirty towel around Wu's head and then rifled his pockets. He found the key tucked in Wu's wallet.

"Got 'em, and, hey, lookie here," the shooter said, pulling several one hundred dollar bills from Wu's wallet.

"Come on," the chauffeur growled, taking the key and unlocking the cuffs. "Quit fucking around and help me get Mr. One Hung Low rolled up in the plastic."

Together they rolled Wu up in the thick plastic sheeting. The chauffeur released the emergency stop and hit the parking level button. As soon as the elevator doors opened, the chauffeur looked around the parking garage. Seeing no one, he pushed the trunk-release button on limo key fob. Together the two men carried the bundle of plastic and deposited it in the trunk of the limo.

"Sanitize the elevator," the chauffeur ordered. "Make sure you pick up your brass and wipe everything down. No finger-prints, no blood. Got it?"

"Yes, sir. I've got it," the shooter replied, holding out an open palm with the two shell casings. "This ain't my first hit."

The chauffeur nodded and opened the driver's side door. "Disappear. The rest of your dough will be wired to your account."

The chauffeur headed for the docks. The Pantelli family owned a fleet of offshore oil rig service boats, and Mr. Wu was scheduled to take a short cruise, one way. The limo pulled into the service company warehouse and stopped. Two rough-looking longshoreman types walked up to the driver's door.

"The package is in the trunk," the chauffeur told the two men. "Put the whole mess in a fifty-five-gallon drum. Seal it and then load it on the *Konny Kay*. She's due to shove off in about an hour."

With Mr. Wu safely on board, the *Konny Kay* put to sea. When the boat reached the one-hundred-fathom contour, the captain cut the engines and signaled to a deck-hand. Two minutes later a single fifty-five-gallon drum rolled off the boat's stern, like a World War II depth charge.

Chapter 65

Chang was worried. He should have had confirmation from Wu by now. He flipped his cell phone open and called Al Pantelli.

"Mr. Pantelli, Lei Chang, here. Has my courier shown up?"

Al wagged his index finger at Pino and silently mouthed the word "*Chang.*"

"No, sir, he hasn't showed up yet."

"That's odd. The charter landed on time, in New Orleans."

"Well, maybe they had car trouble, or an accident," Al said, barely able to control his mirth.

"No, my man would have called immediately."

"Of course. Well, I'll have him call you the moment he shows up."

"Please do so, Mr. Pantelli. And for your sake, I hope there are no problems."

Al looked at the dead courier's aluminum brief-case sitting on his desk.

"Well, New Orleans can be a pretty rough town. Especially if you're carrying a lot of cash."

"I warn you, Mr. Pantelli. You'd better hope nothing's happened to my courier, or my cash."

"You should be careful how you talk to me, Mr. Chang. This ain't Hong Kong, and you ain't Bruce Lee."

Cyrus and I landed at Louis Armstrong in New Orleans and waited in the terminal for Jim's plane to arrive. We'd just ordered a couple of cokes when my cell phone started vibrating. It was Jim.

"We're in the west gate area at the Café Beignet."

"Okay, I'll be there in a couple of minutes."

I looked over at Cyrus. "Jim's on his way."

"Good deal. The sooner we get this done, the better."

"Second thoughts on trouble with the Pantellis?"

"No, it's Chang that keeps bothering me. Why wouldn't he trump IUC's offer. Hell, it's chump change to them."

"Yeah, I know. I'm thinking the same thing. Who knows? Maybe the Pantellis don't like the Chicoms any better than we do?"

Jim walked into the café and over to our table.

"Why the long faces, fellas?" Jim asked.

"Neither one of us can figure out why URAN-China didn't top your offer. Hell, you know Al was on the phone with Chang ten seconds after he got your offer."

"I've got to admit I've been wondering the same thing," Jim replied. "Maybe Chang refused to be worked."

I looked at Cyrus. "Yeah, maybe. But I think Chang wants the Sullivan uranium reserves, and I don't think money is an issue."

Jim nodded in agreement. "Well, all I know is, I've got a cashier's check for five point six million. And it's made out to Albert A. Pantelli, so let's go buy some shares."

We grabbed a cab and headed to the Pantelli's' office building in the French Quarter.

"Does Al know Cyrus and I are coming with you?" I asked.

"Nope," Jim replied. "I thought we'd surprise him."

Cyrus turned from his seat in the front of the cab. "I think it was a good move, Jim. Three witnesses are a lot better than one, in any scenario."

The cab dropped us off in front of the Pantelli's office building, in the Quarter.

"Al's office is on the third floor," Cyrus said, as he handed the cabbie a twenty.

We took the elevator and followed Cyrus down the hall to Al's office. Cyrus knocked and we walked in. Al's secretary was not in the office, and Al's door was open.

"Come on in, boys," Al said, in a booming voice. "I see you brought the cavalry with you, Jim."

"Well, IUC's about to become a major stakeholder in Montana Creek Mining so I thought the CEO should be here. And as Cyrus needs to transfer his proxy, I invited him to come along as well. I hope you don't mind."

"Hell, no. Come on in. Fix yourselves a drink and have a seat. I asked my secretary to take the day off. I don't like to transact serious business in front of the hired help."

"Not a problem," Jim replied.

"Crown and coke okay for everybody?" I asked. Cyrus and Jim both nodded. "How about you, Al?"

"I've got a gin and tonic going, Trace," Al replied. "But thanks just the same."

With drinks in hand, we all took a seat.

"I've got your cashier's check, Al," Jim said, opening his brief-case. Do you have the stock certificates and stock power ready?"

"Yes, sir," Al replied, opening the center drawer of his desk and pulling out a manila envelope.

"Do you mind if I examine the certificates and the stock power?" Jim asked. "I just need to be sure everything is properly executed and that your signature has been properly guaranteed."

"Sure," Al replied, handing the manila envelope to Jim.

While Jim checked the signatures on the stock powers, I figured it was a good time to ask about Chang. "Al, I'm surprised URAN-China Nuclear didn't buy your shares. Surely you must have given them the opportunity to beat IUC's offer."

"I did, but Chang wouldn't budge. And, all things being equal, I'd much rather deal with the Australians than the damn Chinese."

I glanced quickly at Cyrus and then turned back to Al.

"I see. Well I'm glad you took Jim's offer. Acquiring your shares will make IUC a very significant shareholder in our company."

"Second only to you, I'd guess." Al said with a laugh. "So everybody wins, except for the commies."

"Everything is in order, Mr. Pantelli," Jim said, sliding the certificates and stock power back into the envelope. "Here is your check," Jim said, standing up and handing Al the cashier's check. "I think that concludes our business here, gentlemen."

Al rose from his chair, took the check, folded it, and put it in his shirt pocket. "I thought you all might want to have dinner to celebrate. At least have a few drinks in one of New Orleans's finest clubs?"

"Sorry, Mr. Pantelli," Jim replied. "I have to get back to Australia as soon as possible. My board wants an update on our investment in Montana Creek Mining. So it will have to be thank you, and good luck to you in your future ventures."

We all shook hands with Al and left his office. Once in the elevator, Cyrus couldn't contain himself. "Damn fine work, Jim. You certainly took care of business, and got us the hell out of there."

"Well, sometimes you have to do business with the devil, but you don't have to muck about. Get in, get out, and move on."

"Amen, brother," I said, exhaling softly.

The elevator door opened, and we exited the building and hailed a passing cab.

"Eight thirty six, Gravier Street," Jim told the cabbie. "Hope you fellows don't mind a little detour. IUC keeps a securities account with Jackson-Steinman. They have an office here, and I'd like to deposit these shares into our account. It shouldn't take long."

"No worries, mate," I said, in my best Aussie accent. "Take your time. Our plane doesn't leave until late this afternoon."

"Ah, there is one other small detail," Cyrus interjected.

"Oh, yes, the transfer of your voting proxy," Jim said, reaching into his briefcase and removing a second manila envelope. "If you'll just execute this proxy transfer, I have a check made out to you in the amount of two hundred twenty thousand US dollars. I assume a twenty-thousand-dollar profit, is satisfactory?"

"You bet, and thank you, Jim."

*****

Al Pantelli walked down to his brother's office. "Deal's done, little brother," Al said, taking the check out of his pocket and handing it to Pino

Pino whistled softly. "Man, that's a lot of zeros."

"Yeah, and that's exactly what we'll be if we don't get out of here. Is the plane ready to go?"

"I just need to pre-flight and top off the tanks."

Pino had been flying for years and had worked his way up to a multi-engine-instrument rating. Two years ago he'd talked Al into buying a King Air 350 turbo-prop. He'd have them in George Town, Grand Cayman, in time for a late supper.

Both men had told their wives they'd be gone on an extended business trip to the Caribbean. The women knew what that meant. It wasn't their first rodeo, either.

Pino got one of his people to drive him and Al to Louis Armstrong International. They kept the King Air in a hangar in the general aviation section. Ironically, not too far from where Wu had deplaned a few days earlier.

Al and Pino grabbed their gear and told the driver to take the Caddy back to the office and park it in Al's slot.

"Come on, Al. Let's store our gear, and I'll get her pre-flighted and fueled."

"Don't worry, brother," Al said, patting the aluminum briefcase. "If we forget anything, I think we can cover it."

Pino laughed. "Yeah, I would say so. You've got the cashier's check, too?"

"Yep, it's in my pocket. I'll deposit it in our Butterfield account in the morning."

"Are we going to have a problem with Cayman customs?" We're carrying a hell of a lot of cash."

"Nope, I've arranged for one of the senior customs guys to clear us through. He's on our pad."

The two men loaded their gear into the plane, and Pino taxied over to the fueling area.

"We'll top her off, then I'll finish the pre-flight. We'll be wheels up in thirty. How long do you think we'll have to lay low?"

"Maybe six months, maybe less. The feds are going to have a hell of a time tracking the skim. Even if they get to Black

Chip. Hell, it's owned by a number of offshore companies and trusts. They'll have to do a lot of digging to get all the way down to us."

Pino chuckled. "Yeah, I think we covered out tracks pretty damn good. And besides, I could use a little vacation. It's too bad we won't be around to see the look on Chang's face when he figures out he got fucked."

"What's he going to do?" Al replied. "He can't go to the police. Hell, there's nothing in writing, and how does he explain sending five mil in cash to the Outfit? Are you kidding me? It'll smell like a drug deal gone south. Old Chicom Chang, ain't got a fuckin' prayer."

Pino was watching the technician fueling the wing tanks. He turned to Al. "He could decide to play hardball."

"He could. But if he does, we'll hit him so fuckin' hard, he'll no longer be a problem. *Capisce?*"

Pino nodded and glanced out the pilot-side cockpit window at the man fueling the plane.

"Al, lean over here and take a look at the guy fueling the plane. Does he look familiar to you?"

Al leaned over, trying to get his bulk between Pino and the yoke.

"He does remind me of somebody I've seen before. But I can't place him."

The technician topped off the port wing tank and secured the cap. He looked up and saw Pino and Al looking at him. He gave them a thumbs-up and smiled.

"Did you see that?" Pino asked.

"See what?"

"The shit-eating grin that guy gave us. It was the kind of grin you give somebody when you know something they don't."

"Relax, he's probably some kind of idiot. Fueling planes all day long doesn't require a PhD."

The fuel truck pulled away, and Pino got up from the pilot's seat.

"Where you going, little brother?"

"I'm going to check the fuel for water."

"Water? You think that little prick is working for Chang?"

"Hell, anything's possible."

Al scratched his head. "Jesus, I don't think he could be on to us this fast." He paused for a moment. "But go ahead and check the fuel."

Pino went aft, opened the cabin door, and lowered the stairway. As he walked to the port-side wing, he took a small four-ounce glass vial from his shirt pocket. Kneeling at the edge of the wing, he depressed the fuel sump release and drained about three ounces of Jet-A fuel into the vial. He let the fuel settle for a couple of minutes, then held it up against the sky. Satisfied, he dumped the fuel on the tarmac.

He repeated the procedure for the starboard-side wing tank. Al was watching from the co-pilot's side window. Pino looked up and gave him a thumbs-up and tossed the second fuel sample.

"How'd she look?" Al asked, when Pino returned to the cockpit.

"Fuel's good, but something about that guy still bothers me."

Al nodded. "Don't worry, brother. I never forget a face. It'll come to me."

About two hours out of New Orleans, Al punched Pino in the shoulder.

"I've got it."

Pino looked at his brother like he'd gone nuts. "Got what?"

"The guy at the airport. I know who he looks like. He's a dead ringer for Sean Flannigan."

Pino nodded. "You're right. But he bought the farm on Grand Cayman . . . didn't he?"

"Yeah, went out like a fuckin' spy. Ate a cyanide capsule, or so I heard."

"Damn, that fuel guy could be his twin. Flannigan didn't have a brother, did he?"

"You know, I heard Sean did have a younger brother. But, he was supposedly killed by the British in a shoot-out in Belfast."

Al barely got the words out when the starboard engine starting cutting out.

Pino checked the fuel gauge, mixture, and throttle settings and looked over at Al.

"All fuel settings are okay."

Then the port engine started sputtering, rpm's dropping on both engines.

"She's acting like we're running out of fuel," Pino said, tapping on the fuel gauges, both of which showed more than half a tank of fuel left.

"Son of a bitch! The fuel guy, whoever he is, did something to the fuel floats or gauges. We're running out of gas."

Pino clicked his radio mike and called air traffic control in Houston. He declared an emergency, and gave their position.

"Jesus, can you put her in the water, dead stick?"

"I don't know. Without power the controls are going to be very stiff, if not . . ." Before Pino could finish his sentence, both engines quit.

"Take the co-pilot's yoke," Pino said, his voice firm. "I may need your help to fly this tin can."

Pino put the King Air into a series of wide descending spirals.

"When we get close to impact, I'll flare to get the nose up and try and pancake her as best I can. It's going to be pretty rough, big brother. So tighten your seat-belt as tight as you can. When I yell, Flare!', brace for impact."

Al nodded and looked at Pino. "Do you think it was Sean back at the airport?"

"Not unless the FBI faked his death and stashed him to testify against us."

"Damn, I never thought about that. You know, the last time I talked to him, he was pretty cagey. He knew I was pissed about him capping the detective at the strip club."

"Yeah, and he also knew he was the only one who could tie us to bombing Trueblood's plane. Who the fuck knows? Help me with the yoke. Pull back just a tad. Okay, perfect. Here we go."

Their airspeed was too high and the surface of the gulf choppy.

"Flare! Brace!" Pino yelled.

The initial impact was just aft of the wings. The nose of the aircraft then slammed forward into a good-sized wave, and water flooded into the plane. Pino looked over at Al, who appeared to be unconscious. A deep laceration on his forehead was bleeding profusely.

Pino reached behind his seat and managed to get hold of his flight bag. Water was chest high in the cockpit and rising fast as the bird sank deeper into the Gulf. He opened the bag and took out a snub-nosed .38 special.

As the water in the cockpit continued to rise, Pino looked over at his unconscious brother. "We ain't going out like drowning rats, *fratello.* We're going out like *La Cosa Nostra,* made men. See you on the other side, big brother."

Pino raised the .38 and shot Al once, in the side of the head.

He took one more look around the cabin, as the warm, greenish-colored water swirled ever higher around him. Looking aft down the cabin, he smiled when he saw Wu's briefcase floating above the passenger seats.

"Too bad, Chang," Pino said with a soft chuckle. "Looks like we're both fucked."

He switched the revolver from his right hand to his left, reached over, and grasped Al's left hand. He cocked the revolver, stuck the barrel in his mouth, and pulled the trigger.

Chapter 66

Cyrus and I flew back to Spokane from New Orleans. I planned on staying overnight in Spokane and then head up to the Sullivan Mine to check on the drilling. The next morning, Cyrus and I were having breakfast at a little café not too far from his office. My cell phone was on the table and started sliding around from the vibration.

"Uh-oh, it's the fucking big Indians," I whispered, to Cyrus before I answered the call.

"Special Agent Monroe, I had you on my list to call today. You'd asked me to let you know if the Pantellis started selling their shares. Well, they sold all of their shares to International Uranium Corp., Jim Lee's outfit."

"That's good news, Trace, and just in the nick of time."

"How's that?"

"Both Al and Pino are presumed dead. Their plane went done in the Gulf yesterday, about two hours after they left New Orleans, en route to the Caymans."

"A bomb?" I asked, glancing over at Cyrus.

"We don't think so. Pino, who was flying the plane, was in communication with air traffic control. He reported fuel problems and engine failures. His last transmission said they were going down and gave their position. The Coast Guard had a cutter on-site at first light this morning. They found some wreckage but no survivors, and no bodies."

"Damn, I can't believe it."

"Yeah, neither can Mr. Lei Chang. He called us about a missing courier he'd sent to New Orleans to buy the same shares IUC bought."

I took out my pen and scribbled on a napkin, "'Pantellis' dead–double X,'" and slid it over to Cyrus. He read the note and nodded.

"Looks like Al was playing both ends against the middle," I said.

"Yeah, I'm shocked," Agent Monroe said, dryly. "And so is Chang. We think the Pantellis demanded Chang pay them in cash. Then they knocked off his courier and stole the money. All of which is probably now at the bottom of the Gulf of Mexico, which somehow seems kind of fitting."

"Well you were right about one thing, Agent Monroe," I said.

"What's that?"

"We got the shares out of their hands, in the nick of time."

"FYI, Trace, we're going to keep investigating the Pantelli plane crash, and the disappearance of Chang's courier. But between you and me, I doubt it'll go anywhere. Good news is two more killers are off the board. Unfortunately, a couple of civilians went down along the way."

"It's interesting how things kind of even out in the end, isn't it?"

"Yeah, I guess it is, Trace. I'll be in touch, if we need anything else from you."

I put the phone down and looked across the table at Cyrus.

"Did you get the gist of it?"

"Yeah. The Pantellis got just what they deserved, and I think it's pretty ironic they bought it over the Gulf. What goes around comes around. Hell, I'll bet old Malcolm's laughing his ass off."

"From what Agent Monroe said, I think Al and Pino had a lot of time to think about it while they were on the way down."

"Seems only fair."

"Thank God, Jim bought their shares when he did. Otherwise we'd be dealing with the Pantelli heirs. Can you imagine what a feeding frenzy that would have been?"

Cyrus laughed. "Yeah, you can say that again. "So, what's next? Where do we, you, go from here?"

"We'll, I've decided to join the Pantellis."

"What?" Cyrus said with a chuckle. "Don't tell me you're crossing over to the dark side."

"No, no. I mean I've decided to sell my shares to IUC. I've taken Montana Creek Mining about as far as a no-account geologist can."

"I see. Well, it's the smart move, Trace. It's going to take someone like IUC to finance a full-blown mining operation. Hell, you're like me. You enjoy finding the deposit, doing enough drilling to prove up a discovery, and then move on. The fun's in the finding, not in the operations. Trust me."

"I couldn't agree more. By the way, as I'm soon to be cashed-up, do you have any interest in selling your condo, in George Town?"

Cyrus laughed. "Dominic got to you, eh?"

I nodded. "Uh-huh, I guess she did. So what about the condo?"

"No sale, Trace . . . but I'll lease it to you for a year. Provided you look at a concession I've been eyeballing."

"I'll take the lease. What kind of concession?"

"Alluvial diamonds, in West Africa."

"A ground-floor opportunity, I suppose?" I asked, raising my eyebrows.

A big grin spread across Cyrus's face. "Abso-damned-toutly."